D1602474

Picture

Me

A Mystery

Praise for *Summer's Squall*
"The author obviously did a lot of research for the book and it showed, not in boring lists of facts, but in the way the book was fleshed out. In addition, the descriptions were beautifully done, not telling but showing the beauty of the area."
Among the Reads Review

"Good character development, plot, surprises, thought provoking with excellent descriptions of the Colorado mountain country."
Amazon Reviewer

Praise for Award-Winning, *Island of Miracles*
"A beautiful account of the love and the healing support of community!"
Chandi Owen, Author

"This is the kind of story that makes me long to run away from my perfectly fine life for the sole purpose of stumbling upon something magical."
Alex Jacobs, Author, The Dreamer

Praise for Award-Winning, *Whispering Vines*
"The heartbreaking, endearing, charming, and romantic scenes will surely inveigle you to keep reading."
Serious Reading Book Review

"Schisler's writing is a verbal masterpiece of art."
Alex Jacobs, Author, The Dreamer

"Amy Schisler's Whispering Vines is well styled, fast paced, and engaging, the perfect recipe for an excellent book."
Judith Reveal, Author, Editor, Reviewer

Also Available by Amy Schisler

Novels
A Place to Call Home
Picture Me
Whispering Vines
Island of Miracles
Summer's Squall

Children's Books
Crabbing With Granddad
The Greatest Gift

Collaborations
Stations of the Cross Meditations for Moms (with Anne Kennedy, Susan Anthony, Chandi Owen, and Wendy Clark)

Picture Me

A Mystery
By Amy Schisler

COPYRIGHT

ISBN-13: 978-0-692-94619-0
ISBN-10: 0692946190
Published by:
Chesapeake Sunrise Publishing
Amy Schisler
Bozman, MD
2015

DEDICATION

To the people in my life who opened my eyes to the
brilliance of duMaurier, Twain, Fitzgerald,
Cather, Chaucer, and Austen:
My mother, Judy MacWilliams
Sister Sharon, Mr. Hammersla, Mrs. Enrico,
and most especially Mrs. Bizup and Mrs. Wilson who
encouraged my writing.

PART ONE

You can't connect the dots looking forward; you can only connect them looking backwards. So you have to trust that the dots will somehow connect in your future.

Steve Jobs

PROLOGUE
January 4, 2012

Melissa Grant always loved the snow. The thrilling feeling of seeing it fall and cover the ground, like a blanket of white fleece, stayed with her into adulthood. Even at twenty-six, few things excited her like waking up to a world of white. While others complained about the cold, the hassle of getting around, and the shoveling, scraping, and salting, Melissa delighted in trudging through the mounds of fluffy white crystals.

However, when her old alarm clock sounded at 7:00 on the morning on January fourth, Melissa groaned at the announcement on the radio.

"At least six inches fell overnight, and more is expected this morning. Up to a foot of accumulation is in the forecast by the time this storm blows out of the Baltimore metro area this evening."

Melissa closed her eyes and turned toward the wall beside her bed. She had been dreading this day since the phone call she received at two in the morning on New Year's Day. Now, things were going to be even more complicated than she already expected them to be.

Was this storm predicted?

Thinking it through, Melissa realized that she had been so out of it that the many signs of the upcoming storm had never registered—the weather alerts on her phone, the throngs of people going in and out of the grocery store last night on her walk through her old neighborhood, and the salt trucks parked up and down the streets.

Heaving a long sigh, Melissa rolled over and pushed the covers away. She sat up and looked across her childhood bedroom toward the window.

Yep, it's snowing out there. A lot of snow. Just great.

A chill shot through her as she put her feet on the bare wooden floor. She had forgotten how cold this old house got at night. It was like living in a freezer. Why had she not put on socks before going to bed? Melissa shook her head, trying to clear the many random thoughts that blew around in her brain like the snowflakes blowing outside of her window. The last few days had been a blur. She couldn't even remember if she had eaten a bite since the New Year's Eve party she attended with friends.

She stumbled to her old dresser and looked at herself in the mirror. It occurred to Melissa that she looked like she had aged ten years. Her eyes were bloodshot and puffy, and dark blue circles filled the creases beneath them. She looked pale and thin as if she hadn't been outside in weeks or eaten in months. That wasn't the case, so it must have been her imagination, but she supposed grief could do those things to a person.

She reached for the photo that was stuck in the frame of the mirror. Melissa had taken it back in high school. Her parents stood in front of their Christmas tree, their eyes matching the sparkle of the string of lights on the fake pine. Her gaze wandered to another photo, her childhood friends dressed for their Senior Homecoming dance, making faces at her as she aimed and told them to say 'cheese.' Another picture showed her beloved Tucker, the dog she kissed goodbye on the first day of school when she was in sixth grade, knowing he would be gone when she returned home. He was her favorite subject to photograph.

Melissa dragged herself into the bathroom and saw the black suit hanging behind the door. She didn't remember putting it there. Perhaps Tina, her best friend, put it there for her. God knows she was unable to do anything for herself these days. Thankfully, Tina had come home with her and taken charge. She held her hand through all of the decisions and plans that were made, decisions Melissa had thought were still years away from needing to be made— choices about caskets, music, prayers, readings, pall bearers, and more. And now the day had arrived, the decisions were made, and the service was scheduled to take place at eleven that morning.

Hours later, Melissa was exhausted. In spite of the weather, the day went as planned. She made it through the service and then hugged, shook hands, and accepted condolences from the many friends and neighbors she greeted at St. Thomas Aquinas Church. She grew up in this Church and attended the parish school through the eighth grade. Melissa then moved on to Loyola Blakefield High School. It was at St. Thomas Aquinas, however, where her fondest memories took place.

That evening, after the traditional post-funeral meal was over, Melissa wondered what she would do with all of the fried chicken, side salads, and homemade desserts that were left. That was the least of her worries right now. Feeling overwhelmed by the tasks ahead of her, she decided she needed to take a walk to clear her head, despite the snow and her mental and physical exhaustion. Melissa put on her old snow boots and coat and headed out for a walk along the freshly plowed streets of Hampden. Her mother never threw anything away, and though Melissa teased her about no longer needing any of the things left behind in her closet, she was thankful that her boots were still there.

Just a stone's throw away from her alma mater, The Johns Hopkins University, Melissa's neighborhood hadn't changed much since her childhood. She always loved the quaint little houses in Hampden, just inside the Baltimore City limits. Most of her friends had moved away, but many of their parents remained. Melissa could name just about every family on the street as she passed by their homes.

While she walked, she thought about her mother's abounding generosity and her father's penchant for telling bad jokes. What would the world be like without them? She couldn't imagine it. How could one patch of ice change everything so quickly?

Wiping the tears from her eyes, she headed back to the house where she lived for the first eighteen years of her life. She had no idea who shoveled the walkway or the sidewalk on which once walked a couple who was loved by all. She was just grateful that it had been done by the time she returned home from the funeral. She gazed at the only real home she had ever known. What would she do with it now?

Unable to think about sleep, Melissa walked into her parents' room and sat on the bed. Tina had left for her two-hour drive back to Philly right after helping Melissa put all the food away. She needed to return to the maternity ward at Mercy Philadelphia Hospital where she and Melissa worked the night shift. Just a week ago, they thought it a miracle to both have off on New Year's Eve. Apparently, it was. Melissa had needed her best friend that night, and Tina wasted no time in hurrying over to Melissa's apartment after the frantic phone call Melissa made to her in the middle of the night.

But now Melissa was alone. Tina would return this weekend to help her figure out what to do with all the stuff in the house. She made Melissa promise not to even think about it just yet, but that was a hard promise to keep.

Melissa stood and walked to the small closet that her parents shared. She opened the door and fingered her mother's clothes. She pulled out the sleeve of her mom's favorite sweater and rubbed it lovingly on her cheek. This, she would keep. Melissa pulled the faded blue sweater off the hanger and carried it to her room. That night, she slept curled up with the sweater like it was a teddy bear and slept soundly, her body giving into the emotionally draining the day.

One Year Later, January 1, 2013

The first baby of the New Year was delivered just after midnight at Mercy Philadelphia Hospital. It was a long and hard labor, and Melissa was grateful for the chance to sit in the lounge and drink a cup of hot coffee before the next mother-to-be was rolled into the delivery room. Had couples actually planned to try to have the first baby this year? The maternity ward was packed.

That thought brought to mind, once again, something that Melissa had been contemplating for a while now. She reached into her pocket and pulled out the birth certificate she had been carrying around for the past few days. According to the document, Melissa Christina Grant was born on August 10 at Union Memorial Hospital in Baltimore. The document named James and Ann Grant as the adoptive parents, but the actual birth parents were not mentioned.

This was no surprise to Melissa who had always known that she was 'chosen especially' for her parents because 'God knew they would love her the most.' Those were the words she had been told over and over since she was five years old when the truth of her adoption was revealed to her in a gentle and loving way by her parents. But now Melissa had lived for a year without her parents, and she was beginning to wonder if she might not be an orphan after all.

Since there is no time like the present, Melissa decided to start right away on her New Year's Resolution. Once back at the nurse's station, she searched the Internet for information about closed adoptions so that she could see what she was up against. She read about Search Angels, people who assist adoptees in finding their parents. Perhaps such a person could assist her. She clicked on the link and navigated to an online form where she filled in all the information that she knew about her birth. Her hand hovered over the mouse as the cursor sat on the submit button.

"It's now or never," she whispered to herself as she thought about her mother's favorite Chinese proverb, *Pearls don't lie on the seashore. If you want one, you must dive for it.* Her thoughts drifted to the other piece of paper she had found with the birth certificate, one that she had never been shown before. She now carried it in her bag, too, and she resisted the urge to pull it out and read it one more time. It was the only clue she had as to whom she was, and though she didn't take it out and read it, she knew exactly what it said:

Congratulations, Baby Grant. You are a very lucky baby who should know how much your mother loved you. Everything she did, she did for you. Remember her with love. Her name was Meryl Alissa.

Melissa closed her eyes and thought about the mysterious note. The envelope she found it in was mailed from Alexandria, Virginia, on September 1, a little over two weeks after she was born. A chill went down her spine as she thought about how the note ended – *her name was…*

Did that mean that her mother was dead? Did she die in childbirth? If so, her parents had never told her that. Did they even know? Melissa assumed they named her after her mother - a combination of her first and middle names. It was the kind of loving and grateful thing they would do; they were such good people. Was she betraying them by doing this? No, she decided, they wouldn't want her to be alone. She held her breath and hit the button thus setting off an irreversible chain of events.

When her shift ended at 7am, Melissa headed home. She didn't see anything amiss when she opened the door to the dark apartment, and though she hadn't actually entered yet, her sixth sense told her that something wasn't right. The hair stood on the back of her neck, and goose bumps rose on her arms. A slight movement in the mirror just inside the door caught her attention a split second before the small clicking sound and the flash of light bounced out from the reflection. Melissa never saw the flash or heard the muffled shot. The movement was the only warning she needed to duck back out of the door and flee down the stairs of the building.

She could hear footsteps closing in behind her as she narrowly made it out of the building and onto the street. Glancing back, she saw a man dressed in black, a ski mask

covering his face. As he began to run into the shadows of a
nearby alley, fate intervened. A police car happened to
turn onto the street. Melissa flagged the officer down, but
the man had disappeared.

Hours later, after hurling dozens of questions at her, the
policeman dropped Melissa off at Tina's so that she could
rest. She thanked the officer who assured her that she
would be contacted the next day for further questioning.
During the course of the CSI search, the police found a
cheap .38 that, judging by the scuff marks and trail
through the dust, had been hurriedly tossed under a bench
in the apartment entranceway. Based on the professional
break-in and lack of any clues, combined with the fact that
the gun was left at the scene, the officers assumed that
there would be no fingerprints or DNA on the gun and that
the serial numbers would have been filed off. They bagged
the gun and labeled it as evidence. Then the officer in
charge instructed his partner not to touch anything else and
called in Detective Frank Morris and his special crimes
task force. They all wondered why a twenty-six-year-old
nurse would be the target of a professional hit. Unsure of
what this woman might be hiding or who she angered
enough to hire someone to kill her, Detective Morris
decided to keep a close eye on Melissa Grant.

"Does she have a patrol on her?" Frank asked the
officer who had taken Melissa to her friend's.

The officer shrugged, "Refused one, sir."

Frank nodded in annoyance. His team should have been called in ASAP. He hadn't had a chance to question the victim before she was taken to her friend's house, and she had nobody watching her to keep her safe or, if she was involved in something illegal, to catch her in a lie. Frank made a note to get a tail on her right away. He would make a point of questioning her himself as soon as he had a chance to inspect the scene of the crime.

A glass of wine did nothing to calm her nerves, so Melissa decided to take a shower while she waited for Detective Morris to arrive. He had called to tell her he would be there as soon as he finished at her apartment. She dried off and slipped into one of Tina's sweatshirts and a pair of yoga pants and then began towel drying her hair. She could hear the Tina's music playing through the wall at an unreasonable volume. Why did Tina have it so loud? Opening the bathroom door and peeking out through the bedroom to the living room, Melissa's heart began pounding. Through the two open doors, she could make out a man, clad in black, his back turned to her, standing over Tina's limp body. Raising her hand to her mouth to stop her own scream, Melissa slowly opened the bathroom door all the way and eased into the bedroom.

With her heart beating wildly, under the cover of the loud music, she tiptoed toward the bedroom window where the fire escape was. Praying that the man would not turn toward the bedroom, she quietly raised the window while holding her breath and praying it wouldn't make a sound. Not daring to look back, she dropped herself onto the landing, sucking in frigid air and almost choking as her feet hit the icy metal on the fire escape.

Melissa flew down the stairs, slipping and sliding on the smooth, glassy coating of ice. Her bare foot slipped out from under her on the last step sending her reeling back onto the stairs and hitting her head. Looking up, she saw the masked man lean out of the window above her.

Melissa had no time to even check her head for blood as she wrenched herself from the sidewalk and ran for her life.

PART TWO

Every new beginning comes from some other beginning's end.

Seneca

CHAPTER 1

October 16, 2014

The autumn sun hung high above the treetops, glowing like a great flaming fire against the clouds. The migrating Canada geese passed over the trees, their calls echoing through the tiny town of St. Brendan on Maryland's Eastern Shore. October was a quiet time of year in the little town, after the hustle and bustle of the summer tourist season but before the month-long Christmas celebration that signaled the end of another year for the shops and boutiques, some of which closed down for the winter months.

Eric West, owner of Bass & Bucks, put the shotgun back into the cabinet. It was a Benelli 12 gauge, camouflage, with exchangeable barrels for hunting wild game such as the region's white-tailed deer and geese. Eric loved handling that gun, but at almost $3,000, handling it, now and then, to show his customers was all he could afford. While his fishing and hunting store, a dream come true, was successful, it certainly wasn't a cash cow. Money was a bit tight for Eric, especially after spending a small fortune for the store as well as his house just outside of town. But the store was something that Eric owned outright, could manage and make all the decisions about, and set up as he wished. In short, running the store was completely within his control, something he needed more than anything at this time in his life.

Eric locked the gun cabinet as his customer, a newcomer to St. Brendan, walked out. A promise to return had been made, but Eric knew the guy would drive ten miles up the road from St. Brendan to Easton to price the gun at the larger store there, a brand-new sporting goods store that was part of a large retail chain. If not satisfied with the price there, the customer might buy the gun online, though that was becoming increasingly harder to do these days with all of the gun regulations. The customers Eric could count on to buy from him were the boys he grew up with, both the ones who stayed local and the ones who moved away to D.C. or New York but came back home to hunt as soon as the geese started flying south for the fall.

After wiping his fingerprints from the glass on the display case with the rag he kept in his pocket, Eric returned to restocking the fishing lures. While hunting season was about to start, some kind of fishing was perpetually in season, so he made sure he always had an impressive assortment of supplies on hand for anyone who might need them. And being a seaside tourist town with a large commercial fishing fleet and sport fishing industry, there was always someone in St. Brendan who needed fishing tackle.

Satisfied with the display, Eric gathered the boxes from the supply company and flattened them. The town recently started a recycling program, and Eric was doing his part by putting the plastic and cardboard from his deliveries in the

blue recycling can that he hauled to the curb every Friday.
He took the packing materials out the back door, lifted the
lid on the can, and dropped them in. Gunner, his faithful
companion, was at his side. At five years old, the
Chesapeake Bay retriever had ridden life's roller coaster
with Eric since he was a puppy.

Instead of walking back into the shop through the rear
door, Eric and Gunner walked around the side of the store
to the front sidewalk. Standing in front of his shop, Eric
looked up and down the street of his small hometown.
With just over 1,000 people, St. Brendan was nestled
between two interior tributaries of the great Chesapeake
Bay. With a history dating back to before the
Revolutionary War, the town really hadn't changed much
in the past 150 years. Main Street, the only way in and out
of the peninsula, was lined with colonial era houses, many
of them converted into restaurants, tourist shops, and
boutiques. While the hardware store had closed about
twenty years ago, after the large home improvement store
opened in Easton, ten miles away, Eric always believed
that a sporting goods store would fit right in and do well in
St. Brendan.

Just a block outside of the historic district, the local
zoning laws allowed Eric to have more signage and a
fancy exterior, but he knew that his customers didn't care
about that. What they wanted, if they were visitors, was to
know where and what the fish were biting, or where they
could book a hunting excursion. His local customers were
different, and in Eric's eyes, special. They wanted to see
the new line of guns, find their favorite ammo, and grab a

new set of hand warmers. But what they wanted most was to swap hunting tales or tell how many points were on the buck that was spotted running across the road the night before. And, of course, they wanted to enter 'the Contest.'

This was Eric's second hunting season in business, and folks were already talking about the new tradition he started the previous year. Inside the store, Eric hung a large cork bulletin board. Local hunters came into the shop on a daily basis to see the pictures that were posted there each morning. Many locals, young and old, males and females, posted the pictures of their trophies with details about their hunt—the date, time, location, how many points were on the antlers of the bucks, and a story about the hunt.

'The Contest' had become so popular, in fact, that Eric and the other business owners decided to split it in two and offer one prize to be awarded in December and a second one after the entire hunting season ended in April. At the end of each contest period, the stories were all gathered and sent to the local newspaper where the editors would choose the best story and publish it on the front page. Some people were quite creative with their stories while others just gave the facts. Sometimes those were the best ones – fact can indeed be stranger than fiction.

Having grown up in St. Brendan, Eric had many connections. Knowing he needed a catch to bring the locals into his store, rather than the bigger one up the road, he devised 'The Contest' and convinced other shops in town that they could all benefit from it. He was right. Over the summer, when the tourist season was in high gear and business was good in the town, Eric solicited donations for the prize basket that was to be awarded for each contest.

The baskets contained an assortment of hunting supplies that Eric gathered from his suppliers—samples and new products that they were happy to promote to potential customers. The prizes also included gift certificates from local seafood restaurants, favorites of both visitors and locals, and other goodies donated by the shops along Main Street. The Black Market, an old-fashioned general store and butcher, donated one free butchering for the following season. The Sandwich Stop donated a quart of hot soup, and the Coffee Crab donated a heavy-duty thermos that could be refilled for free throughout the season. Other businesses chipped in with fun and fancy items, bringing the value of the baskets to several hundred dollars each. Not only did the Bass & Bucks shop garner more business from 'The Contest,' so too did all of the donors whose generosity was much appreciated by the local hunters and fisherman.

At thirty-five, Eric had a successful year-round business, a mother in good health, a four-legged best friend, and many buddies he could count on.

And that's all I need, he thought as he gazed up and down the street.

He smiled at his neighbors and fellow business owners as they passed by on their morning jog or to pick up their mail at the post office. Yep, Eric was satisfied with his life. At least that's what he told himself every day in order to get himself out of bed. Someday, he hoped, it would actually be the truth.

CHAPTER 2

Julie Lawson pulled over to the side of the road and hopped out of her small, blue Honda. With camera in hand, she looked to make sure there were no cars coming toward her, and then she walked around the car, along the side of the road, to the bridge. Most of the boats had been pulled out of the water and winterized and now seemed to hang in mid-air at the end of the piers along this small creek that ran near the town of St. Brendan.

Julie had never been to St. Brendan, though she had seen signs for it on her drives to and from the famous Ocean City, Maryland's resort town along the Atlantic coast. Julie and her parents often vacationed in Ocean City when she was growing up.

Holding onto her most prized, and almost only, possession, a Nikon D7000 that she was lucky to find and which took exceptional photos, Julie eased herself down the short embankment to the small piece of land just beneath the bridge and squatted down to take a series of pictures. The camera clicked in succession as she depressed the shutter release, rotating the Nikon back and forth in her hand to take the best shots.

Always aware of every movement around her, Julie turned quickly as a Great Blue Heron took off in flight and glided across the water. An expert at capturing a sudden shot at just the right angle, Julie raised her camera back to her eye and followed the heron with her lens as it made its way to the opposite shore. At least one of those shots should turn out nicely, she thought.

Capping the lens, Julie headed back to her car. She took in the scenery around her. She wasn't sure of the name of the creek, but she knew she had to be close to St. Brendan. She drove over the bridge, wishing it was safe to stop at the top to snap a shot of the picturesque view of waterfront homes bordered by red and orange trees along the shoreline.

She drove all the way through the town, not more than a mile and a half she guessed, and pulled off by a ball field at the town's end. She turned around and drove slowly back through the town, looking for a public parking lot, and spotted one about mid-way through the town. She parked and turned off the engine.

Julie grabbed her purse and camera and began looking for a place to eat that was within her budget. There was no shortage of eateries in town, and she soon found a quaint restaurant with an exhaustive lunch menu. She ordered a soft crab sandwich and sipped the glass of water the waitress sat on the table. Her waitress, who introduced herself as Angie, appeared to be in her mid-fifties and was very friendly.

"Passing through?" Angie asked when she returned and placed the plate on the table.

"Kind of," Julie responded. "I'm renting a cottage in town for about a month or so. I'm a photojournalist and am here for the fall."

"Aren't you on the wrong side of the state for fall photos? My niece goes to school in Western Maryland, and that's the place to go for pictures this time of year."

The waitress smiled, and Julie liked her right away. She instantly saw this very pleasant and slightly plump woman with graying blonde hair as somebody's favorite aunt.

"You're right, Angie," Julie smiled back. "That's where all of the photographers will be this time of year, which is why I decided to go in the opposite direction. I like finding the shots that nobody else thinks of."

Angie laughed and winked at her. "Well, you're in luck, sweetie. There's no prettier time of year in this area than the fall. You should check out the dock by the marine museum right around nine in the morning, just as the sun is coming over the trees." Angie closed her eyes, her painted lips curling up in a contemplative bow. She blew a puff of air as she opened her eyes and looked at Julie. "I guarantee you won't find a prettier fall morning than that anywhere else."

"I'll remember that, Angie. Thank you."

Angie told Julie she would leave her alone so that she could eat her sandwich while it was hot, and Julie bit into the best sandwich she had eaten since childhood.

CHAPTER 3

After a delicious lunch, Julie left the restaurant and met the real estate agent at the cottage. It was perfect, just what she'd hoped for. It was small, as the ad described, with one little bedroom, a bathroom with a tub and a showerhead that had been added, and a small kitchen and living room area. Situated at the end of one of the little side streets in town, it gave Julie walking access to the town but also a bit of privacy. She was sure that during tourist season, even this tiny abode would cost a pretty penny, which was another reason she decided to come in the fall when the price of rentals was lower.

After the agent left, Julie tugged on her jacket and went outside to take a walk around the town. She couldn't help but smile at the scarecrows leaning against the light poles and the witches standing guard outside of the local pub which sported window signs promoting a local political candidate. Election Day was just a few weeks away. Julie didn't realize how far she had walked until she came to the other end of town where the buildings were more modern, and the sidewalk only bordered one side of the street. Just a mile or so up the road was the bridge she had crossed earlier on her way into town.

Curious about the amount of traffic coming in and out of a store a little farther up the street, Julie kept walking. A fish and a deer were carved into a painted wooden sign out front with 'Bass & Bucks' written along the bottom. Not her usual haunt, Julie almost turned around but was stopped when she saw a little boy running into the store excitedly waving a piece of paper.

Just walking into Bass & Bucks was a whole new experience for Julie. She gazed at the wall full of fishing lures and was amazed at the large number of colored, feathery objects in the cubbyholes. As she reached for a bright neon yellow lure, she heard a man laugh, and she turned, drawn toward the rich, hearty sound.

Suddenly Julie froze. While half of the store was filled with fishing supplies, the other half was filled with hunting supplies, including guns. Julie began to tremble at the sight of the weapons in the case. Everything else disappeared, and all she could see was the gun display in front of her. All sound ceased except for her beating heart as it rose into her throat with the memory of the 'pifft' sound she tried hard to forget.

"Miss? Can you hear me? I asked if you're okay."

Julie jumped as someone touched her arm. She stifled a scream, and the man saw pure panic in her eyes as she yanked her arm away.

"Are you okay?" he repeated.

The world slowly started to return as Julie stared into his bright green eyes. She calmed her breathing but still couldn't find her voice. She nodded, unable to speak or explain her reaction.

"Water?" the man asked her. Julie nodded again. She closed her eyes and practiced her yoga breathing. Her heart rate began to slow down.

"Here." In a matter of seconds, the man returned. He handed her a paper cup as she opened her eyes. She sipped the cool water as the man continued to stare at her. Then Julie's sixth sense kicked in, and she realized she was being watched. Looking around, she saw the little boy who ran into the store a few minutes earlier and three other men staring at her. She blushed.

"I'm sorry," she whispered and tried to smile. "I was caught off guard by... something...." her voice trailed off.

"It's ok," the man smiled. "Are you alright now?"

Julie nodded. "I think so." She tentatively returned his smile.

"Do you want to read my story?" The little boy reached out the hand that held the paper. "It might make you forget what scared you."

Julie gave the red-haired boy a genuine smile. "If you think it will help, then I should most certainly read it." She took his offering and gazed down at the paper while attempting to hold still her shaking hand and focus on the writing.

On Saturday, me and my dad went hunting for the perfeck deer. I had to be real quiet. It was hard to sit and be quiet in the stand for so long, but I really wanted that deer. I think I fell asleep but then my dad tugged on my sleeve, and I waked up. I looked down and saw a giant buck with lots of points. My daddy aimed his bow and shot but the deer ran away with his arrow still in it. We looked for it for hours until mommy texted daddy to come home for dinner. The next morning my dad found the deer. It will be real good to have it for dinner. By Tommy Wright

Julie handed the paper back to the little boy who she guessed to be about eight. She grinned. "That is quite a story, Tommy. I've never tasted deer, but I bet yours will the best one ever."

"Thanks," he said with enthusiasm. "Here Daddy," he said as he handed it the red-haired man next to him. "Put it on the board."

The man pinned it to the board, and Julie walked over to look. The board had at least a dozen other stories pinned to it, along with pictures. Julie touched one of the pictures, showing a group of middle-school-aged children each holding a goose by its feet in one hand and a gun in the other. The people in the pictures meant her no harm. This was obviously a hunting community, and being around weapons in the hands of good people would only make her stronger. At least that was what she told herself.

"Mommy said I could add a picture after she prints it, but I didn't want to wait."

"I guess not," Julie said. "It's a very exciting story to share."

Tommy looked up at his daddy with pure joy on his face. "See Daddy! I told you it was good. I hope we win."

"I hope so, too, Tommy. But for now, we have firewood to split." The men said their goodbyes, and Tommy and his dad left, followed by the other men.

Julie looked at the man who brought her the water and raised her eyebrow.

"It's a contest," he said.

"Uh-huh. I got that." Julie read some of the other stories. Some were about deer, some about geese, and one was even about a squirrel.

"People hunt squirrels?" She turned toward the man with a look of surprise. It wasn't that she had a great love for squirrels. She just didn't think of them as a meal.

"Yeah, it's a good way for kids to learn to shoot at something small and fast. Mrs. Perkins hands out a pretty good squirrel soup recipe for anyone who wants it. I'd be happy to introduce you." His smile spread across his entire face as he reached out his hand. "But you have to tell me your name first."

Julie's hesitated, but she couldn't resist his warm and honest smile, so she gripped his hand. "Julie Lawson," she said without having to think about it. She was pretty good at that now, telling people her name without pausing to remember it.

"Eric West," replied the good-looking man with green eyes the color of a cat's and close-cut sandy brown hair.

"So, does everyone in St. Brendan participate in 'The Contest'?"

"Everyone *can* participate. They just need to have a hunting or fishing story to share."

"And what do they win?" At that moment, Julie realized she and Eric were still holding hands. She blushed as she pulled hers away.

"Come look," Eric said, seemingly nonplussed by the contact. He led her to a large bushel basket wrapped in cellophane that was behind the checkout counter. A beautiful dog, with fur the color of an old copper penny, looked up at her from a throw rug on the floor. Julie felt her heart tug as she remembered her old pal from years ago. She looked at the contents of the basket and turned back to Eric, obviously impressed by the collection of goodies that awaited the eventual winner.

"Very nice," she said, as she felt heat rise to her cheeks. She realized how close they were standing to each other in the small space behind the counter, much of it taken up by the dog. "Um, I have to go," she said quietly. "It was nice meeting you, but I'd better find my way back to the house before it starts getting dark."

"Are you staying in town?" Eric followed her across the store.

"For a little while, yes. I, uh, I'm not sure how long. I'm, um, taking pictures." She pulled her camera up from where it was hanging around her neck for him to see it. Why was she so nervous all of a sudden? He was being friendly. *He's not trying to hurt you,* she reminded herself.

"For what?" He sidestepped her and blocked the door. She was suddenly confused and self-conscious and had to think about what he was asking. Eric was still smiling, but Julie's nervousness about her inexplicable pull toward this total stranger changed to anxiety. She felt trapped. Seemingly intrigued by her, Eric looked at her like he didn't want her to leave; but then he took a slight step back. Julie wondered if her heightened sense of panic was showing in her eyes. She felt sweat forming on her brow, and her lips began to tremble.

"Um, the pictures are for a magazine. I'm on retainer for a photography magazine." Her breath quickened, and she couldn't think clearly. Eric finally moved out of the entrance of the open doorway, and Julie wasted no time making her exit. Before he could ask her what was wrong, she was gone. She felt him watch her as she walked briskly down the street, and she wondered what had just happened.

*

CHAPTER 4

Julie slammed the door to the cottage shut and bolted it. Like so many houses these days, it had both a lock on the knob and a security bolt. The double lock was one of the very first things Julie noticed when the agent let her in earlier. She leaned against the door and closed her eyes, focusing on her breathing as her yoga instructor had taught her. She couldn't afford a gym membership, but she had lived in St. Louis for a brief time, and was allowed to use a gym in a local community center for free, in exchange for teaching photography to kids.

Though she wasn't a believer in the spiritual teachings of yoga, she did believe in the many health benefits it afforded the student. Clearing her mind, controlling her breathing, and sustaining her level of confidence were all things that Julie valued these days. She continued breathing through her nose, taking deep breaths that filled her chest, then her ribs, and finally her stomach. She exhaled fully until she felt no more breath within her and started on the next breath.

After a few minutes of concentrating only on her breathing, Julie was able to open her eyes and move from the door. She knew that Eric was only trying to be friendly, and she reminded herself that she was safe here. Eric was not after her, not trying to trap her, and not

posing a threat to her. Julie blew out her breath, and
unzipping her lightweight baby blue jacket and sitting it on
the back of a chair as she passed through the small living
room area, she walked to the kitchen.

As she entered the tiny, old-fashioned room, with its
yellow walls and Formica countertop, Julie realized she
forgot to buy groceries before returning to the cottage.
Now she would have to go back out at some point. But the
rush of adrenalin, followed by the deep breathing, not to
mention the long car ride and late afternoon walk, left her
completely worn out. Food could wait.

She wandered through the tiny living space and into the
bedroom. With its sailing décor, the little cottage helped
Julie maintain her calm. The many pictures of water and
sailing vessels added not just charm but peacefulness to
the rooms. Julie slipped off her canvas tennis shoes and
stretched out on the white coverlet. Within minutes, still
wearing her jeans and long-sleeved t-shirt, she fell fast
asleep.

CHAPTER 5

At six o'clock that evening, Eric turned the OPEN sign around and locked the front entrance. He turned off the lights and walked to the back door. He checked one more time to be sure the alarm system was set and headed outside, closing the locked door behind him.

He waited for Gunner to hop into the Ford pickup, slid behind the wheel, closed the door, and headed to his house just outside of town. He waved to the townsfolk he passed who were out for an evening stroll or walking home from work. Turning off the main road, he watched for crossing deer, looking for their evening meal just before dusk.

As he drove down the country road, Eric thought about Julie Lawson, photographer, for at least the twentieth time that afternoon. He wondered about the look he'd seen in her eyes. At some point in the near or distant past, someone or something had scared her, no, petrified her. It was the kind of fear that seared a scar into your heart. He had a similar scar, but his was not from fear. His scar started as heartbreak and moved on to anger, and then acceptance, not a healing, but acceptance nonetheless. From his experience, this kind of scar couldn't be healed by any medicine in the world.

CHAPTER 6

January 3, 2013

Melissa Grant opened her eyes and sat up in the bed. She was fully clothed, disoriented, and unable to place her surroundings. Her heart raced, and fear gripped her. Slowly the images of the past 48 hours came back to her: the movement in the mirror accompanied by a pifft just before the sound of the bullet and the shattering of glass, the masked man running from the building, Tina lying on the floor with blood beginning to pool around her at the man's feet, the same man leaning out the window, unable to pursue her as she fled barefoot down the icy sidewalk.

She closed her eyes and thought about the warmth of the hot cup of coffee she held between her hands at the police station as the officers asked her questions about the day before. Detective Morris and his team had arrived at Tina's apartment to find a dead body, a missing witness, and another gun left at the scene. Melissa had found a sympathetic cab driver who took her to the precinct for free when he saw her bare feet and the fear in her eyes.

Sitting in the police station, Melissa felt as if she were a suspect instead of the victim. So many questions were being hurled at her.

"How long have you lived in that apartment?"

"How long did you know the victim? What was your relationship with the victim?"

"Describe again the man you believe was chasing you. How can you be sure the man who shot at you in your apartment was the same one you saw standing over the victim's body?"

"Did you see the assailant's face?"

"Why do you believe you were the intended target?"

"Why would somebody be trying to kill you?"

"Do you have any enemies?"

The questions went on and on. Melissa didn't know how to answer many of them. She wanted to scream that 'the victim' had a name. She wanted to curl into a ball and disappear. She wanted her mother, alive and well and telling her everything would be okay.

Melissa tried her best to supply answers, but she had questions of her own. Why on earth would someone be trying to kill her? Why would they kill Tina? What had she done to tick someone off this badly? Melissa had many friends and always seemed to be well liked, so why had this happened?

Finally, the questioning, or was it an interrogation, came to an end. Melissa was told, by the detective, that she would remain under police protection for the time being. She was taken to a hotel and checked in, after a quick trip back to her house for a change of clothes and a pair of boots. The only personal thing she grabbed before leaving her apartment was her mother's journal.

Melissa's imagination conjured up an elegantly decorated hotel bedroom with luxurious pillows and a mattress wrapped in Laura Ashley bedding, the kind couple paid extra for on their honeymoon. Except that the man in the next room of the suite was not a groom. He was a uniformed police officer guarding his charge. And the room was a musty-smelling efficiency with peeling paint and out-of-date décor.

As Melissa stretched her arms above her head and arched her back, she heard a noise outside the door. She would never have recognized the 'pifft' if she hadn't heard it as she fled her own apartment the day before. The hair stood on the back of her neck, and she froze in mid-stretch. She closed her eyes and swallowed. *Not again.*

Melissa looked around for a weapon while simultaneously slipping her feet into her boots that she had purposely placed right next to the bed. The doorknob began to turn. Grabbing the lamp and yanking the cord from the wall, she tiptoed to the door. As it opened, she brought the heavy lamp down with a crash, sending the man in black to his knees. As he knelt on the floor and shook his head, she leapt over him. Had the lamp not connected in just the right way, he would have been able to grab her leg as she went by, but she hoped that the hit had caused a ringing in his ears and throbbing of his head that was enough to set him off balance. Luckily, her hit had been right on target and did exactly what she hoped. As the man reached for her, he toppled over and fell back to the floor.

Melissa jumped over the officer's limp body and ran out the door. Screaming for the couple boarding the elevator to hold the door, she rushed inside and watched in panic as the man emerged from the room just as the doors slid shut.

By some miracle, Melissa had done the impossible – by the hand of fate, or more likely, divine intervention, she had escaped a professional hit—not once, not even twice, but three times. She knew without being told that she would most likely not be so lucky again.

CHAPTER 7

October 16, 2014

Julie bolted upright in bed. The room was almost dark as the last of the sun's light sunk behind the little town on the Bay. She was covered in sweat, her body shaking with fright. It took her a moment to remember where she was. She closed her eyes and began her deep breathing.

"It was just a dream. It was just a dream." She repeated her mantra over and over until her body became still and the only thing she felt was her own calm, peaceful breath.

She should have expected the nightmare, but she hadn't intended to go into that deep of sleep. Every time she spent the night in a new place the images re-emerged, as did her panic. Julie wasn't sure she would ever feel completely safe anywhere, and she could never let her guard down. She could never totally escape the terrifying feeling that somebody was always watching. Julie looked around the room and convinced herself that she was alone. She had to keep it together. Her top priority was making sure that Melissa Grant remained dead and that Julie Lawson stayed alive.

CHAPTER 8

October 20, 2014

On Sunday morning, Eric walked down to the dock with his fishing pole and tackle box, Gunner following right behind him. The sun was just starting to rise above the trees, casting its golden glow across the sky that tinged the tops of the trees with oranges and reds that then reflected back from the water. As the sun rose in the sky, the glow crawled across the water until it reached the dock like a sea monster gliding just beneath the current. Eric was thankful every morning that he was able to purchase this piece of property. The big farmhouse was meant for a family, and Eric regretted not being able to fill the many rooms; but he bought it for the location alone. Though he sometimes felt lonely and even a little guilty that he wasn't able to fill the halls with the happy sounds of children, he accepted that this was just not meant to be.

Eric sat on the edge of the dock and let his legs dangle over the side. He continued watching the light show over the trees as the illumination covered the creek, reflecting up like a stained-glass window. The only sounds he could hear were the songs of the geese as they flew overhead in their V formation. This was his church, with all the beauty and splendor of the grand cathedrals he and Elizabeth had visited on their honeymoon in Rome.

While Eric sat there fishing, he knew that his mother would be getting out of bed soon. She would take a shower and put on her Sunday best, and then walk to the Catholic Church a block away from Eric's childhood home. He knew it bothered her that he would not be there with her, but he couldn't walk through those doors anymore.

It wasn't that Eric didn't believe in God. He just wasn't sure that God believed in him. At the very least, he wasn't sure that God heard him. He was certain God wasn't listening two years ago, the last tine Eric tried reaching out to Him. The one prayer that Eric had prayed for almost a full twenty-four hours, over and over, all day and all night, God did not answer.

So, while the rest of St. Brendan got dressed up on Sunday morning and headed to the Catholic Church, the Baptist Church, or the Methodist, Eric headed to his dock. Nobody pushed him to go to church, not even his mother, and he appreciated that they all understood that he needed to work things out on his own.

Feeling the tug on his line, Eric set the hook and reeled in his catch. A six-inch white perch waved to him as he pulled it out of the water, its tail motioning back and forth as it struggled to break loose of the hook. Eric carefully unhooked the fish and threw it back into the water. Most Sundays were like this. It wasn't about catching fish; it was about letting them live. This was his way of telling God, on the day set aside to worship Him, that even a mere mortal could save a life if he wished to.

Watching the little perch glide back through the water and disappear, Eric checked the time. He might not go to church that morning, but he knew his mother expected him to look nice when he showed up for Sunday dinner; so, he would fish a little longer, and then go back into the house and take a shower. His father had passed away ten years earlier when Eric was in college. At the time, Elizabeth had been there to help him get through it. Back then, Eric thought that watching his father being lowered into the ground was the hardest thing he would ever go through in his life. Losing Elizabeth eight years later was worse, much worse.

Knowing he could sit for a spell longer, he checked the bait on his hook and cast his line back out into the water. Gunner raised his ears without lifting his head as his eyes peered at the ripple from the sinker that plopped and disappeared beneath the surface. He slowly closed his eyes again before he lazily rolled over on the dock with the sun on his back. Eric grinned at his dog and loosely gripped the rod while his thoughts turned to the woman from the other day. He guessed she was in her mid-twenties, though he wasn't sure. He wondered what her story was, and then he wondered why he cared. He shook his head to clear his thoughts and tried to picture Elizabeth. Even after all the years they were together, he was starting to have a hard time conjuring her beautiful face in his mind. He knew that was normal. The same thing happened to him for a while after his father died, but the images returned in time. He learned to not try so hard and let it come naturally. That was the hardest part of letting go.

Around nine, Eric reeled in his line, packed up his tackle box, and headed back inside. He left his fishing gear on the back side of the wrap-around porch and went through the mudroom to wash up. The family from whom he bought the house had made many upgrades, including the little room with a sink and changing area. It was the perfect place to enter from the back and wash up without dragging dirt into the house. After Eric moved in, his mother did some decorating, but the house was still sparse with just the few pieces from his D.C. home and the piles of books that were stacked along the walls. There were classics, contemporary fiction, romance novels, political thrillers, legal books, and books on organizing a classroom. He couldn't bear to part with any of them, even though he knew that the romance novels, law books, and teacher resources were just gathering dust. Tossing them out or even giving them away seemed too final.

Eric walked through the living room and passed by the large kitchen, complete with an old-fashioned hearth and fireplace. Every room had a fireplace, some large, some small, but he rarely used any of them. The living room was the only room he really used since his meals consisted mostly of leftovers, courtesy of his mother, and he usually fell asleep on the couch, Gunner sprawled on the floor beside him. On the occasional night he made it upstairs to the master bedroom, he often woke up after a couple hours and moved downstairs to spend the rest of the night. The antique, queen-sized bed held too many memories while at the same time reminded him of too many wasted nights at the office. What a double-edged sword it plunged into him.

Eric climbed the stairs to his room and undressed. A washer and dryer had been installed, at some point, on the second floor, and he tossed his fish-smelling clothes across the hall to the laundry room floor. After showering and shaving, he put a load of dirty laundry from the past week into the washing machine and then left for his mother's house in town.

CHAPTER 9

"Mom," Eric called as he opened the front door that led from the porch into his childhood home.

"In the kitchen," his mother called. Eric could smell the fried chicken she was cooking for dinner.

When Eric was growing up, fried chicken was on the menu every Sunday. Now it was reserved for just a few times a year. Eric's mother was in good health, but his father's heart attack caused her to change her lifestyle completely. Gone were most of the fried foods and the rich desserts. Helen West spent several mornings at the gym, only bought organic food, and subscribed to every health magazine in print. Her husband may have missed out on the best years of their lives, but Helen was enjoying every minute she was able to spend with her grandchildren. Eric's sister, Lisa, lived a few hours away, and the mother and daughter spoke every day. Lisa came home for holidays and special events, and Helen visited the family several times a year.

"Fried chicken?" he asked as he walked toward the kitchen. "It isn't the Fourth of July, and it isn't my birth—" Eric stopped short in the doorway.

"We have company," his mother proudly proclaimed. She turned from the stove, her favorite apron tied around her neck and a pair of kitchen tongs in her hand.

Julie forced a smiled at Eric, but the look on her face told him that she was as surprised to see him as he was to see her.

"Eric, this is Julie," his mother said. "She's renting the Bailey cottage over on Maple." Peter and Shelby Bailey moved to Florida several years back but still kept their house and rented it out to vacationers when their children and grandchildren weren't using it.

"We've met," Eric said with a smile. "Welcome to our home, well, mom's home."

Helen walked over to Eric and kissed him on the cheek. "It will always be your home, too," she said sweetly before returning her attention to the chicken.

"Can I help?" Eric asked.

"I've already offered," Julie told him.

"And I've already declined," Helen smiled. "But you, Eric, can pour us all some iced tea."

Eric took three glasses out of the cabinet and opened the refrigerator to find the tea. This was typical of his mother. She hated for anyone to be alone, including herself, so she always found ways to include others in meals, outings, shopping trips, whatever she was doing or could think to do that could include someone else.

"So where did she find you, and how did she lure you here?" Eric asked Julie as he handed her the glass. "Mom has a habit of bringing home stray people, much to the disappointment of the local stray dogs and cats," he said with a smile to Julie behind his mother's back. He sat at the table in the chair opposite hers and noticed that her

Amy Schisler

hair, in a ponytail earlier in the week, now lay in soft blonde waves beneath her shoulders.

"I was sitting by myself behind Helen at Mass this morning. Helen introduced herself during the sign of peace and asked if I was new to town."

"Say no more," Eric sighed. "It's a story I've heard often." He cast a loving look at his mother as she piled the chicken onto a platter. The look wasn't lost on Julie, and she thought of her own mother. That familiar feeling of loss crept upon her, and she shooed it away like one of those stray dogs Eric mentioned.

Eric was impressed by the fact that Julie had attended Mass while on vacation, or whatever it was she was doing here. While his parents had always insisted on finding a Catholic Church wherever they were in the world on Sundays, most of the people around his age just didn't bother going at all. That was certainly true in his previous life in the city. Things were a little different here in St. Brendan, but not much. For Julie to go to church alone in a strange town that she was just passing through was surprising to Eric, and he felt just a small jab of remorse that he wasn't there beside his mother in the pew. It was the first time he had felt any regret about not going to church in a very long time.

CHAPTER 10

By the time dinner was on the table, there was more food laid out than three people could eat in one meal. In addition to the chicken, there was fresh cornbread, green beans, snapped and steamed to perfection, mashed potatoes, and Helen's favorite, baked pineapple, a recipe passed down to her from her beloved Godmother. Helen made this much food every Sunday, even when she was cooking only for Eric and herself. Helen would lament that she only knew how to cook for a family and what a shame it would be to let it go to waste. Of course, Eric knew this was her way of making sure he was properly fed throughout the week. He was quite good at making a variety of meals out of his mother's Sunday leftovers.

Over dinner, Eric asked Julie about her photography.

"It's just a way to make some money while I travel the country. I don't like to stay in one place for too long, so I take pictures and submit them to a magazine or sell them locally, so I can support myself wherever I happen to be at the time."

"Which magazine?" Eric asked.

Julie's hand froze as she held a slice of cornbread in front of her mouth. She lowered the bread back onto her plate and wiped her mouth with the napkin she pulled from her lap as she contemplated her answer.

"Oh, just a small publication," she said truthfully. "Nothing you would have ever heard of. Would you mind passing the tea, Helen?"

Eric noticed the slight tremble in Julie's hand as she held out her glass and the way she avoided his question.

"Do you always travel alone?" Eric pried, his curiosity piqued. "Who takes *your* picture in all of these places you visit?" He tried to sound playful, hoping she might feel more at ease.

Julie took a sip of the tea and then placed her glass on the table. She looked Eric in the eye as she answered. "I don't get photographed. Ever." She smiled and added lightly with a shrug, "I'm not very photogenic."

Eric disagreed, but he didn't push her. This attractive blonde with her big chocolate eyes and small dimple to the left her mouth was definitely photogenic.

Sensing the shift in the mood, Helen changed the subject to the town's famous legend from the Battle of 1812.

"So, people really lined the docks and boats with scarecrows to make it seem like a vast army was lying in wait?" Julie was fascinated by the story.

"That's what they say," Helen nodded, her smile and twinkling eyes showing pride in the town where generations of her family had lived. "My great-great-great-grandfather was just a boy at the time, and he recorded the whole story in a little journal that's now in the town museum."

"But couldn't the British have just blown everyone away with cannonballs and taken over the town?"

"I suppose they could have, but luckily for us, they thought a whole battalion was waiting for them and would fire back if they took a single shot. The British decided that this little town was not worth a battle. It was a marvelous plan." Helen sighed as she looked at the picture hanging on the wall, a local artist's vision of hundreds of scarecrows, standing guard on the docks and ships around the harbor in the pale moonlight, as a British ship sailed back out into the Chesapeake Bay.

Eric and Julie grinned knowingly at each other. The legend had been in dispute for almost as many years as it had been told, but every August, a celebration was held in honor of the townspeople who fooled the British and saved the town. Julie visited the St. Brendan Museum the day before and couldn't help but wonder at the time if the story was true. When she asked the museum docent about it, the woman was obviously insulted that someone would dare question the authenticity of the town's illustrious history and ingenious role in saving the Chesapeake Bay from the British.

"You should go down to the dock at night to take some pictures," Helen commented. "Some people say you can see the silhouette of the ship on nights with a full moon when the captain returns to see the town in the brighter moonlight so as to not be tricked in the dark."

"I'll have to see when the next full moon is," Julie replied. "That would be some picture, huh?" She smiled at Helen and tried to ignore the way Eric was watching her.

She felt his gaze as he watched her. From the corner of her eye, she thought she saw his slight smile fade and a shadow fall across his face. He blinked and pulled his phone from his back pocket before standing abruptly from the table.

"Eric," Helen scolded. "What's going on? We're still eating and getting to know each other."

"Sorry mom, I've got to go. Fire call."

Eric didn't look at either of the women, and though nobody mentioned it, they all felt the temperature drop in the room. Julie was bewildered. She saw Helen glance at the police scanner that sat silent on the counter. Julie noticed how Eric avoided looking at his mother. She looked at Helen, but the older woman simply bit her lips together as she watched Eric leave the room.

CHAPTER 11

January 4, 2013

Melissa Grant was on the run, but in the twenty-first century, there was no way to hide. An ATM at the Sovereign Bank on Market Street, subway cameras at the 30th Street and Tasker/Morris subway stations, a login at the South Philadelphia Library were just some of the breadcrumbs dropped along the way on Melissa's path.

Melissa thought that she was so smart to sleep in her clothes and keep her wallet on her the night she ran from police custody. She hid in the shadows of the subway until daylight and lingered in a small grocer's store until the library opened. It wasn't until later that she realized she couldn't hide her tracks that easily.

Melissa tried to play it carefully at the library. She had no choice but to use her library card to log onto the Internet and navigate to her Facebook page, but she tried to be smart in her searching. Rather than going straight to the friend she needed, she jumped in and out of people's timelines just as they had all jumped in and out of her life at various stages. She lingered here and there, aware that she needed to complete her task quickly but surreptitiously. She was relieved to see that her friend, Chad, seemed to still be in town. On a recent night out, he mentioned a convention that he planned to attend sometime soon. But according to a post from last night, he had changed his plans.

From the library, she took a bus and then walked to Chad O'Donnell's flat, also the home of O'Donnell Enterprises. Classmates in college, she and Chad had maintained a solid friendship that thankfully allowed him to look past her technical ineptitude. Now, on the verge of creating a search engine more powerful than Google, Chad had a state of the art computer lab and workspace that took up more room in his flat than his living space did.

She banged on the door continuously until Chad opened it, and she pushed her way in.

"Whoa! Where's the fire?" Chad looked out of the door curiously, then shut it and turned around as Melissa grabbed him and pulled him back inside. He looked her up and down, his brow raised in worry. "Oh my God, what happened to you?"

Melissa's hair was a mess, she had no coat, and her face and hands were bright red from the frigid cold that she had somehow been able to ignore until now.

"Lock the door," she commanded. "I need your help, and we may not have much time."

Without asking a question, Chad locked the door and led Melissa into the small, open kitchen area. In the eight years they had been friends, she neither of them had done drugs or been big drinkers. She knew he wouldn't think she was high, but she hoped he wouldn't think she had gone mad.

"You're half frozen. Have some coffee." He placed a large mug in the Keurig machine and popped in a K-cup of the strongest coffee blend he had.

"I appreciate the concern, but I have bigger problems than that, and I may be putting you at risk just by being here." Though she wanted to protest the friendly cup and its invitation to visit, she gladly took the mug and cradled it between her freezing hands.

"I read about Tina in the paper. I couldn't believe it. I'm sorry I haven't called," Chad told her.

"It's my fault that she's dead," she said as her eyes welled up. She looked away and sniffed, blinking back the tears. She turned back and met his eyes. "And I've got to get out of here before they find me again and hurt you, too."

"Melissa, that's crazy. Why on earth would you think someone is after you or that they'd hurt Tina, or me for that matter?"

"It's complicated, but in a nutshell, the guy who killed Tina showed up at my place first." She briefly told him the events of the past few days, concluding with the reason for her visit. Chad shook his head.

"Are you sure you want to do this?"

"Absolutely. Make me disappear."

CHAPTER 12

Sunday, October 20, 2014

Julie strolled down the sidewalk. It was a little after three in the afternoon, but all of the shops were closed. Some had just closed their doors while others had remained shut all day since it was Sunday. The town was quiet, and Julie watched as a leaf was caught by the autumn breeze and skittered down the sidewalk as if out for a stroll itself.

In less than a week, Julie had fallen in love with the town of St. Brendan. Every person greeted her with a smile, whether she had met them or not, and she was treated like she had lived there all of her life. It was the kind of town that was depicted in Hallmark movies and fiction novels, and Julie was fascinated to learn that such places truly existed in this modern world—a town filled with technology and modern gadgets but still faithful to an era that had long passed.

Julie veered off the main road and onto one of the side streets that wound around to a nature trail that ran the length of the town. Part of the trail ran along a creek, and part was shaded by tall pine trees. According to Helen, the trail had been built a few years back to encourage bikers and runners to take advantage of the nature the area had to offer and to help ease pedestrian and bike traffic on the sidewalks and on Main Street. Julie had yet to walk the trail but heard about it from Helen as well as several of the other townspeople. She thought that perhaps she had just enough light left to be able to walk the one-mile trail from its starting point to its end not far from her house on Maple Street.

The walk took longer than she intended, but Julie should have known right away that it would. The trail offered her so many treasures—a large black and yellow spider just beginning its evening work between the railing and roof of a small walking bridge, a heron standing on its nest along the creek (surely not the same one she had seen on the day she arrived, but who knows), the last of the summer flowers in a small garden planted near the trail, a small, centuries old graveyard now neatly hidden from the rest of the world by the overgrowth in the woods by the trail. Julie spent quite a bit of time examining the tombstones, most from the late 1700s. She took several pictures of the setting sun as it disappeared from the horizon and cast a glow around the headstone of Philamon Thomas Hamilton, 1753-1801.

Julie hadn't thought to bring a flashlight with her and now regretfully acknowledged one of the many pitfalls of no longer owning a smartphone. As darkness fell, she picked up her pace, unsure of how much farther she had to go until the end of the trail. Surely it was safe to be out here in the dark at night, right? This was a small town, after all. An owl hooted, and the hair on the back of Julie's neck stood. Once again, she felt that familiar feeling that jump-started her heart to begin thumping in her chest. She was not alone.

Julie began walking faster, gripping her camera by her side, and trying not to lose time by turning around to scan the darkness behind her. The trees seemed to be leaning closer toward her. Were they sheltering her or warning her that danger was close at hand? She suddenly stopped, completely unsure of herself. Had she walked halfway, or was she closer to the beginning of the trail than the end? Should she continue or turn back? She looked up, praying that this would be that night of the full moon they had just talked about that afternoon, but the sky was growing blacker.

Deciding she hadn't walked that far, Julie turned quickly to go back toward the trail's beginning and slammed against something, no, someone.

CHAPTER 13

Julie screamed and tried to run, but he had her locked in his arms. She fought to get away, but he held onto her too tightly. Julie suddenly took the palm of her hand and shot it up into the man's face, ramming it hard into his nose. He loosened his grip, and she kicked him on the shin and ran.

"Dammit, Julie, wait!" a familiar voice called to her.

She stopped and turned back. Eric was bent over, holding his nose. Blood ran down his hand and dripped onto the pavement that marked the trail while the copper colored dog sniffed the red droplets. She ran back to him.

"Oh, my gosh, I'm so sorry, Eric. I'm so sorry."

"Would you stop apologizing and help me?" He lifted his eyes toward hers and continued to catch the blood that was dripping into his hand and dribbling through his fingers. Gunner sat and looked at them, wagging his tail.

"Some watchdog and guardian you are," Eric said. The tail moved faster in agreement.

Julie unwrapped her scarf, thankfully an inexpensive one she bought at Wal-Mart, wadded it up, and handed it to Eric. He held it against his nose and straightened up.

"Where on earth did you learn to do that?" He might have been angry, but his eyes and voice conveyed curiosity as well as respect.

"I took a self-defense course about a year or so ago. A girl can never be too safe," she offered, apologetically.

"I'd say you have nothing to worry about," Eric smiled. Relief washed over Julie but died as she watched him wince in pain.

"I really am sorry. Do you need to go to the hospital? I can drive you."

"No, I just need to sit down, and get some ice. I've broken it before. I don't think it's broken this time. But it could've been," he added as he locked eyes with her.

"Thank Heaven," she breathed a sigh of relief before coming to her senses about the situation. "Wait a minute," she said as she started to draw back away from him. "Were you following me? What are you doing out here?"

"Yes, and no," Eric hesitated. Julie regarded him carefully and backed up a little more.

"Which is it? Were you following me or not?" she demanded.

"Not at first." She waited for him to continue. "I come down here in the evenings sometimes. It's quiet, and it…" he closed his eyes and sighed. "It brings back memories, good ones that I'd like to hold on to."

"I can understand that," Julie said honestly. Eric pulled his cell phone out of his pocket and turned on the Flashlight App. Following his lead, Julie walked with him in the direction of the trail's end.

"I saw you taking pictures. To be honest, I was intrigued. You chose interesting subjects and took pictures at different angles that I would not have thought of. I was enjoying my little photography lesson so much that I didn't realize it was getting dark."

"That makes two of us," she smiled. The night was quiet with just the occasional sound of the owl overhead. Gunner led the way in the zigzag fashion of a dog on the trail of something interesting, his nose bent to the ground, his tail wagging.

"Once I realized you were going to have to go home in the dark, I became concerned. St. Brendan is a great town, a safe town. We don't have much crime or sexual attacks or any of that sordid stuff, but there's always a first time...." Eric's words hung in the air. They both knew what he meant.

"You were worried about me," Julie whispered in surprise, not looking at Eric.

"Yeah, but I guess I didn't have to worry," Eric chuckled and then winced in pain once again. "Over here," he motioned as he turned off the trail and into the trees. "Gunner, come." The dog, who was a little farther ahead, turned around and locked step with Eric.

They left the paved trail and came upon a dirt path. Pushing aside stray, willowy branches here and there, they moved through the trees toward a clearing ahead.

"Where are we going?" Julie asked, but her question was answered as soon as asked. The dirt path ended to the left of the cottage.

"I was so close," she said in amazement.

"Yeah, the trail runs just beyond the trees at the end of the streets on this end of town. You can find a dirt path that leads out to almost every road."

"I guess my sense of direction isn't as good as I like to think," she smiled at Eric, and her heart did a tiny flip, just a tiny one, but she noticed it just the same. She swallowed and tried to push the feeling away.

CHAPTER 14

Julie walked up to the front door and slipped the key out of her blue jean pocket.

"Come on," she waved her arm in a beckoning gesture. "Let's get you cleaned up and put some ice on that nose."

Eric hesitated but then followed her into the house, Gunner at his side. He had never been inside the cottage but had visited it every year as a kid on Halloween.

"This house had quite a reputation when I was growing up."

"Oh yeah?" Julie asked as she took an ice tray from the freezer and twisted it until the small blocks popped out. She piled them onto a dishrag and refilled the tray before putting it back into the older model refrigerator. Eric settled into a kitchen chair.

"Here, I don't have any baggies, so hold it tight, or the ice will fall out."

"Thanks." He took the dishrag from her and tilted his head back with the ice against his nose. Julie's bloodied scarf was sitting in Eric's lap, and he handed it to her when he saw her gaze drop to it. She rinsed the scarf in the sink and let the water run to fill the basin in order to soak it. She thoroughly washed her hands in the flowing water, in the manner of a surgeon, and then took a bowl from the cabinet and filled it with water for Gunner as Eric continued to speak. "The Baileys gave out whole Hershey bars every Halloween. Their house was a favorite stop for everyone."

Julie smiled and sat down next to him. "Oh, the little things. 'It has long been an axiom of mine that the little things are infinitely the most important.'"

Eric moved the ice and dropped his head so that his eyes met hers. "Sir Arthur Conan Doyle."

Julie's grin widened, and her eyes opened in surprise. "You *know* that quote?"

"I know everything he ever said or wrote. Are you a Sherlock fan?"

"Only the *real* Sherlock, the one in the books, not the ones portrayed on TV and in the movies."

"I couldn't agree more." Eric tilted his head back again and put the ice back on his nose. "Though the BBC show is pretty good," he said through the damp cloth covering his face.

"Actually, I do like that show," Julie said in agreement, "but I kind of have this thing for classics, and old movies, and quotes."

He opened one eye and looked at her over his swelling cheek. "Quotes?"

"Yeah, my mom used to have a book she kept, a kind of journal I guess. She always wrote down her favorite quotes. I used to look through it and read them. Many of them I memorized. Those little pieces of someone else's brain that are still stuck in my own are all I have left of her." She looked away, a wistful look on her face.

"I'm sorry," Eric said. He reached across the table and placed his hand over hers. It was so spontaneous that he hadn't even realized he had done it. Julie looked at their hands for a moment, the dried blood dotting his fingers and back of his hand, and then pulled hers away.

She stood up and cleared her throat. "So, how's the patient?"

"I think I'm okay." Eric removed the dishrag and felt his nose. He winced.

"Maybe you should have it checked out," Julie suggested. "A broken nose isn't always obvious and can be serious. Damage to the lining of the septal cartilage can result in blood pooling inside the nose, which can lead to an abscess or a permanent deformity. If left untreated, the tissue in the nose can actually rot and die."

Eric stared at Julie. "Are you sure you aren't really Dr. Watson?"

Julie's eyes widened and her nervously licked her lips. "Just a fan of *ER* reruns," she laughed uneasily and then added, "It's getting late. Are you sure you can make it home?"

"Damn!" Eric slapped the table. "My truck is at the head of the trail."

"I can drive you," Julie said as she jumped up from the table. "I'll get my jacket." She hurried from the room. Eric followed her with his eyes as he wondered what secrets she was keeping.

CHAPTER 15

January 5, 2013

Elaine Smith, no longer known as Melissa Grant, boarded a bus to New York City, dressed in a man's shirt and jacket and wearing a Chicago Bears baseball cap that Chad had reluctantly given to her. Though Chad's clothes were too big for her, the January climate made the extra bulk less noticeable. Her new haircut wasn't quite stylish, but it was short and, thanks to Clairol, a soft shade of red. She already had an efficiency, rented in yet another name, waiting for her in New York that Chad had managed to find and pay for without linking the money to Melissa Grant. She didn't ask how and didn't want to know.

Though nervous and unquestionably afraid, Elaine couldn't stifle the thrill she felt about her new life and the new journey she was starting. She knew that, even if the plan was successful, she would never stop looking over her shoulder, never feel completely safe, and always wonder why she became the target of an unknown assailant, but so far she was still alive, and for that she was immensely grateful.

As Melissa, she and Tina loved to take short trips to New York, and over time, she had learned her way around the city. After exiting the bus station, Elaine headed straight toward Rockefeller Plaza. She pulled the hood of the oversized sweatshirt she wore under Chad's coat up over her head and down in front to obscure her face.

Ignoring the hustle and bustle of the city, Elaine avoided 7th Avenue and the famous Times Square. Quickly glancing toward what was usually her favorite stop in the Big Apple, she imagined the tourists and school groups waving to themselves on the jumbotron. The last thing she wanted was to have her face on a thirty-five-foot-high screen in the busiest district in the world. She kept her head down as she passed through Herald Square; for once, the familiar show tune did not play in her mind. She shuffled her way past the lunch crowd going into the famous Legends restaurant and continued past the Empire State Building.

Oblivious to the cold, Elaine kept up her pace as she passed Bryant Park and the famed New York Public Library. She couldn't help but smile at the memory of the time that Tina and she spent trying on fancy dresses just for fun at Saks Fifth Avenue the prior winter. Passing the building known as The Rock, she remembered skating with Tina in the sunken ice rink that, at this moment, was probably packed with children holding on to skate walkers, couples embracing each other on the ice, and little girls with Olympic dreams, twirling and leaping their way through the crowd. Elaine kept walking until she was standing in front of one of the most famous cathedrals in America, St. Patrick's.

Elaine was raised Catholic, but college, work, and life in general had become more important to her than practicing her faith. She vowed that, from this day forward, that would change. She entered the church and dipped her finger into the holy water, blessing herself as she moved toward one of the side altars where she could pray in private. Surrounded by ninety-four stained-glass windows, depicting scenes from the Bible, Elaine knelt before the altar of Saint Elizabeth Ann Seton. Mother Seton was the first American canonized a Saint by the Catholic Church. Seton had been baptized at St. Patrick's, but her life as a Catholic and the convent that she founded and became her legacy were in Maryland, not far from Elaine's childhood home in Baltimore.

Elaine began to pray, thanking God for allowing her to get this far. She prayed for her parents, who she believed were watching over and protecting her. She prayed that Tina was at peace. She prayed for Chad's safety, and she prayed for forgiveness for the laws they broke to ensure her own safety. Finally, she prayed for guidance and protection. Not until she was finished did she realize she was crying. Her cheeks and chin were wet, and the armrest where her hands were folded in prayer glistened from her teardrops.

Wiping her face and standing up, Elaine made a promise to never again miss her Sunday obligation of attending Mass. She hefted her backpack onto her shoulders and took a deep breath. She remembered an old familiar saying and told herself that this was indeed the first day of the rest of her life.

CHAPTER 16

October 30, 2014

From an early age, Julie had an eye for photography. She had owned a camera for as long as she could remember – the first one was a Christmas present from her grandfather when she was just eight-years-old. It was a Nikon Zoom 300 QD that could fit in her pocket and took surprisingly good photos for a small, auto-focus camera. From that time on, Julie rarely was without a camera, though admittedly she more often used a phone camera throughout high school and college.

After she left her home in Philadelphia and hit the road, Julie bought her Nikon D7000 to avoid having to get a regular job, but also for sights such as this. It was close to 6:30 in the morning, and Julie sat on the dock which overlooked the St. Brendan harbor. The sky was awash with oranges, reds, and yellows. The boats that were tied to the docks glowed with a peach hue that reflected on the still water beneath them. To her left, Julie watched through her lens as the colors traveled up the St. Brendan Lighthouse, bathing it in rich color until its own brilliant white clapboards and red roof shone over the Bay in the sunlight.

Today marked two weeks since Julie's arrival in the little town, and she already felt as if she had always been part of the town's history. Everywhere she went she was greeted with smiles, waves, and well wishes. She ignored that little voice inside warning her that she should remain in the shadows. She was so tired of that voice.

Julie thought back to the previous Sunday. After Mass, Helen West had approached her with a request to come by the church later that day to photograph the collection of quilts that the quilting ministry was getting ready to donate to the assisted living facility in Easton. She tried to turn down the money they offered to her, but they insisted. The pay wasn't much, but it helped. Julie tried to spend only what she earned, knowing that the money she had hidden away needed to be reserved in case of emergency. She had encountered plenty of those in the past couple years.

She delighted in taking the pictures as much as the women delighted in posing with their beautiful works of love, and the edited photos were a testament to their creative abilities. She wondered what it would be like to live in this town, to share in the special bond that all of these people had with one another, to be free to live without fear or secrets and be able to share with others her life and the things she had been through over the past two years. Sadly, Julie knew she would never know the answer. By the time the winter was over, she would need to move on, if not sooner. It was too dangerous to stay in one place for too long. Already she was starting to worry that her face was becoming all too familiar to everyone and that she would be recognized.

Sighing, Julie stood from the dock and stretched. The sun had risen into the sky, and she was ready to see more of the area. She was going to explore some of the back roads today. After seeing the area, she planned to return to the cottage and download the many pictures onto her laptop to see what treasures her camera may have discovered.

CHAPTER 17

Eric was standing in his kitchen, eating a bowl of cereal for breakfast. He was too restless to sit down and ate quickly despite having a couple more hours before it was time to open the shop. He put the bowl in the sink to wash later and looked out the window toward his dock. So many questions ran through his mind.

Over the course of the past couple weeks, Eric spent all day wondering if Julie might wander back into his shop. She had not been there physically since her first day in town, but in his imagination, she was there. And everywhere else Eric went. He felt her presence all the time, and it bothered him. He had no desire to be with her or get to know her. She was just passing through, and he had a business to run and a life he was beginning to become comfortable with.

So how could he explain the urge to see her, get to know her, learn her secrets, and share his own secrets, dreams, and wishes with her? What was it that forced him to spend so many hours on his laptop trying to accomplish what now seemed impossible – discovering just who is Julie Lawson?

Eric's Google search yielded 18,700,000 results when he typed in her name. Of those, there were several college professors, a handful of lawyers, a champion horseback rider, a best-selling author, and even a photographer with a gallery of beautiful photos. However, none of these was the Julie Lawson currently staying in the Bailey cottage. Shouldn't a serious photojournalist at least have a web site? And how come there were no bylines with her name giving her credit for any photos in any magazines, books, or web sites? As far as Eric could tell, there were none.

Adding to his curiosity was the look of panic and fear that he had seen those few times he was with her. That first day in the shop, the night he frightened her on the trail, and later in the cottage when he mentioned her sounding like a doctor. He saw true terror in her eyes on each of those occasions, which was inexplicable to him.

Narrowing his search, Eric looked for 'Julie Lawsons' with a medical background. There were over twelve million hits, but none of them seemed to be the right match. Nor were any of the ones he found on Facebook or Google Plus. The photographer's profile on Linkedin was not hers either. It seemed as if the Julie Lawson now staying in St. Brendan had never existed before she drove into town and began to occupy his thoughts like a ghost, haunting the recesses of his mind. Was she a ghost? An angel? A walking, talking figment of everyone's imagination? Or could she be a fugitive? One of the many mugshots on *America's Most Wanted*?

One thing was certain, at least in the ubiquitous world of the Internet, Julie Lawson, photojournalist and visitor to St. Brendan, did not exist.

CHAPTER 18

Julie drove down several of the winding, country roads that traced the contours of the shoreline of the various creeks and coves around St. Brendan. There was beauty everywhere, from the barren fields where flocks of geese stood, bordered by tall pines and stately oaks, to the little harbors where workboats hauled in the daily catch of the season – Chesapeake Bay oysters. Stopping at a seafood distributor on the edge of a creek, Julie watched the men in tall, white rubber boots and rubber overalls, which she remembered reading somewhere were called oilskins. They lifted the heavy baskets of freshly hand-tonged oysters from the boats and onto the docks.

Grabbing her camera, Julie got out of her car and walked toward the dock.

"Do y'all mind if I take some pictures?" She smiled at the sound of her own voice, a country inflection and dialect that had already begun to creep into her Yankee speech.

"Good mornin' Miss Julie." A young waterman waved with his rubber-gloved hand. Julie recognized him as one of the guys who frequented the Chestnut Street Saloon, a local favorite, known as C-Street, that was half bar, half restaurant – a darn good restaurant, too, Julie was told. Julie often saw the men walking into and out of the establishment when she was walking through the town in the mornings. Once again that little voice warned Julie that her presence was becoming too well known if the men who gathered for breakfast were talking about her.

"You're takin' pictures for a magazine, I hear. Tom Hamilton, nice to meet you." The older gentleman, standing by a conveyor for loading oysters into a large tank, extended his hand to her. Julie wondered if he was a descendant of the same Hamilton whose gravestone she photographed along the trail. There was no doubt this man was the father of the younger man unloading the oysters from his boat. They shared the same square-cut jaw, high forehead, sparkling blue eyes, and welcoming smile.

Julie shook his hand. "Nice to meet you, too, Mr. Hamilton." He blushed.

"Aw shoot, honey, nobody calls me that. It's just Tom." His smile would melt any girl's heart, she thought. "You can take all the pictures you want. We've got a few bushel baskets of crabs in the walk-in if you'd like to take some pictures of those. You missed the height of crabbing season, but this here's when they're at their finest, big and heavy. And we've got boatloads of oysters coming in this morning. At least I hope we do." He winked, and she understood his meaning. Even Julie knew that life as a waterman was getting harder and harder these days as demand grew and supply shrank.

"Thank you," she smiled back. "I'll make myself invisible and take pictures of you'll at work if that's okay."

"Okay by me," his son called as he climbed out of the boat, "but it's going to be mighty hard for you to be invisible." His wink matched his father's, and Julie found that she was the one blushing this time.

For an hour or so, she took pictures of the father and son, unloading several boats as they arrived at the dock. They loaded the trucks with the haul that would be distributed all up and down the coast. The rest were put in the walk-in to keep them cool. While Julie tried to stay out of their way, the men talked and laughed, teasing each other by telling Julie stories about their family and the small town lives they lived and loved. They also talked to Julie about the life cycle of oysters, how they were caught, where they were taken and sold, and the many ways of cooking and eating them.

By the time Julie was ready to move on, her stomach was growling. She wasn't sure if she was hungry because of the time of day or because of the delectable descriptions of the dishes the men described. She may have to stop by C-Street for lunch and see if oysters were on the menu and if the food there was as good as everyone said it was.

After thanking the men for the time and attention they gave her, she got back into her car and headed toward town. Halfway up the country road, she saw no less than a dozen deer standing in a field. They stood as still as statues amidst the stubble that was left from the corn that must have been just harvested. Julie slowed down and carefully pulled to the side of the road. Lowering her window, she reached for her camera and raised it ever so slowly to her eye.

The deer watched her without moving. Their glassy, black eyes met hers, and now and then, an ear would twitch, or a nostril would flare with the rhythm of their breathing. Julie snapped picture after picture until another car drove by, ignoring the deer standing by the road. She supposed that the locals were so used to the deer that the creatures became just another part of the landscape that raced past the windows as they drove by.

In an instant, all of the deer leapt from their stances and ran toward the woods. Julie continued to shoot them until they were gone. The last thing she saw of the deer was a scattered line of waving, white tails as the deer disappeared into the trees.

CHAPTER 19

After a fried oyster sandwich at the C-Street Saloon, which was as good as promised, Julie went home and opened her laptop. Though it was a good quality laptop, and had wireless capability, Julie didn't use the wireless offered as part of the rental agreement. She never went online even though she had been assured that the laptop had been rigged with an untraceable IP address.

She received all her news from television. She had no family or friends back home with whom to keep in touch. For Julie, life was one big train ride with lots of stops along the way and another station always on the horizon.

The only person with whom she ever made regular contact was the photo editor of a small photography magazine. The editor always recognized her photos when they arrived by unmarked envelope. Her paychecks were direct-deposited into a bank account in the Bahamas that, now, only the two of them knew existed. She sometimes shed a tear as she slid the photos into the envelope, remembering the friend they both lost.

Julie looked at the photos she had taken that day. The sunrise pictures she took in the morning were beautiful. They always were. That was one thing that could always be guaranteed—sunrise pictures are never bad or boring. One could take the same pictures of the same landscape every day at sunrise for an entire year, and each day's pictures would be slightly different, but just as beautiful, as the ones from the day before.

After some fine-tuning, Julie moved on to the pictures from the crab house. There were several of the father and son at work, a handful of the crab house inside and out, a few of the crabs that Tom had been insistent on showing her, as well as shots of the oysters in the baskets. Julie thought of sending them to *Chesapeake Bay Magazine*, a publication that seemed to be on the shelves of every store in the town; but she was sure they published dozens of similar layouts and stories over the years, and the magazine may not be interested in more. And then, there was the question of which name she would attach to them and how she would be paid. She shook her head. For now, she would hold onto them and think about what to do with them that would pay tribute to this dying breed.

Pulling up the deer pictures, Julie was amazed at what she had captured. As she went through them, it occurred to her that these were more than just pictures of deer in a field. They told a story of beauty and survival. The tawny colored fur almost blended with the empty field and bare trees, but the black eyes stood out and spoke to the viewer. Julie's favorite photo was the last one. Barely visible among the brown tree trunks were the white tufts that waved like flags just before they vanished into the woods.

Julie saved her pictures to a flash drive and grabbed her purse. Donning her dark sunglasses and Orioles cap, she smiled as she headed to Easton to have them developed. She couldn't wait to send a stack of photos to *American*

Photography. She loved the way these pictures told a story, and she hoped that Earl Mueller would agree.

CHAPTER 20

January 6, 2013

The Housekeeper stood over the mess on the floor of Chad O'Donnell's flat. He surveyed the rest of the apartment to see what other cleaning needed to be done. He was the best in the business. He was also very expensive. Thus, he only worked for the richest and most powerful people, and he had received a call earlier that morning from one of them that his services were needed to fix the mess left behind by another hired hand. He was an expert at cleaning up behind others and ensuring that no trace evidence would remain after he left.

It was well known that O'Donnell was on the fast track to be the next Larry Page of Google fame, though his age was closer to Facebook's Mark Zuckerberg. Facebook and Google, as well as Amazon, had all started in garages before becoming the biggest and fastest growing technology giants in the world. Looking around at the equipment, notes, and prototypes in O'Donnell's computer lab, it seemed that this David was preparing to slay all of those Goliaths. The Housekeeper was not impressed. He had many clients with vast power and prestige. This young man's intelligence and business endeavors held no interest for The Housekeeper, but the information on his

computers might hold some insights for the powerful man
who was paying for this job.

He called his crew to come in and get to the task at
hand. They used the back door, as always. Those who
hired him insisted upon it. Discretion was the key.
Actually, there were three things that The Housekeeper
insisted upon from his crew that kept his clients happy—
haste, confidentiality, and perfection.

The Housekeeper ordered that the heavy garbage bag
and its contents were to be taken out and dumped. The
floors and all other surfaces were to be mopped and wiped
with oxygen bleach, which contains a different formula
than household bleach, enabling it to hide all stains, even
those ordinarily detected by Luminal. No evidence was to
be left that would reveal that anybody had been inside of
the flat other than O'Donnell.

When the entire area was clean, The Housekeeper made
a phone call.

"It is done." He paused for any further instruction but
was asked a question that insulted his intelligence and
competence. "Of course, we were discreet," he snapped.
His obvious annoyance was met with a moment of silence
on the other end before the client finished their
conversation. "Very well," The Housekeeper said and
ended the call.

"We are finished here. A tech team is on the way to get
what they need from the equipment. Leave now."

The team exited through the back door hastily and
quietly, leaving a perfectly clean flat behind them. The

Housekeeper had once again successfully and flawlessly cleaned up after someone else's mess.

CHAPTER 21

October 31, 2014

Julie woke up on Halloween and truly felt like she had awakened in a horror movie, her own nightmares notwithstanding. Looking outside, she could see absolutely nothing but thick, white fog. The ghostly scene was unlike anything she had ever experienced. She turned on the small television in the little sitting room and saw a stream of school delays running across the bottom of the screen. School delays because of fog? Was this normal?

After a quick breakfast of Greek yogurt mixed with fresh fruit (as fresh as could be had this time of year) and green tea, Julie left for the gym. She was willing to spend the small, one-time fee for the yoga class just to keep up her practice. No matter what headlight settings she used, the fog was impossible to see through. She drove as slowly as she could, through the town, and kept a close watch for pedestrians crossing the street. Pulling into the parking lot, she noticed very few other cars. The whole town seemed to have slowed down as if the fog truly had a pea soup consistency that forced everyone to sluggishly wade through it. She understood why schools were delayed.

As Julie was getting out of her car, she heard the siren go off at the fire station next to the gym. No doubt, there was a fog-induced accident somewhere nearby. As she had done since childhood, Julie recited the Hail Mary in her head, praying for the victim and the first responders. She remembered Eric mentioning something about a fire call before he left his mother's that Sunday a couple weeks back. Helen had filled Julie in with the information that Eric was one of the town's volunteer firefighters. Was he on his way to the accident?

Once inside the studio, Julie spotted Helen warming up. Julie grabbed a yoga mat and spread it out beside the limber, older woman. She was very grateful that Helen had mentioned the class after Mass the previous Sunday when she and Julie stopped to chat.

"What is the deal with the fog?" Julie asked as she bent and stretched. "I feel like I'm trapped in a cheesy *Halloween* movie-sequel."

"Oh, this?" she waved toward the window. "Nothing out of the ordinary here. The low-lying fields sandwiched between all of the waterways tend to be the perfect haunting grounds for thick fog. No pun intended," she smiled.

"This is normal?" Julie asked in amazement. "How often does this happen?"

"Only on Halloween," Helen drew out her response in a creepy voice reminiscent of Bela Lugosi. Seeing the look of shock on Julie's face, she laughed. "It happens often. Mostly in the fall, but really any time that the wet ground and creeks are warmer than the night air. You'll get used to it."

Julie wasn't so sure. Something about the fog made her uneasy, and it wasn't because of the ambulance that screamed as it passed by. Julie was sure that her subconscious would incorporate fog into her next nightmare.

CHAPTER 22

Eric looked out the window of the shop later that same day. It was almost five o'clock, and soon the town would be full of friendly ghosts and goblins running up and down the streets on a mission for candy. He flipped the 'Open' sign around and locked the front door. It had been a slow day in the shop, which was good since Eric had been tied up for most of the morning, helping at the scene of the accident. An elderly woman, already nervous about driving to her doctor's appointment in the fog, misjudged the distance of the car in front her and rear ended it when it slowed down to turn. That wouldn't have been so bad if two other cars hadn't followed her lead and continued with the rear-ending as a result of the low visibility. While feeling sorry for the people involved, Eric hadn't regretted the time spent with his mind on something other than a certain female.

Of course, the guilt now plagued Eric as he wandered through the store making sure everything was in its place. The feeling was not a new one. He had felt guilty many times over the past couple years, but this was guilt of a different kind, and he didn't know how to handle it. It was the first time in many years that Eric had thought about another woman.

Standing in the dark room, Eric looked up toward the ceiling and let out a long, heavy sigh. Was Elizabeth up there somewhere in the great beyond watching him? Did she know that this feeling of self-reproach was tormenting his heart and mind? He closed his eyes and clenched his teeth. He'd spent the last two years feeling guilty—guilty that he had worked too much, guilty that he let Elizabeth down, guilty that he hadn't done his job well enough to make her safe. She was gone, and he was still here living a life he never imagined for himself, a life in which he was alone.

And there's the rub, as the Bard would have said. For the first time in two years, he was beginning to think that perhaps he didn't have to be alone. Whether this woman, who had suddenly entered his life, was someone he was supposed to be with or not, she certainly opened his mind to the possibility that there might be someone else out there for him besides the one woman he considered his soul mate. Could lightning strike twice? How would he ever know if he didn't allow himself to face the storm?

Those questions continued to nag him as he left the shop and headed to the grocery store across the street to pick up some candy bars.

CHAPTER 23

Halloween has always been a tradition embraced by small towns across America. St. Brendan was no exception. While the kids saw the holiday as a chance to dress up and parade through the streets, asking for candy, adults saw it as a time to catch up with their neighbors, sit for a while on the front porch with a mug of apple cider (or a bottle of beer), and observe the never-ending circle of life.

Children who once dressed as witches, ghosts, and superheroes seeking treats were now adults, giving out candy bars to robots and rock stars. Many of them grew up right here, watched their children grow up on these streets, and now watched as the offspring of their own children's peers paraded down the sidewalks. St. Brendan was a town where every porch light was on, and old friends were greeted with baked goods and hot drinks as they walked with their children and grandchildren.

Julie couldn't remember ever experiencing a Halloween quite like this one. Thankfully, the fog cleared by mid-morning, and this evening, smiling, laughing children and their parents filled the sidewalks, roads, and yards. Local police strolled the streets, handing out glow sticks and stopping the few cars on the road so that youngsters could safely cross. Everyone waved and called out to one another. Julie felt like she was living in another time.

Remembering what Eric told her about the Bailey cottage reputation, Julie splurged and bought dozens of candy bars. But she now feared that she would run out. She had no idea this many children lived in the small town!

When she had only three candy bars left, Julie began wondering what else she might have in the house to hand out to the many children still coming down the street. She stood up from the swing and was about to go inside when she heard a familiar voice.

"How's the candy supply?" Eric asked as he and Gunner came up the front walk.

"I'm about to break out the oranges," Julie turned and shrugged.

Eric held up a grocery bag that looked like a piñata ready to explode. Julie laughed. "You're a lifesaver!"

Eric ascended the steps and poured the bag of candy bars into the almost empty bowl. "Mind if Gunner and I join you?"

"How can I say no? I imagine you saved me from the toilet paper gang tonight."

"Nah, that's old school," he said as they sat on the porch swing and placed the bowl between them. "These days you'd wake up to find your car completely wrapped in Saran Wrap. It's almost impossible to break through when done right."

Julie just stared at Eric for a moment. "Are you serious?"

Eric laughed. "Yeah. I've seen it happen. It's a popular teen prank around here."

Julie shook her head as Harry Potter, an iPhone, and a box of popcorn appeared. "Trick or Treat!" Julie praised their costumes as she gave them candy.

"The costumes here are amazing. Do they spend months working on them?"

"Some do," Eric said as he snagged a Hershey Bar and started unwrapping it. "Abby, down the street, was a can of Old Bay Seafood Seasoning last year. Coolest costume I've ever seen. Want a bite?" Julie accepted the piece of chocolate as she imagined the little girl dressed as Maryland's famous seafood seasoning. Abby and her mother, Kari, had delivered home baked cookies the day after Julie arrived in town, and Julie liked them both instantly. People who baked cookies for a new neighbor didn't exist everywhere in the world these days, and Julie had been lucky to meet just a few of those special people in her lifetime. Her thoughts strayed to her mother who always welcomed new neighbors with a basket of homemade bread, a bottle of wine, and a canister of salt, wishing the family prosperity, joy, and flavor in their new home.

"My parents would have loved it here," she said. Eric's eyebrows rose with piqued curiosity.

"Where did you grow up?" He asked.

"Um, not far from here." Julie hesitated and began scraping across her lower lip with her teeth as she looked away. "I'm sure you've never heard of it." Why, after having been asked that question so many times over the past few years, was she suddenly finding it hard to lie? Was it this place, this life, or this man?

"Try me," Eric coaxed.

"Trick or Treat!" Saved by a set of salt and pepper shakers, Julie stood and gave them candy. She spent several minutes swooning over their costumes, using the distraction to her advantage.

"Where are they all coming from?" she asked as another group came up behind the shakers.

"From all the farmhouses and little villages between here and Tilghman." Eric referred to the island located at the end of the peninsula. "Where they live, the houses are too far apart, or there just aren't enough houses in the village to make a whole evening of it. Everyone is always welcome in St. Brendan. We're all family here." His eyes met hers, and Julie knew that Eric was not just referring to Halloween.

"So, the fire call you got that day at dinner, what was that about?" Julie asked. "How can you be a fireman and own a business? Who covers the store when you're on duty?"

Eric seemed caught off guard for a moment, but he recovered quickly.

"A lot of us volunteer for the fire department around here. If somebody can't make it to a call, there's usually another guy able to fill in. Most of us try to go on all of the calls, though."

"Volunteer?" Julie raised an eyebrow. "You mean you don't get paid to fight fires?"

Eric laughed. "Not around here we don't. That's the way it is in most small towns. The town can't afford paid firefighters. Most of these guys have been volunteering their whole lives. Some of them are retirees from some big city fire departments. Some of the younger guys end up moving away to a city with paid firefighters to make a career. Either way, small towns couldn't survive without volunteer fire and rescue crews."

Julie nodded, impressed that there appeared to be many layers to this virtual stranger as well as to small-time life. No wonder everyone seemed to be part of one big family. They all depended upon each other for a variety of things. She was still thinking about how nice it would be to have those kinds of connections when the next chorus of "Trick or treat" sounded.

After another thirty minutes of visits from Disney Princesses, a collection of crayons, and various other things, creatures, and celebrities, the street grew quiet. Porch lights were turned off one by one, and Julie surveyed the bowl of candy.

"Just four left. Good guess." She smiled at Eric and motioned to Gunner asleep on the opposite side of the porch. "He looks comfortable."

"He's a good dog. We've been there for each other through thick and thin. Sometimes I don't know how I would've survived without him."

"Survived what?" Julie asked. Eric looked away as the tables were turned on him. He'd obviously said more than he intended. That old enemy, guilt, had returned. Julie sensed his unease and sympathized.

"It's okay," she said. "I didn't mean to pry."

"I know," Eric tilted his head back and blew a gust of breath into the night air. "It's not something I like to talk about."

"I understand. There are things I don't like to talk about either." That was probably the most honest thing she had ever said to him, or anyone, in a long time.

He stood up and walked to the front door. He opened the door and reached inside, turning off the porch light. Gunner raised his head and then lowered it back down. Julie's senses heightened, and she fought back the urge to run into the house.

"We don't have to talk," Eric said as he bent over and sat the bowl on the floor under the swing. "We can just watch the stars come out."

As Eric sat close beside her, every instinct told Julie to get up and say goodnight, almost every instinct. While her mind was screaming to be careful, her heart was rapidly pounding with joy.

Neither one paid attention to how long they sat there in silence watching the stars come out. Eventually Julie yawned and began blinking her eyes.

"Time to go," Eric said quietly. He stood and stretched, and Gunner did the same.

"Where did you park?" Julie asked, looking for his car.

"At the shop. It's safer for the kids if we don't drive through town."

"Do you want a ride back there?"

"No, Gunner and I will just walk away into the moonlight."

"Aren't you supposed to ride away into the sunset," Julie smiled. Eric winked and waved goodbye as Julie watched and wondered what she was getting herself into.

CHAPTER 24

January 19, 2013

Two weeks to the day after Melissa Grant walked into Chad's flat, and Elaine Smith walked out, Chad's parents filed an official missing persons report. They would have filed it sooner, but the Philadelphia Police were slow to suspect that anything out of the ordinary had happened to him.

When Chad lost contact with his family, friends, colleagues, and investors, his mother immediately went to the authorities. However, an inspection of his home and computer pointed to evidence showing that Chad had packed a suitcase and taken a spontaneous trip. Friends who were questioned confirmed that Chad had mentioned a possible business trip recently, though his last Facebook post suggested the trip had been cancelled. The evidence contradicted that. In Chad's line of work, he often left town spontaneously to meet with possible investors.

An airline ticket to the Cayman Islands had been purchased in his name. A return message from emails, sent to both his private and business email addresses, said that he would be out of touch for a few days. While Chad's parents argued that he would never leave the country without telling them and without contacting his business associates, the police had no reason to investigate his supposed disappearance.

When it was confirmed that the airline tickets were not used, and two weeks later there was still no word from him, Chad's father persuaded the Philadelphia Police to start searching for him. Another week went by before Chad's body was found floating in the Delaware River. His car was located with his suitcase and plane ticket inside. His wallet was missing, and the case was closed as a robbery gone bad.

A link to Melissa Grant was not yet suspected. Chad's parents, who lived outside of Chicago, had no knowledge of the friendship with the other missing Philadelphian. Since the flat didn't appear to be a crime scene, and the vacation plans and robbery had been perfectly set up by The Housekeeper and the computer tech crew that followed him, no further investigation was deemed warranted. Had the police searched the computers, they wouldn't have found anything relating to Melissa. Chad knew how to cover his tracks, and even the FBI Cyber Crimes Team could not have followed his electronic footsteps to help his friend. Not even The Housekeeper's tech crew was able to follow her trail.

Within three weeks time, Elaine Smith was full swing into a new life. All the money Melissa inherited from her parents and the proceeds from the sale of their house had been transferred to an offshore bank account and then moved to another account under the innocuous name Mary Morgan, its location unknown and untraceable. And though nothing is truly untraceable these days, by the time

the bank account was located by both Detective Morris
and The Housekeeper's tech crew, the money was gone.

Melissa's driver's license, library card, ATM card, and
all other possible forms of identification had been burned
along with her clothes and most of her hair. With Chad's
help, Melissa was able to obtain not one, but four new
identities. These were purchased from different dealers in
Philadelphia and beyond and could not be traced back to
Chad.

Chad had done exactly what Melissa asked for. He
made her disappear. Little could they have known that it
would end up costing him his own life.

CHAPTER 25

November 2, 2014

Julie spent most of Saturday writing. Putting words together to create a story was something completely new to her. She loved to read and admired those who could concoct an entire plot complete with imaginable settings and believable characters. She never thought she could come close to doing it herself. She looked at her pictures for inspiration.

It wasn't easy. Sometimes the words flowed, but other times, she couldn't find quite the right way to express herself. Not knowing anything about hunting, she tried using her imagination and limited experience to convey her story. Around three in the afternoon, she gave up. Remembering the conversation from the night before about the little girl down the street, Julie went out for a walk, hoping to find her neighbor, Abby.

Julie was in luck. The energetic little girl was in her front yard, still wearing part of her costume from the night before. The ten-year-old was dressed as a dog with big floppy ears. On Halloween, of a box was strapped to her body that was filled with a litter of stuffed puppies.

"Hi, Abby. How was trick or treating?"

Her eyes lit up. "Awesome! I got more candy than ever!"

"That's great! I had so much fun seeing everyone in their costumes." Julie waited a minute and then asked her lead-in question. "Hey, Abby, do you hunt?"

"Yeah, sometimes. It can be fun, but it gets boring after a while." She wrinkled up her nose and shook her head a little. Her brown ponytail swayed back and forth. "I'm going on Opening Day, though, and this time I can actually shoot my own gun." She lit up at the thought.

"Can I ask you some questions about what it's like? I'm trying to write a little story to go with some of my pictures, and I'm kind of stuck."

Abby rolled her eyes dramatically. "That happens to me all the time."

Abby's mom, Kari, came out onto the porch. "Hi, Julie," she called. "You two look like you're having a serious conversation out here. How about some cider and fresh baked pumpkin bread?" She smiled and opened the door beckoning them inside.

Julie spent the next couple of hours with Abby and Kari hearing about experiences in the woods. Kari was not a hunter, but her daughter had plenty of stories to share from her short lifetime of traipsing along after her father.

That evening, after turning down Kari's dinner invitation, Julie sat at her computer, typing until her fingers hurt. Finally, feeling accomplished, she went to bed. Why she had spent so much time on a story that nobody would ever see, she didn't know. It just felt right to imagine herself being a part of the town and its traditions. Julie was so tired of being on the run. She wanted desperately to feel like she belonged.

CHAPTER 26

November 3, 2014

The next morning, as had become her routine, Julie slipped into the pew next to Helen. After Mass, they walked out together, and Julie asked if Helen had a printer at her house. Helen looked at Julie like she had two heads.

"Of course, I do. Who doesn't?"

"I don't," Julie answered with a chuckle and then explained. "I travel light, and a good quality printer is not light. It makes more sense for me to have my photos professionally printed. I usually go to the library if I need to print something, but it's Sunday."

"Julie, you are more than welcome to use my printer any time you need it. And you know how I love cooking on Sundays. Come on." She laced her arm through Julie's as they walked the short distance to Helen's house. Though the past couple days had been the perfect temperature, a sudden chill crept in overnight reminding them that it was now, indeed, November.

Helen set Julie up at her computer right away, insisting that she did not need help in the kitchen. Julie pulled up the story on her flash drive and printed it out. For what reason, she had no idea. It was almost as if she needed something concrete to hold onto to show that she was here.

She was ejecting the drive when she heard the front door close behind her.

"Look what the cat dragged in," Eric teased as she turned around. "What are you working on?"

"It's nothing," Julie said, hiding the paper behind her back.

"Well, now you've really got my curiosity fired up." He took a step toward her and tried to reach around her, but she turned her back to the side moving the paper out of reach.

"Oh, no, you don't." She tried to wiggle away, but Eric put his other arm around her and captured her between them. Her heart caught in her chest as she looked up at him. This time, his blocking her escape did not elicit the same kind of fear as that first day in the shop.

Eric froze, and their eyes locked. They stood still, breathing hard, unable to look away from each other.

Helen cleared her throat from the doorway. "Dinner's ready." Julie could tell, just by the tone of her voice, that she was smiling.

Eric immediately released Julie, and could feel her cheeks redden, and imagined that they suddenly matched the color of the few leaves left on the Red Maple in the front yard. She scooted around Eric and headed toward the kitchen with the paper still firmly in her grasp.

Helen and Eric just looked at each other. "It's not what you think," he started, but Helen held up her hand. Julie observed the scene as she hastily folded the print-out and hid it in her back pocket.

"I didn't say a word."

"Uh huh," he responded. "Don't." Eric walked around his mother and looked at Julie, standing innocently in the kitchen.

Rather than being tense, dinner was truly enjoyable. Helen put a roast in the crockpot early that morning, and it was cooked to perfection. She added beans, potatoes, and carrots, and served warm homemade biscuits. They laughed at the stories she told of Eric's childhood antics, and Julie knew that Helen noticed every look that she and Eric exchanged, no matter how nonchalant Julie tried to remain. Several times, their hands brushed as they passed food, and the electricity building between them was palpable.

Eventually, the stories left childhood behind and centered on Eric as a teen, some of the fire calls he attended while in high school, and his determination to leave St. Brendan and become a big city boy.

"I can't imagine you in a big city," Julie admitted.

Eric shrugged. "It was another time." He looked down at his plate. "It wasn't the right place for me after all."

"Where did you live?" Julie asked

"They lived in D.C.," Helen said as she reached for another biscuit. "They had a beautiful old row house that Elizabeth's-" Eric stood up.

"Mom, I'm sorry to run, but I've got to get to the shop. I had a big delivery yesterday that I haven't finished going through yet." He averted his eyes from both Julie and his mother.

"Oh, I didn't realize…" Helen let the words trail off. "I'm sorry," she said quietly. Julie knew that Helen wasn't referring to the unfinished inventory.

"But we haven't even finished eating," Helen gently protested.

"I'm full," Eric said without looking at her, and Julie noticed the guilty expression on his face. "I need to go. Do you mind?" he gestured toward the table.

"It's okay. I'll help clean up," Julie offered. "I don't mind." Eric turned to look at Julie, and a look of understanding passed between them. His words from Halloween came back to her: *It's not something I like to talk about.*

"Thank you," he said with a deeper meaning than the words conveyed. Julie nodded, and Eric hurried away just as he had the first time they all ate together. Helen and Julie heard the front door close, but neither went back to eating, nor did they make a move to clean up.

After several minutes, Helen spoke up. "Her name was Elizabeth." Julie waited, but Helen seemed at a loss for words.

"Did she die?" Julie asked instinctively. "He doesn't act like someone who was betrayed, and I already know he wouldn't have been the one to do the betraying."

Helen shook her head. "She was shot. She died twenty-two hours later. The doctors did all they could, but…" A tear left her eye and ran along the laugh line at its corner until it gently rolled down her cheek. Julie caught her breath.

"Oh, my gosh. How?" She couldn't help but ask.

"A robbery. She was walking home from work after dark. The neighborhood was safe, but it is a city. Eric never let her walk home alone, but he was working on a case that was about to break. He was stuck in an interview with an important witness, and he called and told her he'd be late. She said she would walk with a co-worker, but she didn't." Helen smiled. "She was the last person in the building and didn't want him to worry. I'm sure that never in a million years did she think…" Her words hung in the warm kitchen air.

Julie stood and walked around the table to Helen's chair. She bent down and wrapped her arms around her. "I'm so sorry. It must have been very hard for both of you."

Helen nodded. "It was eight years after Bill died, but Eric was just then getting over the loss of his father. To lose Elizabeth, too, was just awful."

Julie sat back down. "If you don't mind my asking, you said that Eric was working late on a case. What kind of case?"

"Eric was a prosecutor with the D.C. District Attorney's Office. He worked so hard to put himself through college and law school. After the shooting, he couldn't go back to work. He blamed himself. He came up with every reason as to why it was his fault. If he hadn't been working late, if he had been open to having a second car in the city, if he had a regular nine-five job, if he had done a better job putting away criminals. Nothing I said could change his mind. He quit his job, sold the row house, and moved back home. He was always passionate about hunting and fishing, so he put the money from the sale of the house into buying a restored farmhouse on the water and the old fish market. He gutted the store and rebuilt it into his business." Helen smiled. "It seemed to take months before it no longer smelled like dead fish."

Julie just listened. She didn't know what to say. It was so much to take in. She could relate to what Eric had been through on so many levels. But hers was a story that couldn't be shared. And truth be told, she wasn't sure how she felt about Eric's previous job. Would that help her or hurt her if the truth about her past and her own crimes ever came out?

"Oh, look at me. I must be a mess." Helen wiped her eyes and blew her nose into her napkin. She smiled at Julie and put her wrinkled hand over Julie's. "I'm glad you've become friends. I don't expect anything more than that from you but thank you for being his friend."

Julie covered the older woman's hand with hers. "It's my pleasure." And for the first time in a long time, Julie felt a real connection to someone, and she wondered again just what she was getting herself into.

CHAPTER 27

Eric sat behind the counter in the shop and looked around for something to do. He didn't have any inventory to put away, and the shop was in perfect order as always. He almost wished his phone would signal a call from the fire station, but he knew to be careful about what he wished for. He picked up a catalog and started thumbing through it before flinging it across the room and banging his hands on the counter. Balling his fists, Eric raised them to his forehead and gritted his teeth.

His mind was a jumble of thoughts. Why did he come back home? At least if he had stayed with his law career, he would be working eighteen hours a day, seven days a week. Here, he had too much time on his hands. Fishing, hunting, going to Chestnut Street on an occasional Friday night - there were ways to keep him busy, but only for so long. Every night he returned to a lonely house and a couch or an empty bed, unless he counted Gunner who took up more room in the bed than he did.

And now there was Julie. He was so confused when it came to her. No, his body knew exactly how it felt about her, and at times he had to restrain himself from reaching for her, touching her, wanting to protect her from whatever she was afraid of. But that led to yet another dilemma. His heart was telling him he was betraying Elizabeth, and his mind was telling him that his innate need to turn back the clock and save his wife was his real attraction to Julie.

The bottom line was that Julie was the last thing Eric needed in his life right now. He knew this without a doubt. But he also knew that something about her past was nagging at him. Could he turn back the clock? Could he find a way to help save this stranger to whom he was undoubtedly attracted?

Grudgingly, Eric picked up his cell phone. So many times, he thought about throwing it into the Bay. The phone calls and texts from friends and colleagues offering condolences and support, asking him to return to D.C., and pleading with him to reconsider his resignation were more than he thought he could stand. Then one day, the dozen calls lessened to seven or eight, then dwindled to two or three, then stopped altogether. The texts took a little longer, but they, too, died out. Now, Eric was about to reopen a book he had closed.

He searched his contacts for Jerome Williams, a private investigator who was on retainer for Eric back in the day. Jerome answered on the fourth ring just when Eric was about to hang up.

"Am I dreaming, or has this phone been stolen?" Jerome had to shout into the phone to be heard over yelling and an announcer giving play by play in the background.

"Damn, the Skins are on, aren't they?" Eric glanced at the clock hanging behind him.

"What, you been livin' under a rock? We were supposed to be goin' all the way this year, man, but it ain't going so well. Don't tell me you stopped following my boys."

"I guess I've been a little out of the loop. Unfortunately, the Shore has always been more Ravens country, though that seems to be changing."

"You go there, and our friendship ends."

Eric laughed and listened while Jerome covered the phone with his hand and yelled at the TV. "That was pass interference! Are you refs blind?" After a pause, the noise died down. Jerome must have moved to a different room. "I'm thinking that you calling out of the blue isn't because you want to meet for a beer after the game. What's up?"

It was typical of Jerome to get right to the punch. Never mind that they hadn't spoken in over a year. In their tenure of working together, Jerome was a good employee, but he was also a good friend.

Eric told Jerome everything he knew about Julie, what little there was to tell. Jerome's whole manner changed as he morphed into his professional self.

"This sounds like trouble to me, Eric. She could be a con artist or a mob member. You and I both know those things aren't just in movies."

Eric shook his head. "I don't think so, Jerome. She's scared, guarded, and running. I don't know if it's a man or—"

"The law," Jerome cut him off. "What are you going to do if she's hiding out from the cops? I know you. You're going to have to turn her in. Maybe you should leave well enough alone and just stay away from her."

"I keep thinking the same thing, but somehow I find myself running into her all the time."

"By accident or on purpose?"

Eric didn't answer right away. That was a good question. "Hell, man. I don't know. I just can't seem to stay away."

"Have you asked her yourself? 'Cause if you have feelings for her, you're already blowing it if we go any further than this phone call. Maybe you should talk to her first."

Eric thought about that. He knew Jerome was right, but he was pretty sure that talking to Julie wouldn't get him any answers. And confronting her might send her running. That was the last thing Eric wanted.

"There's nothing between us, Jerome. I'll always love Elizabeth. I'm just making sure there's nothing going on that I should be worried about. She and Mom are becoming awfully close."

Jerome waited a minute before he answered. "How's Helen doing?"

Eric smiled. "Same as always. Ornery."

Jerome laughed. "Some things never change." He paused and sighed. "I'll see what I can find out."

"Thanks."

"Don't thank me, Eric. You might not like what I find."

Eric sat in the dark, silent shop for a long time after ending the call with Jerome. Jerome was the best in the business. If anyone could find out what Julie's story was, it was him. Eric just hoped his friend was wrong and that he wasn't making a big mistake.

CHAPTER 28

February 2013

Detective Frank Morris did not like coincidences. In fact, he didn't believe in them. Call it years of experience, a gut instinct, or just plain intuition, but Morris knew that the so-called botched robbery of a computer genius and the disappearance of a one extremely lucky nurse had to be related. Nobody escapes three hits and then disappears without a trace. It wasn't unheard of, in big cities, for two professionals to be working the same area at the same time, but it wasn't exactly the norm unless the mob was involved. And he had no doubt these were both professional hits, and the inquiries he had made with the Organized Crime Unit had yielded no connections to the mafia or to any gangs. Add to that, the many photos of Grant and O'Donnell together online, and he knew, beyond a doubt, this was no coincidence.

Just a block from where Chad O'Donnell's car had been found, a gun was recovered from a dumpster. It would never have been found had Morris's gut not told him to look for it. The robbery scene was too clean, too manufactured. And according to the coroner, O'Donnell had not killed himself. He had no water in his lungs; he was already dead when he went into the Delaware River.

And of course, there was the hole between his eyes. Not the kind of shot made by your average every day mugger.

None of it added up. Morris would have the rear-ends of the officers on the scene who closed the case without tying up the loose ends.

Having done his research, Morris made the connections that should have been made weeks ago.

1. O'Donnell, Grant, and their friend, Tina Marsh, had all graduated from Hopkins in the class of 2009.

2. Based on their Facebook postings and pictures, O'Donnell, Grant, and Marsh remained in touch after all three moved to Philly.

3. All three were victims of a professional hit (though Melissa's whereabouts were still unknown, Morris assumed her body would turn up soon, unless, of course, she was in on it).

4. The last time Grant was seen was the day of O'Donnell's disappearance, and her last cyber print was at a library not far from O'Donnell's flat.

When put together, there were no coincidences here. The deaths of Marsh and O'Donnell were directly related to the attempted hits on Grant. The real question was whether or not Melissa was a victim or part of the scheme all along.

The bullets were in the process of being matched, identified, and traced, using IBIS, the International Ballistics Information System, but Morris was sure they would all be from the same lot. Guns were discarded at all three scenes. The barrels were drilled out and electrically charged, meaning they were completely untraceable.

Altered and electrically charged guns, discarded after use, verified that this was a professional at work.

Unlike in the movies, no silencer was attached. Those were only used in Hollywood. The subsonic ammo would have made almost no sound, just a faint click as the bullet was released from the chamber. How could Melissa, someone with no experience with weapons, have possibly identified the slide and click of the chamber closing on the gun or the faint noise the shot made in time to escape the bullet? And how could she have escaped the shooter without help or training?

There were too many unanswered questions, and Morris didn't like unanswered questions. He ordered the men and the one woman on his team to find out everything they could about Melissa Grant.

CHAPTER 29

November 7, 2014

Eric and Gunner walked along the nature trail on a breezy Wednesday evening. Though Eric told himself that he came here to be alone, he found himself looking for Julie around every bend. He picked up a stick and threw it into a field along the trail. Gunner retrieved the stick and dropped it at Eric's feet. He threw it a few more times until Gunner became bored with their game and started following an interesting scent he came across. Eric watched Gunner but found his thoughts drifting to Julie.

Who was she? Where did she come from? What was she hiding? And why did he care? Every time he thought about her, he felt himself being torn in two. Ever since Halloween, when he felt so at ease sitting next to her on the porch swing, he couldn't stop thinking about her. On the other hand, it still felt like he was betraying Elizabeth.

For almost three years, Eric shunned all thoughts of other women. Friends and family tried to fix him up with a few women, some of them very nice, even beautiful. Eric wasn't interested in any of them. What was it about Julie that attracted him to her? He could admit that much. He was attracted to her, but why? He couldn't shake the question that kept plaguing him—was he just trying to fix the past?

Watching Gunner run around in circles sniffing the ground, Eric decided that the answer was no. Elizabeth was gone and was never coming back. It had taken a long time, but Eric was finally beginning to accept the fact that he could not have saved her. Some people are just so good, so loving, so special, that their goodness transcends this world. Those are the people who Billy Joel sang about when he said, "Only the good die young." Elizabeth was one of those people.

He and Elizabeth spent little time talking about their future, but they both knew what it would be. Until it wasn't. Perhaps that was the catch with Julie. Was she also caught between her past and her future? Was her vision of the future suddenly snatched from her grasp?

Eric whistled to Gunner. "Come on, boy. Time to go home."

As they walked back to the truck, Eric decided that he might as well go with his gut. If Julie was the first woman he was attracted to since losing his wife, then who was he to fight it? Perhaps it was time to get to know her and see where it would lead. Into the storm he would tread, lightning or not.

CHAPTER 30

November 8, 2014

That evening, Julie took her camera and slipped
through the wooded doorway onto the dirt path leading to
the nature trail. Soon the days would grow too short for
evening light, and Julie wanted to capture the last
remaining rays over the creek before the window between
day and night became too small an opening for anyone to
notice. The creek was on the opposite side of the harbor,
so Julie had the advantage of being just several yards from
the setting sun once she reached the trail.

She wasted no time along the way as she headed
straight toward the dock she had spotted the first time she
was here. Several boats were tied to docks scattered
around the creek. They bobbed in the twilight, rocked by a
gentle breeze, and reminded Julie of a cradle rocking a
baby to sleep. If boats could think or feel, she knew that
those tied to the docks would be content as they drifted off
to their slumber. Julie smiled at the thought as the
camera's shutter opened and closed like the drowsy eyes
of the rocking baby. Lowering her camera, she sighed as
an image of her mother suddenly came to mind.

It was then that she felt his presence. For the first time
in recent memory, her heart raced with something other
than fear. In that moment, she felt a connection between

the two of them, for how else could she have known, not only that she was being watched, but by whom? Without turning to look behind her, she beckoned him with a hushed tone.

"You're welcome to join me for lesson two."

Eric walked the rest of the way to the end of the dock with Gunner just a step behind him.

"I didn't want to disturb you," he said as he took a seat beside her, his legs dangling over the water next to hers.

"I'm almost done. I just wanted to take advantage of the bit of light that was left."

"You seemed very…content," Eric told her. Julie glanced sideways at him wondering how he knew what her thoughts had been just moments earlier.

"It's this place," Julie admitted. "It's like I'm finally…" She caught herself when she realized what she was about to say, and Eric let the moment pass as they looked out at the last of the reddish glow on the horizon. She wondered if he knew exactly what she meant.

"Red sky at night," Eric said. Julie turned toward him.

"What about it?" she asked curiously.

"The old saying, 'red sky at night, sailor's delight; red sky at morning, sailors take warning.'"

"Hmm," she thought for a minute. "That saying, it sounds familiar. I think my dad may have said that when I was little." Eric noticed a faraway look in her eyes and a hint of sadness in her voice.

"Was he a sailor?"

Julie laughed. "Not even close. He was a professor. English Lit."

"Ah, so that's who introduced you to Sir Author Conan Doyle." He noticed the way her eyes lit up when she laughed. Suddenly she straightened and raised the camera to her eye.

"Look," she whispered as two swans glided across the creek just as the moonlight stretched across the water.

"They're called tundra swans," Eric told her. "They're not usually in this close to the shore, but every now and then, you get lucky and see them in here. They're migratory. These are the first ones I've seen this winter." Julie nodded in understanding as the swans gracefully glided out of the cove and back toward the more open waters of the Bay. The night was quiet, and the scene contributed to the peaceful feeling in the air.

They watched the swans in silence and Eric thought back a few years to the battle over the mute swans that once lived along the Bay. The fight to rid the area of the nonnative birds was a long and contentious one. In the end, the entire species was eradicated from the state, and the surrounding states followed suit.

"Julie," Eric said quietly after the swans swam out of sight. "I have two tickets to the Annual Waterfowl Festival in Easton this weekend. It's a huge, huge deal around here. Almost 20,000 people attend the festival to see or buy waterfowl carvings, paintings, and sculptures or watch the bird-dog contests or hunting and fishing contests and exhibits." He turned to her. "Would you like to go?"

"Thanks Eric," she smiled weakly, trying to conceal the constricting panic she felt in her chest and the rapid beat of her heart. "It's a lovely thought, and I'm sure it's a wonderful festival, but I don't think I can make it."

"Come on," he nudged her arm with his elbow. "You should go, if for nothing else, but to see the photography exhibit. You might even decide to enter something next year."

Julie stood up quickly and busied herself with wiping off the back of her jeans. "I really do appreciate it, Eric, but I can't. Thanks for asking." She kept her eyes averted as she turned to leave. "I'd better go."

Eric sat and watched as Julie hurriedly walked the length of the dock back to the trail. He certainly wasn't going to push her, though he did feel a small pang of disappointment. The truth was, he really was hoping she would say yes, and he wondered, not for the first time, just what, or whom, it was that Julie was hiding from. At that moment, Eric's fire pager sounded. After listening to the call, he stood and hurried toward the trail.

"No time to wallow in self-pity," he said to himself as if Julie were still there, and he headed to help put out a kitchen fire in the town of Neavitt.

CHAPTER 31

November 10, 2014

Julie avoided Eric all weekend. In fact, she avoided everyone, unsure of how many of those Waterfowl Festival attendees might decide to take a side trip to St. Brendan. She decided to play it safe and stay inside, despite the beautiful weather. She kept herself occupied by alternately editing the photos she had taken over the past week and reading some of the books in the cottage. There were many that dealt with local lore, and Julie found herself drawn to them. She enjoyed learning about the rich history of the area. She only ventured out once—early Sunday morning—to drive to Mass two counties away. Then she quickly headed back to her hideaway on Maple Street.

It was Abby who convinced Julie to go to Bass & Bucks that Monday. They ran into each other earlier that morning when Julie emerged from the cottage to go to yoga, and Abby was outside getting ready to head to school. She was full of excitement about her goose hunt with her dad that past Saturday.

"I'm going to write a story about it just like yours!" She beamed with pride.

"That's a great idea, Abby. I bet it wins."

"I don't even care if it wins. I'm just going to have fun writing it like you did."

Julie could tell she had an admirer, and to tell the truth, the feeling was mutual. Julie was quite smitten with Abby.

After all of Abby's talk about 'The Contest,' Julie's thoughts ran to Eric as she left the gym later that morning. Though she knew it was better to stay away from him, she found herself crossing the parking lot and passing by the fire station to the entrance of his store.

Eric was busy with a customer when Julie walked in. He glanced at her, when she entered the shop, but continued talking to his customer. It was like a jolt of electricity traveled across the room, connecting them with its current.

Julie smiled and greeted the hunters who were in the shop, swapping stories from their busy weekend of duck hunting. They talked about the Waterfowl Festival some, but many of the men avoided the crowds and took advantage of the time that their wives were volunteering at or attending the Festival by heading to their duck blinds. Julie had learned were small floating structures built out of, or covered with, old tree limbs, sticks, and brush to hide hunters from their flying prey. Julie lingered by the fishing lures and discreetly observed Eric go from one customer to the next, answering their questions and helping them with their purchases.

A teenaged boy was usually here on weekends, but Julie didn't see him today. She recognized him at church on Sunday and had seen him around town. He seemed like a good kid. She guessed he worked for Eric on Saturdays and after school. Eric obviously worked alone the rest of the time.

Julie felt Eric come up behind her but pretended not to notice.

"Going fishing?" he asked.

She continued looking at the lures. She ran a finger lightly across a neon pink one before turning her gaze toward Eric.

"Maybe. Believe it or not, I've never been."

"Well, maybe we'll have to fix that." His smile sent an arrow straight to her heart, and Julie reminded herself, once again, that she was playing a dangerous game and should just stay away from this man.

"Hey Eric," a voice called. Julie recognized Craig Black, owner of the Black Market Deli. "You got any waders left in stock? My son keeps growing out of his."

"Excuse me," he said to Julie.

As Eric helped Craig, Julie wandered around the store in spite of the voice in her head telling her to leave. It was a large store, and Eric must have paid quite a fortune for it. Real estate was no doubt expensive in this area.

When Craig was ready to pay for his son's waders, Julie watched Eric ring up the waders and say goodbye.

She walked over and leaned across the counter to look at the pocketknives, digital compasses, and other small but pricey wares under the glass. "So...how've you been?" she asked casually.

"Busy," he answered as he walked around and leaned his back against the front of the counter beside her. "It's really just the beginning of hunting season—geese, ducks, deer; and Rockfish season runs from April until the middle of December. It's not tourist season for St. Brendan, but it's the busiest time of the year for me. Not to mention, we've had three calls in the past few days, two fires and one accident. That's a lot for an area our size."

Julie listened to Eric as she picked up a wooden object that looked like a thick whistle from a display box on top of the counter. "What's this for?"

"It's a duck call."

She examined the device then lifted it to her mouth and blew into it. The sound it made caused her to jump. She and Eric both laughed.

"What kind of duck would that be?" she asked Eric as she turned toward him. Eric took the call from her.

"One that I've never heard before," Eric exclaimed with a laugh. "You're not blowing into it right. Here, like this," he demonstrated.

"Okay, that sounds more like a duck." She said as Eric handed it back to her.

"Now you try." Their fingers grazed as she took it from his hand. They looked at each other, and Julie raised the call to her lips. She blew into it.

"Like that?" she asked quietly, noticing how close Eric's face seemed to hers all of a sudden and how he stared intently at her mouth.

"Yeah, just like that," he swallowed and raised his gaze to meet her eyes. Julie felt as though she couldn't breathe. The sound of the shop door slamming shut caused them both to jump.

Julie pushed herself away the counter. "Well, I guess I should be going."

Eric straightened and cleared his throat. "Yeah, uh, I need to get back to work." He waved to the man looking at the collection of shotgun shells, but neither he nor Julie moved.

"You got more of these in the back?" The man held up a box of shells, and Eric and Julie turned to look at him.

"Let me check," Eric answered. "I'll be right back," he said to the man, and then turned his eyes back to Julie as if to send her a message – *Please stay*. He went into the back to find the new case of shells, walking quickly and glancing back at her. Feeling guilty, but not sure what was happening between them, Julie quietly hurried to the door and left before Eric returned.

CHAPTER 32

February 28, 2013

Elaine was working at Terry's Deli on River Pier near Battery Park. It wasn't exactly her dream job, but it paid the bills.

On Tuesday night, when things were slow, Elaine actually made it home in time to see the eleven o'clock news. The opening story stopped her in her tracks.

"Philadelphia Police have confirmed that up and coming computer entrepreneur Chad O'Donnell, who had been reported missing back on January 19th, was murdered. O'Donnell's body was found on January 26th in the Delaware River. His death was originally thought to be the result of a mugging, but sources now tell us that his death has been linked to the death of college friend, Tina Marsh, and the disappearance of a third Johns Hopkins graduate, Melissa Grant. Police are asking for help in locating Grant."

Elaine sat on the edge of the bed in the tiny, one room apartment and cried at the news of Chad's death, but only for a moment. The picture of Melissa Grant was from a girls' night out the previous fall that had been posted on her Facebook page. Elaine stood and walked to the bathroom to see how much she still resembled that girl. The face in the mirror was streaked with tears. The red dye-job she maintained looked good, and her hair had grown out into a rather cute bob. But she still looked like herself.

Obviously, New York was way too close to Philly for Elaine to be safe. She left the bathroom and quickly changed out of her pajamas. She pulled her backpack out from under the sofa bed and stuffed her clothes into the bag. She returned to the bathroom and retrieved her toiletries.

Once she was packed, Elaine pulled the middle drawer out of the dresser. Turning it over, she ripped the tape off of the Manila envelope, which she had secured to the bottom of the drawer. She slid out a wad of money and the open-ended bus ticket she had purchased the same day she arrived in New York. She looked at the number on the index card that was inserted into the rubber band that held the money. Putting the card in her pocket, she slid the rest of the items back into the envelope and stuffed it in between her clothes before zipping the back pack and hoisting it onto her back.

Elaine took the subway from Bowling Street to Penn Station and made the necessary transfers to JFK Airport. Walking into the baggage claim area, Elaine pretended to be looking for someone among the crowds of people just arriving from destinations unknown.

Following Chad's advice to only make phone calls from an airport pay phone, Elaine searched for a bank of phones. She located several pay phones and was surprised to see people actually using two of them. She pulled the card from her pocket and made the collect call to the number Chad had given her.

After hanging up, Elaine sought out the information desk and asked where she could find a bus to Chicago. Though the woman behind the desk gave her a quizzical look, she provided the necessary information. Elaine left the airport for a bus, heading to Chicago, to pick up her next set of identification papers.

She didn't even have time to properly mourn for the man who saved her life.

CHAPTER 33

November 13, 2014

Julie pulled her long blonde hair into a ponytail and slipped on her tennis shoes. She didn't have the spare cash to join the small gym just down from Bass & Bucks, and she would have spent a small fortune in one-time use fees in order to come regularly, but Helen had a guest pass that was good for a full month. Most likely meant to entice someone to become a member, it was just what Julie needed to refresh her mind and body with regular yoga classes.

She met Helen in the parking lot, and they spent the next the hour focusing on nothing but breathing and opening up their joints and muscles as well as their lungs and minds.

"I can't thank you enough," Julie told Helen as they left the gym.

"It's my pleasure," Helen told her. "I was really thrilled when you mentioned your love of yoga. Most of my friends don't understand how wonderful it is. For me, it's not about being one with the divine, as they say. It's about the way my mind and body feel when we're finished."

"I know exactly what you mean," Julie said as they reached their cars. "There were times over the past few years that I know I wouldn't have survived without the breathing techniques I learned in yoga."

Helen opened the car door and looked over the roof at Julie. "You know, I've been told I'm a pretty good listener if you ever want to talk."

"I really appreciate that, Helen. I'll let you know. See you later." Julie got into her car and waved as she put it into reverse and backed out of her spot.

Helen stood and watched Julie turn onto Main Street, then closed her car door and walked across the parking lot. Cutting across the grass and through the fire department lot, she opened the door of Bass & Bucks and looked around. She found Eric in the back corner of the store rearranging hunting boots. He turned and smiled.

"Good morning, Mom. What brings you in here today?"

Helen wasted no time in sharing her concerns about Julie with Eric.

"I can't explain it," she continued. "There's something off about her, and it bothers me. She's hiding from something or someone. Do you know she doesn't even own a phone?"

"At all?" Eric asked.

"At all," she reiterated.

They headed to his small office in the back of the store. Eric handed his mother a bottle.

Helen continued, "For a young woman today, don't you find that strange?"

Eric nodded thoughtfully and took a drink from his coffee. "Yeah, I guess I knew that. The first night I saw her on the trail, it was dark, and she didn't have a flashlight or a phone. At least, not that I could see. I used my phone to walk her home." He shrugged. "I guess she doesn't want to be bothered while she's on vacation." The bell over the shop door rang. "Saved by the bell," he winked as he walked back into the storeroom.

"I'm not through with this," his mother called after him.

"I know, mom. I know." Eric greeted his neighbor, Jim, and waved to his mother as she left the shop. He knew more than he telling her, but she wasn't going to give up until she knew who Julie was and what she was hiding.

CHAPTER 34

November 13, 2014

Eric's conversation with his mother replayed in his mind all day. As he closed up the store, he decided to pay Julie a visit. Stopping by the pizza place across from his store, he picked up a pepperoni pizza, figuring everyone likes pepperoni. Then, he swung by the liquor store and bought a six-pack of light beer though he preferred the heavy stuff.

When he rang the bell, he saw Julie's shadow move through the house. He could make out her figure as she peered through the window, obviously trying to stay hidden behind the blinds. She tentatively opened the door.

Right away, Eric knew something wasn't right. Julie was smiling, but her expression wasn't genuine.

"Did I come at a bad time?" he asked through the screen door between them.

"Not at all. Did you need something?"

Eric held up the pizza box in one hand and the beer in the other. "Just some company." He gave her what he hoped was a persuasive smile.

Julie hesitated for a moment and then pushed the screen door open. "Come on in. I was just about to reheat the pot roast that your mother insisted I bring home with me last night, but I never turn down pizza." Her expression was less forced as she beckoned him inside with a toss of her head.

"That must be a tough piece of meat she gave you," Eric raised his eyebrows inquisitively when he noticed the sharp butcher's knife in her hand.

"Excuse me?" Julie asked. Eric motioned to the large knife, and Julie's face reddened.

"Oh, that. It was just the first knife I grabbed when I took out the roast." She smiled in an obvious attempt to cover the truth. Eric decided to let it go for now.

Over pizza and beer (two for Eric, one for Julie), they talked about the citizens of St. Brendan, the places in and around town that she had photographed, and other places nearby where she could take pictures. Julie was intrigued by the Oxford-Bellevue Ferry, the oldest operating ferry in the United States, which was just a short drive away.

"It's closed for the winter, but perhaps I can convince you to stay until spring?" Eric put down his beer and looked at Julie.

"Eric, there are things that you don't know…" Julie picked up her paper plate and started to rise from the table, but Eric gently put his hand on her arm and eased her back down.

"I get that. I can see it. You're obviously running from something, but at some point, you have to stop running."

Julie shook her head, tears forming in her eyes. "You don't understand." She closed her eyes and took a deep breath through her nose.

Eric reached over and wiped away the teardrop that slowly trickled down her cheek. "Then make me understand. Tell me what you're afraid of."

Julie opened her eyes and looked at him. "It's not that simple. I, I don't know who I can trust, or—"

"Me," he fingered a piece of hair that had fallen into her face and tucked it back behind her ear. "You can trust me." He traced her cheek and slid his finger down to her chin, tilting her head up so that their eyes met. He repeated, "You can trust me."

Without thinking about what he was doing, Eric leaned across the table and gently pressed his lips to hers. He drew back and looked into her eyes again. "Trust me."

Before she could respond, Eric stood, took his jacket from the back of the chair, and slipped it on. He wanted to give her something to think about without pressuring her. He hoped he had made his point.

Julie sat as he got up to leave, and Eric wasn't sure if she would stop him. He kept walking but sensed when she stood and followed him. He saw her reflection in the framed picture above the couch and watched as she stopped in the kitchen doorway.

When Eric reached for the doorknob, Julie called out his name. He turned back and looked at her, leaning against the doorframe. He waited.

"I do," she said quietly. Eric felt that little tug at his heart and acknowledged to himself that he did have feelings for her. In fact, his heart had been hooked on Julie Lawson since the day she stepped foot in town.

"Tomorrow? Dinner out this time?" he asked. Julie nodded. "Okay, then, I'll pick you up at seven." He opened the door then stopped and turned back to her. "Wear a dress, and I'll leave my phone at home." He smiled and walked out into the night.

CHAPTER 35

November 13, 2014 - San Francisco, CA

Earl Mueller was a photo editor for *American Photography* Magazine. It wasn't a big publication, but it was somehow managing to survive the downturn in the magazine publishing industry, so Earl had no complaints. The January issue of the magazine was going to press, and Earl was torn between two different shots to use for the cover.

His favorite photographer had taken both pictures the previous winter. As always, the pictures were unique and breathtakingly beautiful. They were both taken in St. Louis and both had the famous Arch in the background. The theme of that month's publication was Taking Advantage of the Weather, and that she had done.

One photo was shot through the branch of a cherry tree, its first buds just beginning to show their bright pink color as spring attempted to arrive. Beyond the branch was the Arch with snow falling around it. The second photo, taken earlier in the year, showed the Arch in the background while branches covered with icicles framed the monument as it bent in the sky.

Earl chose the cherry blossom picture for its ability to stand out among the teasers that would be printed on the cover. This was the first time he had chosen one of her works for the cover. It wasn't the norm for such a prominent spot to be occupied by someone who wanted to remain anonymous. For at least the twelfth time in the past year or so, Earl wondered why such an incredibly talented photographer would want to remain unknown to the world.

Questions aside, Earl went online and completed the transaction to send payment to Mary Morgan's Bahamian bank account. Whoever she was, Earl always looked forward to seeing her photos. He was already thinking about the ones that arrived the day before. He had never been to the Eastern Shore of Maryland, as the label on the back of the pictures identified the area, but the shots of the watermen at work captured a way of life that he knew was slipping away. The ones of the fall foliage and the sunrise and sunset over the various bodies of water were exquisite. Whoever this Mary person was, she had a real eye for beauty and knew how to convey it.

PART THREE

A ship in harbor is safe, but that is not what ships are built for.

John A. Shedd

CHAPTER 36

March 2, 2013 - Dallas, TX

Elaine Smith stepped off the Greyhound bus in Dallas. She pulled the piece of paper out of her pocket and looked for the address of the hostel she had located, using a public computer at a coffee shop near the Chicago O'Hare Airport. Her short trip to Chicago had been like a scene from a spy movie.

Obeying the instructions given to her over the phone in New York, she arrived at O'Hare airport in the early morning hours. She went to baggage claim and looked for the carousel for incoming flight 1308 from San Diego. While pretending to wait for a traveler arriving on that flight, she kept her eyes out for a blind man with a cane and guide dog wearing a red doggie vest. She was told to ask the man if she could pet the dog. The man replied that petting a guide dog was not allowed, but could she please check to see that the vest was not too tight. Elaine complied, and discreetly pulled the envelope out from inside the vest on the underside of the German Shepherd.

After retrieving her new driver's license, passport, and birth certificate, Elaine walked to a bathroom on the far side of the baggage claim area. She silently thanked God for her girlfriend, Misty Stevens, from high school. Misty was an aspiring hairdresser who often used Melissa Grant

as a guinea pig. Christina knew that the bleach kit hidden
in the bottom of her bag wouldn't take out the red, but it
would change the shade and create a combination of light
red and pink hair with some white streaks.

Christina Stewart emerged from the bathroom with a
very chic pink and white hairstyle, looking like a younger,
hipper person. After depositing Elaine's papers in an ash
can outside of the terminal where they would smolder and
burn (and hopefully not burn down the airport), she
boarded the El and rode the train to the Madison/Wabash
stop in downtown Chicago. She walked two blocks to
Millennium Park where the famous bean-shaped sculpture
is located. As she became one with the crowd, she
marveled at the amazing sculpture and the surrounding
architecture. How she wished she had a camera!

Perhaps it was fate intervening, because as she walked
to the nearest bus station, she noticed a Going out of
Business sign on a Ritz Camera store. Christina entered
the store and began looking at the cameras, all priced to
sell quickly. A sales associate approached her and asked if
he could help.

"Hi, Mike," she addressed him by the name on his shirt
and pointed to a camera on display behind the counter. "Is
that a good camera? I've always owned Nikons but
haven't bought a new camera in years."

"It's a great camera," Mike answered as he went around
the counter and took the model from the shelf. He
explained the specs of the camera and let Christina hold it
and play with it a bit.

"How much?" she asked, mentally calculating what she could afford to spend out of the cash in her bag.

"It's priced at the lowest you'll ever find one." He smiled and whispered conspiratorially, "And just to stick it to these jerks selling us out, I'll make you a real sweet deal."

Christina walked out of the store with the camera. No more waiting tables and creating a regular routine for herself. This new persona was going to be a freelance photographer. She walked to the bus station with a smile on her face, feeling a bit like herself for the first time in months.

By the time the bus came to a stop in Dallas, she had read the entire manual and practiced taking pictures from the bus and various stops along the way. Borrowing someone's smart phone, she researched what she would need to do to sell pictures on the street in Dallas. Just a simple form and a $50 fee, and she would be in business.

CHAPTER 37

November 14, 2014 - St. Brendan, MD

Julie woke up, feeling like a teenager. She was sure she would never make it until seven o'clock that night, but she did have some things to keep her busy. After a quick shower, she pulled on her jeans, a long-sleeved T-shirt, and a sweatshirt. She grabbed a yogurt and ate it while pulling on her imitation Ugg boots she had picked up the week before at Wal-Mart and tied her hair into a ponytail.

The drive to Ocean City was just over an hour and a half. Julie parked and headed to the Boardwalk. Most of the businesses were closed this time of year, but she wasn't interested in shopping. Snapping pictures of the waves, crashing onto the empty beach, and the lonely benches waiting for beachcombers, Julie lost herself in her lens.

She wandered along the boardwalk taking pictures of the giant Ferris wheel that was up the beach from the crashing waves. The wheel stood still and silent, keeping watch over the waters and the resort town. There was an almost eerie feeling in the small waterside amusement park that sat, longing for summer. Julie could feel the ghosts of happy children from generations past, laughing as they lined up for the old-time funhouse and screaming as they emerged from its shadows. If she closed her eyes and inhaled, she could smell the caramel popcorn, taffy, and famous boardwalk fries doused with vinegar and sprinkled with Old Bay seasoning.

She stepped onto the soft sand and remembered the feeling of the scorching summer sand on her bare feet. She walked to the water's edge and watched the waves carry one lone surfer, clad in a thick wetsuit, far off toward the end of the beach. Vague but comforting memories glided through her mind of a little girl in a red, white, and blue bathing suit holding her father's hand while he held her up against the force of the surf as it crashed into their bodies. The little girl laughed through her fear as the cold water splashed all around her. Julie wiped away a tear and continued down the beach, listening to the waves and the call of the gulls as they flew overhead. The camera, abandoned for the time being, hung loosely around her neck.

Around noon, Julie climbed the steps, from the beach to the boardwalk, and ventured down the boards in search of a generic ATM machine. It had been almost two years since Chad had given her a crash course in staying anonymous. "The most important thing," he had told her "is to stay off the grid. Leave no electronic footprints, ever." The one exception to the rule had been an anonymous debit card tied to a bank account in the Bahamas. Chad had handed her the untraceable laptop as an afterthought, just before she left him, and assured her that it was safe to use, but going online was a chance Julie wasn't willing to take. The only time she dared to expose herself was to get money, and she prayed each time that the transaction could not be traced back to Melissa Grant.

Chad had explained that the debit card worked like a regular ATM card but could not be tracked back to any bank or any person. More secure than a regular ATM, it could hold as much or as little money as desired and could be linked to an off-shore account, set up to add money to the card at pre-set intervals.

The first time Julie used the card, she was petrified that her unknown assailant would be hot on her trail. Thankfully, she was able to log into her account and get the amount she needed and still arrive in a new city, alive and in one piece. Not willing to push her luck, though, Julie never used the card more than once every two or three months and only to take out amounts less than $1,000.00.

Thanks to the few photo gigs she had done since coming to town, and the money she still had from her last identity's photography shoots, Julie didn't need to take out anything today. She would wait until she was ready to move on. However, she believed in the old adage, 'better safe than sorry.' She needed to scope out the location, and make sure that she could quickly and easily access the machine without bringing attention to herself. Once she had the money, she could easily take Route 113, either North toward New England or South toward Florida, and make her escape.

Finding the ATM and making a mental note of where it was located, Julie kept walking for a few blocks, and then turned around and casually headed back down the boardwalk in the direction of her car. She snapped a few pictures of the gulls, walking on their stick legs across the sand, and of the businesses along the way, their storefronts boarded up for the winter. The smiling face of the chef mascot hovering over Tony's Pizza reminded her of another childhood memory, and she wondered if the debate still lived on—Tony's or the Dough Roller—which had the best pizza in town? Her mother always voted for Tony's, but her father preferred the Dough Roller. They usually ended up eating at both before their trip was over.

It was just past two o'clock when Julie pulled onto the highway after making a quick stop at the Route 50 Bridge Outlets. She began the drive back to St. Brendan with a feeling of anticipation. She would have plenty of time for her date with Eric, and she had an escape plan in place to remind herself that tonight was all about having a good time and nothing more. There was no telling when it would be time to move on.

CHAPTER 38

Julie's stop at the outlets had been fruitful, and she left with a new pair of leggings and a cobalt blue sweater that showed off her petite figure. She made it home in time to shower, put some curl in her normally straight hair, and apply a little makeup. By six-thirty, Julie was sitting in the living room, reading the latest Nicholas Sparks novel that she had borrowed from Helen.

At six-forty-five, Julie saw Eric's headlights as he pulled up out front. Unsure as to whether to go out and greet him or wait for him to come get her, she took a minute to check her lipstick in the mirror. Eric exited the truck and walked up to the porch. He rang the bell just as Julie opened the door.

"I'm/You're early," they both said at the same time. They laughed, and Eric held the door open for Julie to come out. He led her down the walk with his hand on the small of her back. Opening the passenger side door of the truck, he helped her climb in before shutting the door and walking around to the driver's side.

They chatted the entire drive to The Island Tavern, a restaurant on Tilghman Island. Eric ordered a bottle of wine, and Julie looked at the moonlight as it beamed onto the water outside of their window. When Julie had gathered her courage and began to speak in a hushed voice, Eric looked up from his menu.

"My best friend and I used to go to a place like this."

Eric closed the menu and gave Julie his full attention.

She continued to look out at the water as she spoke. "There was a restaurant just outside of the city, on the Delaware River. We would go there on our birthdays or to celebrate something," she paused, and took a deep breath as she composed herself before going on.

"I remember when we both found out we'd gotten the same job, our dream job, in the maternity ward. We spent over one hundred dollars of our hard-earned money at The Landing that night."

The waitress returned with their wine and asked if they were ready to order.

"Not just yet," Eric told the waitress, but Julie waved at him to go ahead.

"Please," she said, "go ahead and order for us. You'll know what's good better than I will." Julie looked away and dabbed her eyes with her napkin.

After the waitress walked away, Julie took a sip of her wine. She felt Eric watching her. "I miss her." She turned and looked at Eric. "I miss her every day."

Julie wanted to tell Eric what she was really feeling, that it was her fault that Tina was gone, but she couldn't bring herself to form the words. Eric reached across the table and took her hand.

"What happened?" He asked quietly. Julie just shook her head even though the desire to confide in him was almost overwhelming.

"I'm here whenever you're ready," Eric told her. They sat in silence, holding hands and gazing out at the water, until their salads arrived.

CHAPTER 39

Eric and Julie walked hand in hand on the nature trail.
It was a warm and sunny day, and life felt perfect.
Rounding a bend, Eric noticed a fog suddenly creeping in
out of nowhere. It swirled around them, enclosing them in
its thick grey cloud. Eric felt Julie's hand slip out from his
grasp.

"Julie," he called to her, but she didn't answer. The fog
was so thick, he couldn't see. He began to panic and
shouted for her.

"Over here," she screamed back. "Help me, Eric. Help
me." Her panicked voice seemed far away as the fog
thickened even more.

"I can't find you," he yelled, becoming frantic that he
couldn't get to her. He swung his arms out in front of him
as though he could clear the fog.

He could make out a woman's figure up ahead. "Julie!"

The woman turned, and he saw Elizabeth standing
before him as alive as she had ever been. He reached for
her, but she vanished before his eyes. He could hear her
voice in the fog.

"Find her, Eric. Help her. She needs you."

"Elizabeth," he called. "Come back." But she was gone.
Her voice echoed in the air. "Help her, Eric. Help her."

Eric sat up in bed. He was panting, and his sheets were drenched with sweat. Gunner stood up on the bed and went to him, rubbing his nose on his cheek. Eric took a deep breath and thought about the meaning of his dream before getting out of bed and moving to the couch.

CHAPTER 40

March 2013

"Yes, I have some information about the girl on the news, Melissa Grant." The manager of Terry's Deli in New York City held the line and waited for the investigating officer to come on.

"Yes, sir, what kind of information do you have for us?" the voice on the other end of the line asked.

"Well, I'm not sure, but I think she may have been working here for the past few weeks." The manager was nervous and not overly confident that he was correct, but he felt obligated to call the number given in the news report.

"Why do you think, that, Mister…"

"Parks, Dave Parks."

"Go on Mr. Parks. What can you tell me?"

"There was a girl who was working here. She said she was studying at Manhattan University, but she didn't act like a college kid. She seemed older, a little wary maybe."

"And what makes you think she was Melissa Grant? Did she tell you that was her name?"

"No, officer. She said her name was Elaine Smith, and she had a driver's license, social security number, and all. She was real dependable in the short time she was here, then all of a sudden, the day after that news report aired, she disappeared. It's been a couple weeks, and I ain't seen her since."

"And you suspect she might have been Miss Grant because she suddenly disappeared?"

"Well, that, and the fact that except for the red hair, she and that Grant girl could'a been twin sisters."

"Thank you, Mr. Parks. You have been very helpful. Can you please give me a phone number where I can reach you in case we have any more questions?"

When the phone call ended, the investigator made another call.

"Yes?" said the voice on the other end.

"The missing package is being tracked."

"Any word on where it ended up?"

"Not yet, but we may have a positive ID."

"Let me know when you locate it." The call ended. The man on the other end brushed a piece of lint off of his outrageously expensive Alexander Amos suit before returning to the daily briefing on the status of world affairs. His boss would be very pleased with the news obtained from the intercepted phone call.

CHAPTER 41

March 2013 - Philadelphia, PA

"Adopted?" Detective Morris said as he stared at Officer Mindy Berman's report.

"Yes, sir." Officer Berman motioned toward the file. "James and Ann Grant were her adoptive parents, but her birth parents are unknown at this time."

"Who do we know in Maryland who can get us a subpoena?" Morris asked. "I want those records, and I want them immediately."

"Sir, you don't think this has anything to do with the shootings, do you? I don't see a connection."

"Berman, right now I'll take anything I can get. I'll call Baltimore PD and see if we can get their cooperation. We need to question their neighbors, friends, anyone who knew the family well. Does anyone know anything about the adoption and if Melissa knew about it?"

"I'll find out, sir," Berman said as she exited. Morris had served on the force for almost forty years, and his intuition had never failed him. They were on to something. He could feel it.

CHAPTER 42

November 16, 2014

It was the night of a full moon, and Julie was taking Helen's advice. She parked in the lot at the town marina and walked out onto the dock, carrying her camera and a blanket from the cottage. She sat down on the edge of the dock, wrapped the blanket around her, and checked the camera to be sure it was on the right setting. She took a couple of preliminary shots to ensure that the pictures would be good. When she heard the sound of the truck pull into the lot, a smile tugged at her lips. She turned and watched Eric stroll toward her with a bottle of wine and two glasses in his hands.

Julie began to ask how Eric had known she was there, but he cut her off and motioned to the moon.

"I decided to take a chance," he shrugged. "I thought you might need backup in case the British ship shows up."

"I think I can handle myself, Eric." She waved her arm in front of her. "There isn't another soul around, dead or alive."

"Okay, but what's a ghost hunt without a good bottle of wine?" he asked as he took a seat beside her.

"I wouldn't know. This is my first ghost hunt." Julie grinned and gave in as Eric popped the cork on the wine.

He poured them each a glass and raised his in a toast. Julie
matched his glass in the air.

"To full moons and ghostly legends," he toasted, and
they each took a sip before turning their attention to the
harbor.

While they sat on the dock, with the moon illuminating
the harbor and casting an eerie glow on the water, Eric
told Julie some of the other local lore. She was particularly
intrigued by the history of Perry Hall, an estate once
owned by William Perry, President of the Maryland
Senate in the 1790s.

"My sister, Lisa, loves riding by the house when we go
out in the boat. She eats up the legends. According to one
story," Eric began, "an ancestor of Perry's wife was struck
by lightning while calling out the window to a servant.
The force of the electric shock caused the door on a
grandfather's clock to swing open, and the clock's gold
pieces flew across the room. Nobody knows what
happened to the woman, whether the pieces killed her or
whether she just disappeared.

"Then there's another legend that a great treasure exists
somewhere at Perry Hall that has lured treasure hunters
from around the world, to no avail, and another one about
a slave by the name of Ned who still walks the plantation
grounds." Eric continued as Julie listened without
speaking, mesmerized by his tales.

"A more captivating tale is that of the Frenchman's
Oak, a giant tree on the water's edge, which served as the
meeting place for two lovers. According to the story,
during the Revolutionary War, a young French soldier in

Lafayette's army met his mistress under the oak tree. The two were discovered by the young woman's betrothed who slew the French soldier with a sword right in front of her. Watermen, sea captains, and leisure sailors along the Miles River have long told of seeing the lovers kissing under the tree by the light of the full moon."

"The full moon legends go on and on around here, don't they?" Julie asked with a smile.

"It's an area full of both history and mystery," Eric said as he split the last of the wine between their glasses. "But you have to be here for several more full moons to hear and see them all." He cast a sideways glance at Julie who ignored him and picked up her camera, wordlessly shooting images of the moonlit harbor.

After a few minutes, Julie capped the lens and started to stand up, pulling the blanket tighter around her shoulders. "I'm getting pretty cold," she said. "I think it's time for me to call it a night."

Eric stood next to her, and they gazed out onto the water. "Okay, but promise me something," he waited for her to look at him. "Promise me that someday, you'll let me take you out on the boat to see Perry Hall under the full moon."

"I can't make that promise, Eric, but please know that I wish I could." She turned and walked back to her car. Eric stayed on the dock and watched her leave. Julie wiped a tear, squashing any hope that her story would have a happier ending than any of the tales he had shared with her that night.

CHAPTER 43

April 1, 2013 - Washington, D.C.

"We've tracked the package to Chicago and believe it has been re-routed to Denver."

"How soon until it is found and destroyed?"

"It should be done by tomorrow night."

"Very good," replied the man. Today he wore a $47,000 Desmond Merrion suit. "Anything else?"

"We may have a problem in Philly."

"Go on…"

"That police detective has gotten a subpoena for the birth records. He's digging pretty deep."

"Eliminate him."

The man in the suit ended the call and looked out his office window onto Executive Avenue Northwest. He could just make out the North Lawn Fountain in the yard across the street at 1600 Pennsylvania Avenue.

He had paid his dues for many years to work in this building and to stand in this office. His boss had even higher aspirations than this for the two of them, and he'd be damned if some mistake from almost thirty years ago was going to get in the way.

CHAPTER 44

April 7, 2013, - Philadelphia, PA

It was a spectacular Easter morning in Philadelphia. Though long divorced and somewhat of a loner, Frank Morris never missed a holiday with his daughter and grandchildren. They were just leaving the Easter service at the First Presbyterian Church on South 21st Street when Morris's cell vibrated. Ignoring the call, he picked up his youngest granddaughter and swung her onto his shoulders. A minute later, the caller tried again.

Annoyed with being disturbed on a rare day with his family, Morris checked the number. It was blocked. He answered the call.

"Morris."

"I have information about Melissa Grant. Meet me in ten minutes in Rittenhouse Square by the giant frog."

"You've got to be kidding me. Who is this?" Morris demanded.

"A friend." The call ended, and Morris looked at his cell as if it contained a clue he was missing.

"Dad, what's wrong?" Are you coming?" His daughter stood by the family car, looking anxiously at her father.

"Yeah, I have to make a stop first." He motioned for her to get in the van as he opened the door on his Taurus, parked in the next space.

"Are you sure everything's okay?"

"Yeah, yeah, positive. It's nothing. It will only take a minute. Don't start the Easter egg hunt without me," he said as he closed the door.

Ten minutes later, he was sitting on a bench near the frog statue, watching the families in their Easter clothes hunting for eggs or just out enjoying the sunshine. On the way over, he considered calling Officer Berman, as she was Jewish and probably not celebrating Easter, but he didn't want to intrude on her weekend. He would just see how this played out.

After another ten minutes went by, Frank gave up. The kids would be having a fit if he didn't get over to the house soon. He walked away in disgust, wondering how some prankster had gotten his private number. He didn't notice the blinking red light under the carriage of the car. He was silently cursing the caller as he turned the key in the ignition and set off the explosion that shattered the peace of that quiet Sunday morning.

Two days later, Officer Berman received a manila envelope in the mail addressed to her attention with no return address. As far as she knew, she was the only one who suspected why her former boss had lost his life. No, it wasn't just suspicion, she was certain. An explosion was not a message to the person it killed. It was a message to those left behind. Mindy's sixth sense kicked in, and she hid the envelope in her bag until after she made it home.

Opening it with trepidation, she used tweezers to pull out the letter contained within the packet. Her gloved hand began to tremble as she read the information that had been sent to her.

The paper looked like a kindergarten project with its clipped magazine page alphabet. Mindy was surprised. After six years as a city cop and detective, she had never seen an actual clue made of cut-out letters, glued to a piece of paper. Neither the envelope nor the paper gave any indication as to where it had come from or who sent it. There was nothing special about the materials, and the letters could have come from any magazines on the market. Though it was probably a waste of time, she would take it back to work and dust it for prints. The possibility of finding DNA on either piece was doubtful. The envelope was of the peel and stick variety. Whoever sent this seemed to have thought of everything.

The message was clear:

BACK OFF
GRANT = TROUBLE

Sliding the paper back into the envelope, and closing the flap with trembling hands, Mindy sat at her desk unable to move. She thought about the message and the fact that it had been sent directly to her. Then she sat in dread and tried to figure out what to do next.

CHAPTER 45

April 10, 2013 - Bethesda, MD

Meg Gallagher was nervous about going to work that morning. She had done something that she might forever regret, something that could even get her killed. She looked both ways before crossing the street to the metro and nonchalantly watched the other subway passengers with a wary eye. Anybody could be on to her.

Meg was forty-five, attractive in a suburban, working mom kind of way—brown hair neatly cut short, trimmed and manicured nails, nice suit from Nordstrom (but from the bargain rack of course). She used her maiden name at work and used Gallagher for family and school events. She worked hard to get to where she was and had everything going for her. She married a wonderful, caring man, had three terrific kids, a nanny to take care of her children and home while she worked, and a job that most would envy. Like many working moms, she valued her job, but not because of the reasons one would think. A graduate of American University, she studied hard and beat out a lot of others in her department to get an internship in the Nation's Capital that she knew would put her on the right track. It wasn't the job itself, the money, or even the clout that she desired. It was one particular man she needed to be close to. Though it sickened her to be near him, knowing what she, and she alone, knew about him, she swore many years ago that she would watch his every move and that she would never again let him get away with murder.

The envelope she mailed from the blue mailbox in Union Station should have arrived today. She hoped it reached the right person and that the receiver heeded the warning it contained. Though, Meg admitted to herself, a part of her hoped that Officer Berman would continue digging. If anyone deserved to be found out, it was the man responsible for a killing spree that started twenty-six years ago.

CHAPTER 46

November 19, 2014

As the days grew shorter, and November waned toward December, Julie found herself thinking that maybe she could stay in St. Brendan through the winter. She was torn over what to do since she knew that coming back to Maryland was taking a chance in more ways than one. Not only was she in greater danger, being this close to where people knew her, but she was beginning to remember all the things she loved about the Mid-Atlantic area. There were few places in the country where there were truly four distinct seasons. Though Maryland had somewhat of a reputation for going right from summer to winter and sometimes right from winter to summer, Julie had traveled enough in the past couple years to know that wasn't true. She had come to appreciate the temperate fall and spring weather that could be found here.

She had also forgotten how great it was to be in a state where, in less than five hours, you could drive from the ocean with its warm sand and salty air, to the mountains with their crystal-clear streams and fresh pine scent. Called 'America in Miniature,' Maryland had cliffs in the south, farm fields in the east, and rolling meadows in the north, all as spectacular as its flowing ocean and majestic mountains. How Julie longed to be able to travel across the entire state and photograph every scene without fear of being chased by an unidentified pursuer.

For today, Julie was content to photograph some of the most important sites in Maryland's history. For the past twenty-one months, Julie felt like a passenger on a runaway train, someone trapped in a world out of her control, running and hiding with nobody to trust. Feeling akin with one of Maryland's most famous historical figures, Julie made the half hour drive to Cambridge, nestled on the Choptank River, a finger of the Chesapeake Bay. It was not far from here that Harriet Tubman worked on the most famous 'railroad' in American history, when she had little control over her life, and spent much time in hiding and helping others to run and hide.

Julie walked down High Street, taking pictures of the historic buildings, including the Dorchester County Courthouse. According to a book that Julie found in the Bailey house, this was where Tubman's niece escaped from a slave auction, was smuggled from the county, and escorted to freedom by her Aunt Harriet. Julie continued on to Race Street where she toured the Harriet Tubman Museum. She wasn't sure how long she stood and gazed at the famous portrait of Tubman with a bright green shawl draped across her shoulders.

"It's quite beautiful, isn't it?" asked the volunteer museum guide.

"It takes my breath away," Julie answered. "She was a remarkable woman. I hope I have half of her strength and courage if I need it."

"Let's hope you never need it, my dear," the woman smiled. Julie smiled back and thought *if you only knew*.

Julie left Cambridge and drove to the small town of Church Creek. She had hoped to be able to take pictures of the new Harriet Tubman State Park, but construction and restoration of the area was scheduled to continue for a couple more years before the park would open. Julie wasn't disappointed with the drive, however, and stopped numerous times to photograph the colorful fall foliage before crossing over onto Taylor's Island.

Julie drove around the small island, taking pictures of the nearly leafless trees along the water and the piers and small coves. She drove to the south side of the island where she found a family campground, closed for the season. She thought briefly about what it would be like to have a family to bring here to this secluded site. She imagined Eric teaching their children how to fish while she took pictures and then immediately shook the vision from her head. What conjured up that image? She turned the car around and headed back toward St. Brendan.

It was dark by the time Julie returned to the little cottage. She emptied a can of Campbell's soup into a saucepan and heated a mug of hot chocolate in the microwave. The rest of the evening was spent curled up in front of the gas-heated fireplace reading Catherine Clinton's *Harriet Tubman: The Road to Freedom*. Julie fell asleep and dreamt that America's Moses was leading her to safety. However, in her dream, it was Eric who waited for and held his hand out to lead her home when she crossed the line to freedom.

CHAPTER 47

November 20, 2014

It was the perfect night for roasting marshmallows. The air was crisp, the sky was clear, and the outdoor fireplace in Eric's back yard was roaring with glowing flames. It was one of the many upgrades that the previous owners had installed, and after considering it nothing but a nuisance every time he cut the grass, Eric was actually happy to have it tonight.

"This really is the first time you've ever used this?" Julie asked.

She and Eric snuggled together, wrapped in a blanket, on an old chaise lounge he had pulled from his mother's shed. She wasn't sure why she accepted his invitation for dinner at his house, but ever since her dream the other night in which Eric and Harriett Tubman led her to safety, she found herself beginning to let her guard down.

"Boy Scout's Honor." Eric held up his fingers as he made the hundred-year-old promise. "I've never had a reason to use it before, or the desire to use it. Tonight, it just felt right to give it a try."

Julie couldn't agree more. For the first time in a long time, everything felt right. She watched the smoke as it curled up into the night sky and became lost in the twinkling stars.

"One more?" Eric asked. Without waiting for an answer, he reached out from the blanket for two more marshmallows and slid them onto the prongs on the roasting fork.

"Why not?" Julie answered as she unwrapped two miniature Hershey bars and picked up four graham crackers, a set for each of them. "I just won't eat for the next week," she laughed.

Eric held the marshmallows just above the flames, and they sat in silence and watched him rotate the sugary concoctions amidst the swirling smoke. She watched as he turned the marshmallows so that they toasted evenly, a soft golden-brown tinge with a little dark brown on the edges. Just as one of the marshmallows caught fire, he pulled them from the fire and gently blew on them, putting out the small flame. He sandwiched them between the chocolate and graham crackers that Julie handed to him. He gave Julie one of the sticky, sweet treats and then made his own.

"Elizabeth could eat a dozen of these in one sitting," Eric said quietly, a smile on his lips as he looked at the s'more.

"Tell me about her." Julie asked tenderly.

Eric was quiet for a few moments.

"Well," he began. "There's a lot to tell."

They finished their s'mores, licking the sticky marshmallow residue from their fingers, and settled back down under the blanket on the lounge. Once they were both comfortable, Eric began to speak.

"She was beautiful, not Miss America beautiful, but the kind of beauty that comes from deep in her soul and radiates for everyone to see." Julie rested her head on Eric's chest and looked at the starry sky as Eric lost himself in the past and took her with him.

"We met in college, and I knew from the minute I saw her walk into my math class that I wanted to know her. She had an air of confidence that turned every head in the room, but a kindness that emanated from every part of her as she spoke to others and truly listened to what they had to say. She made everyone she spoke to feel like they were the center of her attention. She was beauty and brains and compassion all rolled into one. I loved her more than anything in the world." Then he chuckled, "But she wasn't perfect. She had a heckuva temper. Make her angry, and the 'you know what' would hit the fan. It's what made her a good teacher. She looked out for her students like a mother bear protecting her cubs, but if a cub stepped out of line, she was on them faster than they could blink." Eric laughed and shook his head.

"She sounds like a good match for you."

"She always said we were soul mates," Eric sighed and smiled sadly. "But we made our share of mistakes. We worked too hard, put our jobs before our marriage, and made stupid choices about life. We lived like we had all the time in the world. Even poor Gunner suffered from our stupidity, locked up all day in a house in the city with only the dog walker we hired to play with him once a day. Now that I can see what a train wreck we were heading toward, it's too late to go back and fix things."

Julie turned toward him. "But you were happy, right?" Julie had assumed Eric's life with Elizabeth was perfect, but his words made her think otherwise.

"We were happy," Eric affirmed, "but my life with and without Elizabeth taught me several things. First, happiness is fleeting; appreciate it while it's there. Second, don't put a higher paycheck before family. All the money in the world can't buy back a life once it's been taken from you and can't give you a life you never took the time and care to create. And when you have the chance to right the past, you should take it." He paused and took a breath. "I'm beginning to see that it might be possible for lightning to hit twice."

Eric wrapped his arms around Julie and squeezed her tighter as he kissed the top of her head. They remained on the lounge in each other's arms until the fire went out. Eventually the chill of the night air forced Eric to take Julie home. And though it was cold out, the warmth that radiated from Eric's hand to Julie's, as he walked her to her door, spread straight up her arm and into her heart.

CHAPTER 48

July 2013, - Phoenix, AZ

Christina knew Phoenix would be hot in July, but she had no idea it would be this hot. She took her bandana out of her pocket and wiped her brow. Even at nine o'clock in the evening, it was still close to one hundred degrees, but the sunsets here were perhaps the most amazing she had ever photographed. And the cacti, which she had always assumed were all green, were actually a blend of the most beautiful colors one could imagine.

After having 'Elaine' buy a ticket to Denver from Chicago, Christina took a bus to Dallas. She liked Dallas, and she felt safe there, but she didn't want to take any chances. She kept the same alias but thought it best to move on. She didn't want to become too familiar a face. During her time in Dallas, she photographed sites at the Trammell Crow Park, White Rock Lake, and the Arbor Hills Nature Preserve. Her favorite place to take pictures, though, was Bachman Lake Park with its beautiful lakes and winding creeks. It was quite the contrast to the high-rise buildings in the City of Dallas.

The first thing Christina did when she arrived in the 'Big D' was to sign up for the Dallas Photo Walk, but she much preferred finding spots where she could shoot her own personal choices of pictures. She had plenty of photos

of AT&T Stadium where the Cowboys played, the Dallas
Fountain Place, and the Margaret Hunt Hill Bridge, but
they were just typical tourist shots. It was the parks outside
of the city that called to her. With her photographer's
license, she was able to make some money by
photographing the many tourists visiting the city, but she
was most at peace in the parks.

She discovered a small magazine called *American
Photography* and managed to convince the photo editor to
publish her pictures anonymously. She arranged to have
her payments sent to the bank account in the Bahamas that
Chad had helped her set up. Christina only made one
withdrawal, a small amount she retrieved just before
leaving Dallas. Chad had been insistent her that the
account could not be traced, but she didn't want to take
any chances, and she was still doing okay as far as money.
She rarely ate out, stayed in hostels or economic rentals,
and watched every penny. By now, Christina was getting
good at being on the run, but she prayed that someday she
could stop running and learn to enjoy life again.

CHAPTER 49

November 22, 2014

"Hold the line steady as you reel it in." Eric had his arms wrapped around Julie as he helped her reel in the rockfish. He could feel here shivering beneath him and knew that it wasn't from excitement or from fear. He was sure shew as freezing. The couple of crisp evenings they spent on the dock and in his back yard had yielded to a cold weekend as the month of November neared an end. Now they were in a boat, running up and down the middle of the Bay. Julie's lips quivered, and her teeth chattered, and Eric worried that his idea of spending the morning on the Bay had been a bad one.

Julie reeled in the fish, and Eric measured it and put it in the cooler, but not before Julie snapped a few pictures. Though it was typical for the person who caught the fish to pose with it, Eric didn't argue with Julie when she insisted that he be the one in front of the camera. Putting the rod back into the shaft on the side of the boat, he told the captain they were taking a break. The other passengers could watch the lines. Eric took Julie's hand and led her into the boat's cabin.

Julie grabbed the heavy-duty thermos Eric brought for her and poured a cup of the steaming hot chocolate. He watched as she blew on it and took a sip.

"Why on earth would anyone want to fish this time of year?" she asked.

Eric laughed. "This is actually a really popular time of year for charters. The fish are huge right now!"

"I'd rather catch a small fish on a warm day." She sat on a cushioned bench, leaned her head back, and closed her eyes.

Eric sat on the bench beside her and put his arm around her, pulling her to him running his hands up and down her arms to bring her warmth.

"Are you having any fun at all?" he asked.

Julie smiled. "I am having fun. I'm just half frozen."

All kinds of ways to keep her warm starting running through Eric's head, but he kept them to himself.

They were spending a lot of time together despite Julie's insistence that she would need to leave town sometime soon. The night before, Julie cooked Eric a Southwestern dish she learned to make in Dallas while on a photo shoot, and then they made it an early night and bid goodbye since they had to get up before dawn on Saturday. Somehow Eric had talked Julie into joining him on this fishing trip. He left Nathan, his teenaged employee, in charge of the store for the day and picked up Julie at five in the morning to head to Tilghman Island to meet the boat. In spite of the cold, Eric knew it was hard to deny the thrill of reeling in a thirty-six-inch rockfish. He had seen the excitement on Julie's face and was familiar with the rush she was experiencing.

Eric checked his watch. "It's almost time to head in," he told Julie, and she leaned toward him and rested her head on his shoulder.

"I wish…" she stopped and sighed.

Eric tilted his head and brushed his lips on her forehead. He didn't ask her to continue her thought. He felt exactly the same way. The images from his nightmare, of looking for Julie in the fog, came back to him for what felt like the thousandth time, and he wondered what he could do to help her and to make their situation permanent.

CHAPTER 50

On his way home from dropping off Julie, Eric's radio, which was clipped to his belt, sounded the tones that designated a working fire in town. The tone was familiar to him, and he could feel his heart racing as the voice over the radio said, "Box 64, Station 60, Station 20, Station 40, Paramedic 96. Working house fire, 46728 Ashby Rd. Smoke showing."

Without hesitation, he turned the truck around and raced toward the fire station to get his gear and meet up with the truck.

The sounds from the radio indicated a house fire out of control just outside of Easton, over which Station 60, in Easton, had domain. The St. Brendan Volunteer Fire Department was Station 40, but because it was a house fire, backup was needed and expected. Eric wasted no time getting back to town and turned into the lot at the station along with several other volunteers. After pulling on the his overalls, he jumped into the truck with his matching coat and helmet in his hands. He was suited up and ready when they reached the scene. As he had been doing since high school, Eric said a quick prayer to St. Florian, Patron Saint of firefighters, as he jumped from the engine and secured his helmet. That short prayer was the only one he ever said anymore, and it was truly more out of habit than faith.

Taking in the scene around him, Eric saw the three stations called to the fire. Easton was the first responder, but the nearby station in Oxford was present as was Cordova. Flames roared through the roof and out the windows of the one-hundred-year-old wooden structure that was the perfect collection of kindling. Eric had witnessed fires like this before, and they seldom ended with the building still standing.

He stood with the other fighters from his engine, alert and ready to go inside if the command from Station 60 gave the order. The family that lived in the house was already safely outside, and Eric was thankful. Though he was away from the department the many years he lived in D.C., he was still among the most experienced due to his years of service as a teenager and the time he had served since returning home. He had no desire to go into a burning house tonight, and it occurred to him that his reluctance was not the norm. Most firefighters relished those few minutes where adrenalin took over as they rushed into a burning building. But as he stood watching the flames consume the house, he realized that there was a reason he had joined back up when he moved home. If somebody needed to go into a burning house, he would be the first one to volunteer because he hadn't cared if he lived or died. Now, for the first time since he buried Elizabeth, he cared.

In time, the fire was under control, but the men continued to hold the nozzles on the flames to keep the scene secure. Firefighters from each station would man hoses, aimed at the house as well as the nearby trees, until the fire was completely out. If any one of the pines surrounding the house ignited, the entire wooded area could go up. The displaced family watched in horror as the monster that took their home, but thankfully not their lives, consumed everything they ever owned.

The air was thick with the smell of smoke, and Eric thought about the different odors that came from a fire. A home contained wood, plastic, fabric, food, and chemicals. All of those things had their own unique smell, but with a house fire, the smoke became a thick, heavy cloud that burned one's eyes and throat and made one's head dizzy with the choking stench of all those things burning at once. Again, Eric was grateful that he was on the outside of the house and not on the inside.

Glancing over at the now homeless family as they climbed into their car and left with nothing but the nightclothes they were wearing, Eric felt the need to make some changes in his life. He would go home and shower and then join Nathan at the store until closing time. After the early start, he'd be more than ready to go to bed early, and then he had a Sunday morning obligation to meet that he had neglected for far too long. It was time to stop dwelling on the regrets and anger in his past and time to start living his life thankful for what he had and what could still be.

CHAPTER 51

November 23, 2014

The processional was just about to start the next morning when the door to the church opened. Julie and Helen were standing with their hymnbooks open when Eric genuflected by the pew and nudged Julie to make room for him. Julie and Helen both picked up on a hint of smoke lingering in Eric's freshly washed hair and knew that he must have been at the fire in Easton the previous afternoon. Helen lifted her eyes upward as they began to sing *The King of Glory*. Julie felt that Helen had been praying for this day for a long time.

Over their Sunday dinner, Eric told the women about the fire, and Helen and Julie planned the menu for their Thanksgiving dinner. There was never a question that Julie would be spending the day with Eric and his mother.

"Don't forget Lisa's crew," Helen said. "She would be insulted if we didn't ask her to bring something."

In the weeks since she arrived in St. Brendan, Julie heard Eric's sister mentioned several times in the tales about his childhood, but she never really made a real-life connection between the two siblings. Eric was thirty-five, but his older sister, Lisa, was in her forties. It was a bit of a surprise when Helen discovered she was pregnant with

Eric after long giving up on having another child. Though Julie had seen her in pictures and knew Lisa called her mother regularly, she hadn't really thought of her as being part of this family that Julie had come to know.

Julie turned ghostly white as she remembered something Helen mentioned one time a few weeks back. Lisa's boys were going to Hershey Park in the Dark, a Halloween celebration at the famed chocolate-themed amusement park, with their Cub Scout Troop. At the time, Julie thought nothing about it. People from all over the mid-Atlantic went to Hershey Park. But now, her heart began to race at the implication.

"Where did you say Lisa lives?" Julie asked with a tremble in her voice. Eric looked at her with concern, and Julie knew that he recognized the look of panic in her eyes.

"Lancaster, Pennsylvania," Helen answered as she picked up another bite of lasagna, seemingly oblivious to the change in the atmosphere.

Julie swallowed the sick feeling that rose in her throat and grabbed the edges of the table. She thought she might pass out. Her ears roared with the echo of Helen's words, and her head began to spin. She held onto the table to steady herself and felt the warm Italian food roll in her stomach.

"Helen, I have to go," she managed to say. "I think I'm coming down with something. I think, I think I'm going to be sick." Helen looked up in alarm as Julie, feeling ill and unsteady, stood and shakily ran from the room.

After she left, Helen turned toward Eric. "What was that about, do you suppose?"

"I don't know, but I have a feeling that her mysterious past is somehow tied to someone or something in Pennsylvania." Eric stood up and laid his napkin on the table. "I'm sorry to run, mom, but I think it's time I got to the bottom of this."

Helen couldn't agree more.

CHAPTER 52

August 1, 2013 - Bethesda, MD

"Mommy, why are you cutting up your magazine?"

Meg jumped when her youngest daughter walked up behind her; it was well past bedtime. She quickly pushed the scraps of paper into a pile to obscure what she was doing. Little Emily was her surprise baby, born just five years ago when Meg was forty-years-old and convinced that her baby making days were over. That's what you get for going on a romantic getaway to celebrate your fifteenth anniversary, her friends teased her. Surprise or not, Emily was the apple of her mother's eye, and Meg never regretted a moment of her life after the spot on the strip turned pink.

"I'm just clipping coupons, honey," Meg told her. "What are you doing out of bed?"

"I couldn't sleep," she pouted. "I need another story."

"I think two stories are enough for one night. How about a cup of warm milk instead?"

The little girl nodded and toddled up to the barstool at the kitchen counter. Meg lifted her into the seat and poured her a cup of almond milk that she heated for forty-five seconds in the microwave. When Emily was finished drinking her milk, Meg scooped her up and carried her back to bed. Emily slid between the Little Mermaid sheets, and Meg kissed her on the forehead. She couldn't imagine life without her girls. What would she have done if she'd had to give one of them up, or what would their lives be like if they were being raised by someone else, and Meg was completely out of the picture, perhaps even dead? She shook the question from her mind and wiped the tear that slowly trailed down her cheek before Emily could see it.

"But Laurie and Betsy don't have to go to bed yet," she protested through a yawn, her eyes getting heavy.

"And when you are in high school, you will get to stay up late, too. But for now, it's lights out young lady, or no park after school tomorrow." Emily nodded sleepily and rolled over, hugging her teddy bear.

Meg closed the door and hurried back out to the kitchen. She hastily finished gluing the letters onto the piece of copy paper she took from the printer and slid it into the envelope before anyone else decided to venture from their bedrooms. While part of her hoped that Officer Berman of the Philadelphia Police Department would keep looking for answers, part of her was afraid that the end result would be another death she could have prevented. She would try warning her again and hope that neither of them was caught.

She hid the envelope in her briefcase and cleaned up the mess. Her husband was out of town, and she wanted no evidence left behind when he returned the following day, not to mention when her teenage daughters woke up in the morning. She knew that she was playing a dangerous game, but she made a vow many years ago to protect an innocent child, and she would not go back on her promise.

CHAPTER 53

August 3, 2013

Mindy Berman looked at the note on her desk. She glanced around to make sure that nobody was looking before she slipped the envelope into her bag to take home and place with the other one. For the past four months, she had been quietly looking into the life and disappearance of Melissa Grant. She kept the cold case investigation from her Sergeant, from the new detective in charge of their task force, and even from her partner. She tried to concentrate on her other, more pressing cases until it was time to go home, but her mind kept drifting back to the envelope hidden in her bag. Frank's death had been attributed to one of the gang-related cases he had been working, but Mindy was certain it was tied to the Grant case. She was determined to solve the case and bring Frank's killer to justice.

On her way back to her apartment, Mindy decided it was time to consult with the best. Her uncle was retired now but was once a big shot in D.C. law enforcement. The stories he told were wilder than a James Patterson novel, and she often wondered what it must have been like to be a cop 'back in the day' before technology and government rules and regulations had changed the game in so many ways. Mindy looked up the number on her phone for his retirement home on Lake Michigan. She started to hit the Call button, and then stopped herself. Feeling rather paranoid, she slipped on her shoes and grabbed her purse. She headed to the drug store down the street where she could buy a burner phone. Officer Berman was taking no chances.

Later that night, she sat sipping a glass of wine as she tried to decide what to do. Her Uncle Jack listened to everything she had learned but had no suggestions as to where to turn for more information. He concurred that Frank's death was connected to Grant but firmly believed that whoever planted the bomb had some mighty powerful connections, and there was no way for Mindy to continue her investigation without leaving a trail. She assured him that she had been careful. By questioning some of Melissa's neighbors in Philly, her former co-workers, and some of her neighbors in her old Baltimore neighborhood, her uncle warned her, she had already put herself in too much danger and needed to back off.

"Burn the letters and move on," he told her. "Whoever is behind this knows what he's doing. Melissa Grant is most likely in the belly of a shark by now."

Mindy knew that she wouldn't be able to stop until she discovered what happened to Melissa and who killed Frank Morris. She looked down at the letter sitting next to her on the couch, the magazine letters taunting her with their hidden message, and she knew she was getting close.

PLEASE STOP
I CAN'T HIDE YOUR TRAIL FOREVER

CHAPTER 54

November 24, 2014

Eric had not seen nor heard from Julie since Sunday afternoon. He went straight to her house that evening after she left the dinner at Helen's, but she did not answer the door. Her car was gone, and Eric gave her the benefit of the doubt that she was still in town, but his heart raced wildly with the thought that she may have fled. By Monday night, he was beside himself with worry. She hadn't met Helen at yoga that morning, and she didn't answer the door later that evening when Eric stopped by. He'd hoped she would drop by the store that day, but she did not. By Tuesday afternoon, he decided that he was going to go to her house and wait for her and was not leaving until she returned. He continued to hope that she had not run, that she would not leave him that easily.

He took Gunner home, fed the dog some dinner, and let him out for a quick run before he drove back into town. He parked his truck on the next street over and planted himself on her porch swing to wait. It was almost midnight when the sound of her car woke him up. He sat as still as a statue and was grateful that it was a dark night.

Julie got out of the car and closed the door. She walked up to the house, glancing all around before climbing the steps to the porch. Eric silently watched her swing open the door and glance inside.

"There's nobody in there," he said. Julie screamed and dropped her keys as Eric rushed to her side. He threw one arm around her body and covered her mouth with his hands. She didn't try to fight him, but the look in her eyes told him she was ready for a brawl. Eric pulled her inside the house and closed the door.

"You scared the hell out of me," Julie yelled at him. Instead of fear, Eric saw only fury in her eyes.

"You scared the hell out of me," he shouted back. "Where have you been?"

Julie went to the window and looked outside. She turned back to Eric. "Let's not wake up the neighborhood," she said through gritted teeth.

"We're probably too late for that," Eric spat back.

"What are you doing here at this time of night?" Julie asked heatedly.

"Trying to talk to you," his eyes flashed with anger. "I thought you were going to run... again."

"Oh, and I'm the only one running from something? Look in the mirror, Eric." Her accusation hung in the air between them. Eric said nothing at first and then shook his head. Taking a deep breath to calm down, he locked eyes with Julie.

"I'm not running anymore, Julie. Don't you know that? Can't you see it? Feel it? The only place I want to be is here. With you."

Julie collapsed on the couch and put her head in her hands. She looked up at Eric with tears in her eyes.

"Eric, I don't want to fight with you."

Eric sat beside her on the couch and turned toward her. He took her hands in his.

"Neither do I, but I don't want to be shut out anymore either. You need to level with me. Now." He enunciated his words, "Let me help you."

Julie pressed her lips together between her teeth, closed her eyes, and took a deep breath. She opened her eyes and looked at Eric. Her eyes were full of pain, of fear, and something more. Her eyes were full of love.

"What if telling you the truth could get you killed?"

"If you run, I *will* die without you." As the words tumbled from his mouth, Eric admitted to himself, as well as to Julie, the extent to which he had come to care for her. His heart felt heavy, as if pumping was a chore. A lump formed in his throat, and he implored her with his eyes to trust him, to open up to him, and to let him love her.

Julie sat silent for several minutes with her mind and heart at odds. Her best friend and her dear friend and companion had died because of her. A trained police officer was killed in the line of duty while trying to protect her. She had escaped death three times in Philadelphia, and evaded capture and probably death in San Diego. After all that she had been through and the care she had taken for the past two years to protect herself, was it worth the risk to confide in Eric? Julie's mind continued to wage war with her heart, counting off dozens of reasons why it was a bad idea to open up to anyone. However, her heart couldn't get past the look in his eyes, the feel of her hands in his, the yearning to unburden herself of her secrets and wrap herself in the warmth of the feelings that pulsed through her body when he was near. Julie took a deep breath and pushed aside the warnings that flashed in her head.

And for the first time in almost two years, she talked about her past.

CHAPTER 55

November 2013 – San Diego, CA

Brandy Holmes stood on the deck of the U.S.S Midway. She joined the tour group, so she could see the famous aircraft carrier docked in the San Diego Harbor. She had been taking pictures of it from the shore for the past couple months, and her curiosity finally got the better of her. She had never been on a military ship, and she was excited to be part of a group, even if it was only temporary at best. Brandy had been alone for almost a year now, and her solitary life was becoming depressing. She tried to make the best of it every day by reminding herself that she was still alive.

"Welcome to the most visited Naval ship in the world," the young female officer touted as the group gathered. "The Midway is the longest-serving Navy aircraft carrier of the 20th century, and we are proud to have you all on board."

Brandy listened as the guide listed the rules of the tour—stay together, do not enter restricted areas, do not touch anything unless given permission, or instructed to do so, etc. Brandy was amazed by the size of the ship, enthralled by the primary flight control room, and stunned by the sleeping quarters, bunks that resembled metal

shelves with blankets stretched on them and no doubt felt
as claustrophobic as a coffin. That was certainly a
sensation she could have done without.

After the hour-long tour, Brandy spent quite some time
in the gift shop. Although she had a degree in nursing, she
always had a keen interest in American history. She ran
her fingers over the souvenirs and read the backs of
several books about Naval history and major victories at
sea. She walked back out onto the deck, before
disembarking from the ship, and gazed out at the ocean. It
was a far cry from Phoenix, and Brandy was happy she
made the decision to move on. Her intuition told her that it
was time to morph into her next persona and make a clean
break, and she chose to spend the fall in California, a state
she always hoped to visit. She was trying to decide where
to go next and was preparing to leave the West Coast
before winter. She had her heart set on seeing snow. The
previous winter seemed as if it had been years ago, and
she longed to be closer to home.

CHAPTER 56

November 2013 – Washington, D.C.

The man in the Brioni suit used all the restraint he had not to throw his cell phone across the room. Just because he wore the same suit as James Bond didn't mean that he was happy about this continuous undercover plot he was orchestrating. He was tired of this messy covert operation that required lying to government agencies and using National security resources to cover up a personal problem, though he admitted that wielding that power gave him a rush better than sex. He worked with only top-notch professionals, men who knew their stuff and didn't make mistakes, mostly former military and highly trained. Why had this gone on for almost eleven months now? How did an average nurse from Baltimore keep eluding them? The only thing that kept him from completely losing control was that things were finally looking up.

He paced back and forth in his office as he recalled this latest conversation. The most sophisticated facial recognition software (FRS) that Homeland Security employed had identified Melissa Grant in four states over the past eleven months. She managed to leave New York before being found by his men back in February, but he was now able to trace her steps. After leaving New York, she was spotted at O'Hare Airport in Chicago and then on a street corner in Dallas. Ironically, the camera that logged her appearance there was a security camera outside the Texas Book Depository. Too bad it hadn't been there on November 22, 1963 when Lee Harvey Oswald made his way to the sixth floor of the building. Perhaps many of those conspiracy theories could have been laid to rest.

Melissa was spotted in Dallas as late as July, but when his man arrived in the city, she was nowhere to be found. A few people thought her picture looked familiar, but nobody knew for sure. She had certainly learned to remain anonymous since leaving New York. But as fate would have it, she was identified by the FRS arriving at a bus station in Phoenix a week later. After that, she disappeared...until today.

Grant had been very smart up until now. Today, a woman named Brandy Holmes, who looked an awful lot like Melissa Grant, had taken a tour on the U.S.S Midway. That was a big mistake. Security cameras were everywhere on the military vessel, and one in the museum gift shop had filmed Holmes without her sunglasses and hat on. There was no doubt—Melissa Grant was in San Diego. Now they just had to get to her before she disappeared again.

PART FOUR

*Trust is to human relationships what faith is to gospel
living. It is the beginning place, the foundation upon
which more can be built. Where trust is, love can flourish.*
Barbara Smith

CHAPTER 57

November 27, 2014

Julie came clean to Eric. She told him everything, starting with the morning she walked into her apartment and her entire world turned upside down in a split second. She cried in his arms when she described seeing Tina's lifeless body. She shuddered as she told him about the night she fled from the police after a third attempt on her life in as many days. She wept over her role in Chad's death and the guilt she felt that, by saving her life, he lost his own.

Julie documented the cities she visited over the past twenty-two months: New York, Chicago, Dallas, Phoenix, San Diego, St. Louis, New Orleans, Mobile, and Miami. She told Eric she had grown weary of moving from one city to another and longed to just go home. The Eastern Shore was as close as she dared to go, and now she was afraid that she had made a mistake.

"I should have stayed away from the Mid-Atlantic altogether but especially Maryland. I had hoped that maybe they stopped looking for me, that maybe I could live a normal life, but what if I'm wrong?" She wrapped her arms around her chest and rocked like a child. When she looked up at Eric, he saw in her eyes the vulnerability she always tried to hide.

"Maybe they have stopped. How do you know they haven't?" he asked.

"How do I know they have?"

Ignoring her question, Eric asked one of his own. "And you have no idea why they're after you?"

Julie shook her head. "No idea."

"Did you see something or hear something you shouldn't have? Did you somehow come across information—"

"No," Julie was emphatic. "The police asked me the same questions, and I've asked myself those and more for the past two years. If I knew why, don't you think I would have found a way to end this by now?"

Eric looked at her without answering. He encircled his arms around her and pulled her close to him.

"I think you're the strongest person I've ever known," Eric whispered to Julie. "How have you kept going all this time with nobody else to lean on and without giving up?"

Julie raised her head and looked at Eric, the small hint of smile played on her lips. "I remind myself of one of my mother's favorite quotes, something she read by the philosopher, Cicero: 'While there's life, there's hope.'"

She laid her head back on Eric's chest and closed her eyes. While Julie was afraid that she made a mistake by confiding in Eric, she was relieved to have shared the truth with someone she trusted. In a couple hours, it would be daybreak, but Julie that Eric was not in a hurry to leave.

After reliving the nightmare that was her reality, she didn't want to be alone.

🎴

Exhaustion finally took over, and Julie struggled to keep her eyes open. Eric picked her up and carried her into the bedroom. He eased her onto the bed and managed to pull the covers down around her as drowsiness overtook her. They had abandoned their shoes long before, so he tucked her feet under the sheets and pulled the covers up around her. He walked around to the other side of the bed and stretched out beside her on top of the quilt. He pulled her to him and held her. He listened to her gentle breathing and, in spite of everything she told him and the fear that coursed through him when he thought of her being in danger, he felt, for the first time, as if he were truly at home. He closed his eyes and held onto her, and they slept until long after the sun appeared above the trees.

CHAPTER 58

That evening, Eric called Jerome. For the past two weeks Jerome had met dead end after dead end. He was no closer to discovering anything about Julie Lawson than he was to finding the cure for cancer.

"You believe her." It wasn't a question, but Eric assured him of the answer.

"I do."

"What do you want me to do?" Jerome asked.

"There has to be a reason why she was being targeted. I'd like to know what that is. I'd also like to know if they're still after her or discovered any of her other identities."

Eric gave Jerome the list of names Julie used and in what cities she used them. He promised to be back in touch.

"And Jerome, be careful. I have no idea who or what we're dealing with here."

"Always am, my friend. Always am."

CHAPTER 59

November 2013 - Mount Vernon, VA

Meg took advantage of Betsy's field trip and used the blue, U.S. Mail drop-off box to send her latest note to Officer Berman. The Philadelphia Police detective was not giving up, and Meg knew she would keep digging until she dug her own grave. It was time to give her a solid clue. The decision was easier than she thought it would be. An item on last night's local news broadcast reminded her about that morning so many years ago, a day that would stay stamped on her brain forever.

It was the morning she returned home from visiting her parents and found her best friend lying in a pool of her own blood...

Judging by her appearance and the state of the apartment, Meg knew exactly what happened to Lissa, but when she came to, her friend refused to tell her the truth or involve the police. It wasn't until six months later that Meg confronted her.

"Don't shut me out, Lissa, I'm your best friend. You might be the one in medical school, but I know a pregnant woman when I see one, especially when we're living in the same house and she's as far along as you are."

Lissa broke down in tears and collapsed onto the couch. She held her head in her hands and sobbed while Meg sat beside her, stroking her hair.

"Oh, Meg, what am I going to do?" She shook her head and sniffed. "I can't have a baby, I just can't; but I can't just, just..." The sobs turned into wails as Lissa thought about all the classes she had taken on human growth and development, the ones where students argued over what constitutes a life. She never allowed herself to think it through before; she absorbed both sides of the argument and decided to stay undecided, but now... now that she could feel the baby kick and turn and saw in the books and on the sonogram what she looked like...

"Shh, honey, it's okay. You don't have to do either. I can help you. We'll go to one of those agencies. They'll help you find a nice couple."

Lissa nodded her head but continued to hold it in her hands and cry.

"What about the father?" Meg asked quietly. Lissa looked up and met her friend's gaze.

"You know as well as I do that there is no father, only a monster who would rather I kill this baby than—" Lissa suddenly stopped talking and looked at Meg with sheer terror in her eyes. "I've made a terrible mistake."

"What have you done?" Meg asked with trepidation.

Lissa swallowed and then continued. "I contacted him. I wrote to him and told him I needed help. I told him I'd go to the press if he didn't help me. I was desperate, but now... now I think I might be in danger."

Meg's heart began to race. What was Lissa talking about? Who was this man? Why would the press care, and what kind of danger could she be in now? Meg hesitated to ask, but she had to know the truth if she was going to help her friend.

"Lissa, it's time you tell me the truth, the whole truth, and don't leave a single detail out."

An hour later, Meg was exhausted, and her mind reeled with the story she had just been told. How could this be real? These kinds of things only happened in movies. Surely, he wouldn't actually try to hurt Lissa...

"Promise me," Lissa grabbed Meg's hands and held them tightly in desperation as she looked her friend in the eye. "Promise me that if something ever happens to me, you won't let anything happen to this baby. Don't ever let him get her. As far as I'm concerned, you are her godmother, even if I give her up to someone else and we never see her. I'm depending on you to keep her safe."

Meg swallowed hard and slowly nodded her head. The promise seemed unreal, like something she could never really keep but had to vow to in order to please her friend. It was like a pinky swear on the playground. Were you really bound to that?

"I promise." The oath came out as more a breath than words, and Meg felt the weight of

everything pressing down on her—the knowledge of how the baby was conceived, the fear that her friend might indeed be in danger, and the fact that she was going to have to move out, leaving her troubled friend and their home. Lissa insisted that if Meg stayed, he would know, or at least assume, that Lissa had confided in her. Either way, Meg would be in danger. Meg would need to move out the next day and go back home to her parents' house in Maryland. They would break all ties and have no further contact except through letters, addressed to each other and mailed surreptitiously from mailboxes all around the state, the country even. Their imaginations went wild throughout the night as they devised a plan to keep Meg safe in order to protect Lissa's baby. As soon as the baby was born, and Lissa graduated, she would move far away and never look back, and maybe someday, they could meet up and be friends again, maybe.

Four months later, on a dark night, when nobody else was around, Meg stood by herself in the Fair View Cemetery in Lissa's hometown of Roanoke, Virginia. It was a breezy night, and a cold front swathed the mountains with damp and chilly air. Meg wept quietly as she laid the bouquet of pink asters, Lissa's favorite flowers, on the fresh grave. She reminded herself about the promise she made to protect her best friend's child, and she swore she would spend the rest of her life making sure that no harm came to Lissa's little girl.

CHAPTER 60

November 2013 - Philadelphia, PA

Mindy Berman couldn't believe it. It happened again. She exhausted every avenue and still had nothing. But this time, the letter gave her a glimmer of hope. Maybe there was somebody up there answering her prayers.

When Mindy got home, she retrieved the envelope from its hiding place at the back of her freezer and emptied the contents onto her kitchen table. She now had three letters from an anonymous source. The first two warned her to end her investigation. However, this one did just the opposite, and Mindy wondered why. Was it a trap, or had the tipster finally decided to help? Come hell or high water, Mindy intended to find out.

She put all the letters into the envelope and slid the envelope into the plastic freezer bag. She sealed the bag and replaced it in the back of her freezer. She would dig out that burner phone and call her uncle tonight to ask him to help her figure out a way to conduct a search off the grid. In the meantime, she hunted in her refrigerator for something to eat and thought about the words glued onto the latest letter.

LOOK FOR LISSA MARSHALL
QUIETLY

CHAPTER 61

November 27, 2014

Julie liked Eric's sister, Lisa, right away. Though still nervous that she would be recognized, Julie tried to push aside her fears and enjoy the day. Several times, throughout the meal, she caught Helen looking at her inquiringly, but Julie just smiled and acted like the events of the previous Sunday's dinner had never taken place. Eric did not tell his mother anything other than he was helping Julie sort some things out. He told her that they would tell her more when the time was right.

"So where are you from, Julie?" Lisa asked as she passed the mashed potatoes.

Ready for the question, Julie responded with a smile, "Oh, from all over. I've moved around quite a bit in my life."

"Oh?" Lisa's husband, Mark, spoke up. "Military brat?"

Julie laughed, "Something like that," she answered.

"Oooh, a mysterious one." Lisa winked at Eric and nudged him with her elbow.

"So, Lisa, tell us what's been going on at work," Helen said, stealthily patting Julie's knee under the table as she settled her napkin back in her own lap. "How are things at the school these days?"

Lisa entertained them with tales from her third-grade classroom while they ate. The twins sandwiched Mark across the table from Julie, Eric, and Lisa while Helen sat at the end. The other end was left open in the spirit that Eric's father was still with them. When it was time to clear the dishes, Lisa volunteered for her and Julie to clean up.

"So, tell me, Julie. Have you ever been to Lancaster?" It was the moment she dreaded. Julie nonchalantly began loading the dishwasher and braced herself for Lisa's revelation that she knew who she was.

"I don't think so," Julie said casually.

"It's really beautiful. You and Eric should come up at Christmas. Eric says you're a photographer, and Longwood Gardens looks so amazing during the holidays. You really should come for a weekend and take some pictures. You'll find downtown Lancaster just charming with its carriage rides and old-fashioned decorations." Lisa rambled on as they worked.

"That sounds really nice," Julie answered, relieved that she had not been recognized. "I'll have to talk to Eric. He's really busy this time of year."

"Then you and Mom come." Lisa's eyes twinkled with delight. "We can get a hotel room and make a girls' weekend of it."

Julie thought of Tina and the weekends they used to splurge and get a hotel in New York, Boston, and yes, even Lancaster.

"I'll think about it," Julie said. As Lisa continued talking about the things they could do, Julie noticed Eric standing in the doorway, leaning against the doorjamb, watching her. He wore a contemplative expression on his face, and Julie couldn't help but smile, both inside and out.

Later that night, Eric and Julie sat on her porch swing, wrapped in a blanket, watching the stars come out.

"This was the best day I've had in a very long time," Julie said as she snuggled closer to Eric. He squeezed her closer to him and closed his eyes.

"Me, too," he whispered. "Me, too."

CHAPTER 62

November 29, 2014

It was 4 o'clock in the morning on Saturday when Eric tiptoed into his bedroom and stood looking at Julie lying in his bed. An overwhelming combination of arousal, tenderness, and protectiveness consumed him, and he had to take a moment to remind himself why she was here, in his bed, after another night on the couch for him. He went to the bed and tugged on her arm.

"Time to wake up, Sleeping Beauty," he told her quietly.

"It can't be time already. I feel like I just went to bed," she groaned.

"Get dressed, and I'll grab something to eat. Don't forget your camera."

Julie sighed and pulled herself out of bed. She could not believe she had actually agreed to get up at this ungodly hour and go traipsing through the woods with Eric.

First, fishing at the crack of dawn in the freezing cold, and now this?

She reached over and turned on the bedside lamp and looked around his room. There was nothing special about it, except that it was his. Eric's clothes hung in the closet, his shoes were neatly lined up along one wall—one pair of dress shoes, a pair of tennis shoes, and a pair of dress boots. His hunting and work boots were in the mudroom, she knew. She walked to the dresser and fingered the few masculine, grooming tools that sat there—a comb, a nail clipper, and a clean, folded handkerchief.

Did men still use those?

A wedding picture sat on the dresser, and she picked it up and looked at the handsome couple. The bride wore a modern, A-line, white satin dress with a small veil down her back, and the groom, a much younger Eric, looked dashing in his black tux. They gazed at each other with such palpable love that Julie's heart ached just a little.

She placed the picture back on the bureau and got dressed. She went downstairs to the kitchen, where Eric handed her a bowl of Raisin Bran.

"I know it's not your usual yogurt, but this will keep you satisfied longer."

They ate breakfast while Eric filled himself a thermos of coffee and filled Julie a thermos of hot chocolate.

"I honestly don't know how you talked me into this," Julie said.

"Because you know that you'll be able to get pictures unlike any you've ever gotten before. Besides," Eric added, "you know you're curious."

Julie couldn't deny that some innermost, and obviously somewhat morbid, part of her actually was curious. She pulled on the heavy camouflage jacket that Eric handed her, along with the matching gloves and orange vest and hat, and grabbed her camera as they walked out the door.

When they reached the site of the hunt, Kari's husband, Rich, was already there.

"I almost suggested we ride together," Rich said.

"I figured we had better ride separately," Eric said. "Just in case." He winked at Rich and nodded his head toward Julie. She stuck her tongue out and rolled her eyes at him.

A very groggy looking Abby tumbled out of the truck, hauling a sleeping bag and a pillow. She perked up when she saw Julie, waved, and walked excitedly to her side. The rest of the men were in the process of deciding who would hunt in which tree stand. It was beginning to dawn on Julie just how big a deal the opening day of deer season was around here. Eric explained to Julie that, while the black powder and bow seasons had come and gone, this was the day most hunters considered the first real day of deer hunting—the first day of rifle season. Seeing the men in their camouflage and listening to them discuss the day's plans, she was starting to understand. Though she was still uneasy at the sight of the guns the men were carrying, she felt safe with Eric at her side.

Eric made the introductions quickly, and Julie learned most of the other hunters were members of the fire department with Eric and Rich. Though she and Abby were the only females, the other men welcomed her. One of the men, a nice-looking, dark-haired man in his late twenties, reached his hand out to Julie.

"I'm Jeff, and I'm very pleased to meet you." He smiled as she shook his hand. "I'm glad this bum finally has a woman in his life. The rest of us at the station were beginning to wonder why he spent more time with us than with a member of the opposite sex." The men suppressed their laughter, trying to maintain quiet in the woods, and Julie blushed; but then it was back to business.

Once the hunting locations were decided, Eric pointed out the direction in which they would be heading. Abby protested just a little when she realized that she was not going to be hunting with Julie, but Julie winked at her and mouthed, *See you later.* Eric and Julie headed off to their assigned stand, while Rich and the pouting little girl headed in the opposite direction. They moved from the faint, pre-dawn light in the clearing, into the dark woods with the aid of a flashlight.

After climbing up into the tree stand, about twelve feet off of the ground, Eric began making preparations for the morning. He unpacked their thermoses and a few snacks as well as the book he brought for himself. Julie looked at him curiously.

"I can read, you know," he whispered.

Julie smiled. "I just didn't expect you to bring a book with you on this most important hunt," she quietly teased back.

"If it wasn't for the many hours I spent in deer blinds after law school, I never would have passed the bar. Where else can you study completely undisturbed except by the sounds of nature?"

"Good point," she grinned as she uncapped the lens of her camera and took a few shots of their stand, the surrounding woods, and Eric making goofy faces at her. When she giggled, Eric gently shushed her.

"Remember, nothing but the sounds of nature."

Julie nodded and settled into the small seat that was attached to the stand. There were two metal, cushioned seats bolted to the metal floor of the stand. A ladder led down to the ground, and a thin railing was pulled down around the stand that reminded Julie of the bars on a roller coaster in the way that it maneuvered down and around them. After an hour or so in the stand, Julie was already starting to feel cold. She reached for the hot chocolate and sipped it slowly as Eric sat, watching her. She looked up and caught his gaze.

"I thought you were going to read," she whispered.

"Too dark still. Besides, I'm enjoying the view," he whispered back with a smile. Julie grinned and dug into her bag to bring out a book of her own. Eric raised his brow.

"Uh huh, thought you were going to get bored, huh?"

"Must be the company," she goaded.

They fell into a companionable silence as they watched the sun come up over the trees. Julie sighed with contentment, and Eric smiled. Who know, Julie thought, that the first day of deer season could be like this?

CHAPTER 63

Eric tapped Julie's outstretched leg lightly with the toe of his boot, and she roused herself from sleep. She looked over just in time to see him slowly raise his rifle. Following the barrel of the gun, she spotted a deer, about one-hundred-and-fifty yards away, slowly making its way through the woods. She moved ever so slowly, as Eric had instructed her the night before, and raised her camera to her eye. She began shooting pictures of the deer as it walked, and continued snapping away for several moments before she realized the deer was still moving and was almost out of sight. She turned to look at Eric. He had quietly lowered his gun and was watching her. Julie eyed him curiously and gave him a quizzical look. Eric shrugged.

"I'll get the next one," he said so softly it was barely a whisper. "I didn't want to spoil your fun."

"Isn't shooting the deer the whole point of us being up here?" Just as she whispered back, they heard a shot from another stand.

Too Late, Eric mouthed.

Abby? Julie mouthed back.

Eric shrugged and mouthed, *Maybe.*

Julie held up crossed fingers and lowered her camera to her lap. She stretched and drank some more of her hot chocolate. She opened her book, another romance novel, and began to read. In her former life, Julie might have been reading a James Patterson or David Baldacci thriller, but those sometimes hit way too close to home.

They spent the rest of the morning alternately reading and looking for deer. It looked as though Eric had missed his only chance and would have to be content with the photos Julie took. That was fine with him. Sometimes, it wasn't as much about the hunt as it was about just being out there in the stand amid the sounds of Mother Nature's children. Now and then, Eric motioned for Julie to listen as he opened his old, beat up copy of *Birds of North America* and pointed to a picture of the species they heard: a Downy Woodpecker, a tree swallow, a pine warbler. Julie was amazed at Eric's knowledge of the local avian whistlers. The more time she spent with him, the more she was impressed by him, and the more she longed to know about him.

By the time they broke for lunch, Julie was stiff from sitting in the stand, and she was pretty cold in spite of the bright, late-morning sun overhead. The group of hunters gathered in the clearing and listened to each other talk about the deer they had seen. There were a couple of does, a button buck (a young male deer with no antlers), and an eight point that was too far away to shoot. It turned out that Abby's first deer was the only prize of the morning. Julie took pictures of her with her trophy, and Abby beamed at the camera as she held up the head of the doe and posed. As Julie understood it, finding the deer so quickly after it was shot was rare, as they usually took off with an adrenaline rush and had to be tracked, sometimes at a great distance. She was happy for Abby's sake that the deer had dropped quickly, and she was ready to call it a day. It was fun to be part of the gang, but she was ready to go back to shooting deer that were running free and not the glassy-eyed, limp variety. Julie was all-too familiar with the feeling of being hunted.

CHAPTER 64

December 1, 2014

"You're not going to like what I found."

"Try me," Eric told Jerome. It was early Monday morning, and Eric was on his way to the store. He drove carefully as Jerome's voice poured through the car speakers.

"Everything she told you adds up; her past, the death of her parents, and then the murders of her friends and the cop. All three look like professional hits."

Eric gripped the steering wheel. "Are you sure?"

"Absolutely. I haven't been doing this all these years for nothing. Someone wanted, or wants, her dead."

"Are you sure they're after Julie, I mean Melissa?" Out of habit, Eric lifted one hand off of the wheel and waved at his neighbor as they passed each other on the road.

"I'd bet money on it. After she ran from police custody, a Philadelphia detective, by the name of Frank Morris, took over the case. He's the one who made the connection between her and O'Donnell and started asking questions about her past. Morris was killed when his car exploded on Easter Sunday, 2013, shortly after obtaining a subpoena for her adoption records. The explosion was ruled a gang hit, but who knows."

Eric wiped the sweat from his brow and maneuvered his car onto the road that ran through the peninsula, eventually becoming Main Street. He found himself glancing in the mirror more than usual as he listened to Jerome.

"Adoption records? She was adopted?" Eric reeled.

"Must've been. She didn't tell you?"

"No," Eric said quietly.

"Maybe she didn't think it mattered. She was gone when the cop was killed and might not have known he was looking into it. Maybe she didn't even know she was adopted."

"Maybe," Eric conceded, but he sure as heck was going to ask her himself.

Jerome told Eric that he was going to do some poking around into Melissa's birth records himself. Eric warned his friend to be careful. He pulled into his space behind Bass & Bucks and cut the engine. It was all he could do to get out of the truck and open the store instead of continuing on to Maple Street. He spent the majority of the day trying to figure out, what on earth could have happened in Julie's past that was so bad that someone wanted her dead, and how he was going to protect her.

CHAPTER 65

December rolled into town with a message: winter is here. The wind howled through the little cottage as Julie tried to cover her face with the pillow. She pulled the covers up higher in an attempt to block out the cold. The gas fireplace in the living room added a beautiful ambience to the room, but it did little to heat up the house. Giving in to her bodily needs, Julie heaved herself out of bed and into the bathroom.

Dinner at Helen's the previous afternoon had consisted of Cornish game hens, sweet potato casserole, broccoli salad, and homemade Southern-style biscuits. They topped off the meal with pecan pie that Helen made, using pecans from her own backyard. If Julie kept eating like that every week, she was going to need a new wardrobe. She smiled at the thought. She hadn't even considered running away since that night before Thanksgiving. She prayed that she wouldn't have to because, honestly, she wasn't sure she could. Although when the thought came to her, she was hit with the realization that she could be putting Eric and Helen in grave danger.

Pushing that possibility as far from her mind as she could, Julie brushed her teeth and turned on the shower. She was trying to decide what to do with her day while at the same time thinking back on the previous night. After watching a movie with Helen on Netflix, Eric and Julie returned to her cottage and stayed up late, playing a board game in front of the fire. Late was relatively speaking since Eric insisted on being in bed by eleven so that he could get up early in the morning, work out at the gym, return home to shower and dress, and then open the store on time. Being in bed meant being in his bed, alone, asleep. Neither Eric nor Julie had broached the topic of him staying the night, and both were comfortable with their current arrangement. Julie had made it clear that she was no prude, but that sex was sacred to her, and Eric was in favor of taking things slow. He and Elizabeth had gone to college together, and of course, they spent most nights together. This time, though, he was willing to do things the right way; though, like any male, Julie was sure he would easily change his mind if given the chance.

Julie dressed and pulled back her hair. She had missed her yoga class and felt guilty about sleeping in, but her one-month membership was up, and she was going to have to figure out whether or not to pay for her classes. She was starting to run low on cash, after being in town for almost two months, and she didn't want to use her debit card until she was ready to move on. Eric told her he was calling his investigator this morning, and she hoped that the man had find something that would mean she could stop running. Her gut, however, was telling her that she needed to think about a clean break. A change in the wind was never a good sign, Julie thought, as she watched the bending and swaying of the trees along the trail behind the house.

CHAPTER 66

January 1, 2014 - St. Louis, MO

Julie Lawson had existed for a little over a month and, so far, was hidden away in a seedy hostel in St. Louis. She let her guard down in San Diego, but she knew better now. She thanked God every day that the grocery delivery kid at the corner deli had a crush on her. It was two days before Thanksgiving when she found him waiting on the doorstep of her hostel after a day of photographing the beach and pier at Scripps Pier in La Jolla. She had just rounded the corner when he jumped up from his perch and grabbed her arm.

"You gotta get outta here, Brandy," he said as he tugged at her.

"What are you talking about, Scott? Is something wrong?" She tried to act casual, but her eyes darted up to the window of her room. She swung her head from side to side trying to identify shapes and faces on the street and in the shadows. Scott continued to tug at her arm.

"Some guy, real creepy looking, military buzz cut, Army tattoo with a big X through it on his arm, ugly sneer. He came to the deli asking questions."

"Wow. What a witness you'd make."

Scott puffed out his chest and pulled himself up taller as her compliment sunk in. He smiled, and Brandy reminded him why he was there to begin with.

"This guy," she whispered, as she became the one doing the tugging and pulled Scott into a nearby alley. "What did he want?"

"I don't know. He had a picture of you. It looked like it was from a security camera, judging by the angle. He was asking Mr. Weisman if he knew you. The old man's so blind he wouldn't know his own dog. I stopped the guy and told him I knew you."

Brandy's eyes widened with horror.

"Don't worry," Scott said, waving his hand. "I told him you'd skipped town. I even said you owed me money and I was real ticked, just for effect."

"What did he do?" Brandy asked as her heart raced and her blood ran cold.

"He left," Scott shrugged. "But you should still go. Just in case. Do you need me to go inside and get anything for you?" He motioned with his head in the direction of the hostel.

"No, but thanks. I keep everything with me all the time." Brandy blew the breath she realized she'd been holding. "I don't know how to thank you, Scott."

"It's cool," he said. "I've known for a while that there was something going on with you. The backpack you're never without, the hat and sunglasses you never take off, the way you're always looking behind you. As soon as that creep showed up, I knew he was looking for you. I didn't even need to see the picture."

"Scott, if you're ever unsure of what to do with your life, become a PI."

Scott grinned. "I'm a Criminal Justice major at San Diego State."

"You're going to be very successful." She hugged him and turned to go but looked back over her shoulder and winked. "You're a lifesaver, Scott. Thank you. I'll never forget you." With that, she started running.

Brandy wasted no time getting to the bus station. She bought a ticket to Las Vegas where she met the last of the shady characters Chad had set her up with. Unless she was willing to go back to the tattoo shop in Philly, where she picked up her first new identity, she was out of luck. Thinking ahead, she asked for additional documents from this cohort—whatever paperwork she would need to be able to purchase a car, if the opportunity presented itself, and advice on how to keep from registering it. It was becoming increasingly tiresome to travel by bus, and she wanted the option of buying a car. Not for the first time, she wondered if these other women, whose identities she assumed, existed somewhere. Were they in the system? Were they paying for her mistakes in some way? Federal charges of identity fraud, forging of documents, and covering up crimes were the least of the things that she felt guilty about. What worried her most was the harm she might be doing to innocent people. For all she knew, these other women might have become victims, just like Tina and Chad.

From Vegas, she crisscrossed the Western U.S. and then the Mid-West. She tried to blend in with the holiday travelers, mostly college kids taking the bus home for Thanksgiving break. She kept her head down and her eyes peeled. By the time she reached St. Louis, she had assumed her last available identity and felt like she aged ten years. Her back was stiff from the many long hours on the bus, and her entire body felt tense with fear and exhaustion, but thus far, Melissa / Elaine / Christina / Brandy / Julie was still alive.

From now on, she had to avoid any place where there was even a remote chance of a security camera. In a bathroom in Montana, she pulled out her emergency box of dye and went to work on her hair. She had been bleaching it little by little in Phoenix and San Diego, and now she was going to a dark blonde shade. Nice 'n Easy number 104 promised to look natural. She so hoped that her hair wasn't going to be permanently damaged by everything she had put it through over the past year.

Julie took a bus to the Gateway Station and joined a group of college girls heading to Grand via the metro. Judging by their sweatshirts, they attended the University of St. Louis, and Julie made every attempt to look like part of their group by engaging them in a conversation about the college and chatting with them as they walked to the train. She rode with them to the stop at Grand Station and joined them as they walked up out of the station and onto the street.

When Julie exited the metro station, she was immediately slapped in the face by the cold wind. She certainly wasn't in Southern California any more. She wished she hadn't abandoned Chad's coat and gloves when she arrived in Dallas, but the need to travel light was greater than the need for a coat and gloves in Texas. The Chargers sweatshirt she found at a Good Will in San Diego did little to protect her thin frame from the frosty air. She hugged herself in an attempt to hold in the warmth and asked the girls where she could find the closest thrift shop. Always eager to share their shopping secrets with a fellow bargain hunter, they gave her directions to their favorite places to find used clothing. An hour and a half later, Julie was dressed for the weather and ready to look for shelter.

Within a couple weeks, Julie had adjusted to the cold, found reasonable housing at another hostel, and gotten a part time job, taking Santa pictures at a small toy store. She was rethinking her way of life and decided that she needed to make some changes in order to stay further off the radar. She started watching the classifieds for a reliable car that she could afford to buy with cash. She had made sure to get plenty of money from an ATM in Boulder. She was through with buses and through with hostels. After a week in a hostel, that was infested with roaches, she decided that from now on, she needed her own accommodations. That would mean leaving the anonymity of the city, but the bright side would be fewer security cameras, she hoped.

CHAPTER 67

March 29, 2014

Meg sat at her desk and chewed on the end of her
pencil, a habit that hadn't plagued her since middle school.
She stared out the window of her office in the nation's
capital but noticed nothing, not the helicopter that
patrolled over the city, not the piles of gray snow that had
been plowed up onto the curbs and sidewalks, not the rows
of cars on the streets or the pedestrians hurrying through
the cold wind toward their destinations. Her boss was out
of the country, attending a meeting with many of the
world's dignitaries, and Meg was holding down the fort, as
usual. She had already decided that it was time to send
Officer Berman another clue, but what to say? What could
she tell her that would lead her in the right direction
without giving away Meg's own identity?

Pushing her chair away from the desk and standing,
Meg reached her arms behind her and arched her back.
She tilted her head from one side to the other to get the
kinks out of her neck. How long had she been sitting there,
lost in thought? She glanced at her watch and realized
almost an hour had gone by since she first started thinking
about the next step in her plan. Did she have a next step?
What had started as an attempt to stop Berman from

poking around and getting herself killed, had steamrolled into an undercover investigation that could get Meg fired if not killed herself.

For twenty-six years, Meg had listened, observed, and learned. She had figured out how to best help her goddaughter to stay alive by using the same means that the professionals around her used. She worked her way through an internship with the FBI, an entry-level position at the NSA, a position as an Investigative Records Technician with the Secret Service, and ended up in this prime office overlooking Executive Avenue. She used her double major in Political Science and Criminal Justice to her advantage to have both an interesting career and the opportunity to keep tabs on Melissa.

So far, Meg had been successful in keeping her contact with Officer Berman a secret. Using everything she learned at the NSA and the Secret Service, she placed optical bugs in the office of her boss and his chief accomplice. On the guise that she was backing up their files, she installed keystroke repeaters in both of their computers, which sent copies of everything they typed to her computer. She tapped into their office phones, overhearing conversations concerning Melissa Grant and the other victims. She intercepted the written correspondences between the men who were giving and carrying out the orders. Finally, Meg hacked into their computers to see the security camera footage and surveillance photos of Melissa each time she heard or saw reports that they had spotted her.

Meg was at a crossroads, and she decided it was time to cross that street. No more beating around the bush. Tomorrow, she would send Berman a clue that she hoped would send her in the right direction. She packed her briefcase and straightened her desk. Drawing the blinds, as she did every night out of habit, after years of working in intelligence, Meg pulled on her coat and gloves and wrapped her scarf around her neck. She turned off the light and locked the door before heading down the hall toward the elevator. She was planning an early dinner that evening. A stack of magazines, scissors, construction paper, and a glue stick were waiting for her at home.

CHAPTER 68

April 1, 2014 - Philadelphia, PA

Mindy's uncle called at ten o'clock that night on the untraceable phone he had sent her. He knew somebody in the government he could trust to find answers without arousing suspicion. He was looking into one angle, and Mindy was looking into another. Using a computer at the public library, Mindy did a Google search on Lissa Marshall. Though the police computers were supposedly secure, Mindy was taking no chances. The only mention was of a Meryl Alissa Marshall in an obituary from September of 1987 – just a few weeks after Melissa Grant was born. According to the paper, Lissa was the victim of a mugging. Like Chad O'Donnell's had been at first, her case was declared, death by shooting during a robbery. Coincidence? Mindy thought not. Could this be Melissa's mother? The name alone made sense. Maybe that was all the information the adoptive parents had about Melissa's mother and wanted to honor her for giving them a child. She hoped her uncle could answer that question.

Within the cold case file, was an official envelope from the Maryland Clerk of Courts. The subpoena for the adoption records was returned with a refusal to grant access. The stamp on the document read, *Information Classified.* The records were inaccessible to her. Access to them was denied by one of the highest courts in the land. But the news her uncle gave her made matters worse, and even more suspicious.

"The records aren't just sealed," he told her when he called. "They're gone."

"What do you mean they're gone?" Mindy asked as she stared at the latest letter.

"According to the United States Government, Melissa Grant's adoption never took place."

"But we know that isn't true. We have her birth certificate. She left it behind the day she disappeared. It clearly shows that she was adopted."

"I didn't say she wasn't," her uncle corrected her. "I said that, according to the U.S. Government, she wasn't. Clearly, somebody has been working very hard to cover his tracks."

"Wouldn't he have to be pretty high in the food chain to change that without getting caught or looking suspicious?"

"Yes, he would," her uncle agreed. "Very high in the food chain."

"Can you see if you can find anything out about Meryl Alissa Marshall? I've hit a dead end here. I only have an obituary."

"I'll see what I can find," he told her.

Mindy looked down at the letter and wondered how much more help this anonymous source was willing to give and when she would receive it. Whoever this person was, he or she must have known about the cover-up.

BIOLOGICAL DAD - RESPONSIBLE

CHAPTER 69

December 1, 2014 St. Brendan, MD

Eric and Julie sat on the couch in the cottage looking at the flames in the fireplace. Julie held a glass of wine, and Eric nursed a beer. With hunting season in full swing, and just one false alarm involving an automatic fire alarm, it had been a busy week at the shop and a slow week at the fire department, allowing Eric and Julie to spend a calm, uninterrupted evening together.

Over dinner, Eric told Julie that he had some news, but it might come as a shock to her. She assured Eric that she was ready for whatever he had learned. Julie was certain that nothing could shock her anymore.

"Julie," he said quietly and took her hand. "I don't know how you will react to this, but Jerome found out something about your past. Something that might be a shock to you and might bring you a great deal of pain."

"Okay," Julie said, gripping the table, literally bracing herself for the news. "I'm ready."

"Julie, apparently, you were adopted. Well, Melissa Grant was adopted."

Julie blew out her breath and shook her head. No news was good news, she guessed.

"You knew," Eric said, and Julie nodded.

"I've always known. What I don't know is who my real parents are. I had just decided to start looking for them the day…" Julie stopped speaking and looked at Eric as the realization hit her. "Do you think that's the reason? Do you think it was supposed to stay a secret, where I came from, who I really am?" Her heart began to race.

"I don't know, but it's a possibility, I suppose. Jerome is looking into it."

"Why didn't I think of that before?" Julie shook her head and closed her eyes. After a moment, she shook her head and looked back at Eric. "No, Eric, it just doesn't make sense. It was too fast. I had only started looking that very day. How *could* it be related?"

"I guess that's just another missing piece to the puzzle," Eric said as he finished his beer.

Julie nodded and tried to remember if there was ever a time her biological parents were mentioned or if the circumstances of her birth were ever discussed. Absolutely not. She knew she would have remembered that, but then again... there was something strange about that note she found in her mother's quotation book after the funeral. Just who was Meryl Alissa?

CHAPTER 70

December 2, 2014

Dressed in a sweatshirt and jeans, Julie sat in the front seat of Eric's truck on an unseasonably warm day for December. The air was still, the sun was out, and it was predicted to reach sixty degrees that afternoon before plummeting into the thirties that night. That was the Maryland weather Julie remembered. Predicting the weather here was rather, well, unpredictable.

Gunner grudgingly lay on the back seat of the truck's cab, and Eric's right hand moved back and forth between the gearshift and Julie's hand that rested on the seat between them. He was quiet as he drove down the country road leading to his house. In an unusual move, he had taken off from work that day at noon. That was when Nathan's day at school ended and his job requirement began. As a senior, having earned all his graduation credits, he was allowed to attend school for half a day as long as he worked a steady job in the afternoons. Julie had observed the reserved youth on several occasions and had come to know him as a bright young man with a solid work ethic and an eagerness to please his boss. He had his eyes set on attending a state school, to earn a business degree, and then moving back to the Shore to open his own canoe, kayak, and small boat rental shop. He was learning firsthand what he needed to do to succeed.

"Why won't you tell me what you're up to?" Julie asked as they neared Eric's house.

"Because I don't want to scare you away."

Julie glanced at Eric with a raised eyebrow. He smiled. "Don't worry. It's going to be fun."

They turned into his driveway and came to a stop in front of the old farmhouse that Julie had fallen in love with the first time she'd seen it a couple weeks back. She imagined a whole brood of kids hanging out in the big front yard while their parents looked on from the porch swing. The large yard, surrounded by trees, the waterfront dock, and of course the outdoor fireplace, made this the perfect place to raise kids, and she could see why Eric jumped at the chance to purchase it. She knew that he was eaten up with guilt about not having a large family to bring the place to life, and it broke her heart to think that he might have had a wonderful life here with Elizabeth had they put family first and work second. Julie could understand why Eric had made a vow to never let that happen again. She wished that she could witness this house filled with children one day, but that was still too much to hope for.

Eric led Julie around to the side of the house where he had set up what vaguely resembled a collection of small carnival games. There was a large black box with a bull's-eye target sitting on the ground. Several feet away was a fake deer that also had a bulls-eye target, and a little farther from there, two wooden structures each holding a

pyramid of cans. One had gallon-sized cans and the other
had soup cans. Several yards back, a black paper, hanging
from the trees, portrayed a target in the outline of a
person's torso. Julie swallowed hard before turning to
Eric.

"What is this?" Her voice trembled as she realized
Eric's motives for bringing her here.

"Just what you think it is." He turned to Julie and
placed his hands on her shoulders forcing her to look him
in the eyes. "You're not going to be afraid of guns any
more. You're not going to be afraid of anything. You've
done a remarkable job of taking care of yourself and
keeping yourself alive, but there may come a point when
you're going to need more than a lamp, or your fine
martial arts moves, to help you get away."

Julie breathed deeply through her nose and thought
about what Eric had said and what he was proposing. She
slowly nodded and firmed up her resolve. She had gotten
through being surrounded by guns on the opening day of
deer season. She could do this.

"Let's do it then," she said after a moment's hesitation.
Eric pulled her into his arms.

"You're gonna be fine. I'm here, and I will never let
anything happen to you, but I need to know that you can
protect yourself if I'm not with you."

Eric released her shoulders and took her hand. He led
her to a nearby table where he had a handgun ready for
her.

"Okay, I'm gonna be honest here. What I'm doing is
illegal. You can't get a permit, and I can't legally give you

a gun, so this little 9-millimeter pistol is mine that I may accidentally forget to take home sometime."

Julie put her hands up. "Eric, I don't want that in my house. I can't—"

"You can, and you will. If my mother can handle having one of these in her nightstand, so can you."

Julie's jaw dropped as she looked at Eric in shock. "Your mother has one of these?"

Eric nodded in answer.

"My mother could take the head off a sparrow if she needed to."

Julie continued to stare at Eric in disbelief.

"May I continue?" he asked.

Julie swallowed, and Eric explained how the gun worked, showed her the hollow-point bullets they were going to use for it, and demonstrated the safety techniques she should use when handling the gun or keeping it safely stored.

When Julie felt ready, Eric had her stand in front of him, holding the gun in both hands, her arms outstretched. He reached his arms out around her and grasped her hands, that held the pistol, in his hands.

"We're going to start big and easy," he told her as they faced the deer.

"What about that big box?" she tilted her head toward the first target.

"That's next year's lesson—using a bow."

"Ha ha," she replied dryly.

Eric instructed Julie on how to properly stand and hold the gun. When her hand began to shake, he told her relax and loosen just a bit.

"That's actually just what you want to happen when you first learn to hold it. You'll get used to the feel of it and how tightly to grip it." Julie didn't think she would ever get used to holding a gun.

Eric helped her to lightly grip the gun with her other hand and position her thumbs along the side of the pistol without endangering them by putting them on or too close to the hammer that could easily 'bite' her thumb.

"Make sure your feet are shoulder-width apart, and stand firm," Eric told her as she positioned her legs between his but made sure to keep her own balance.

He showed her how to align the front and rear sites and aim at her target.

"Keep the front site in focus and let the target get a little fuzzy."

That sounds safe, she mused sarcastically, but she kept the thought to herself. Eric talked to her about the right pressure on the trigger and follow through. He stressed the importance of not dropping the gun or letting go of her stance too quickly.

Once Eric felt like Julie had her stance down pat and understood how to aim and shoot properly, he loaded the ammunition. Without giving her time to second guess herself or the situation, he aligned her body back into position and gently placed his hands on hers to steady her.

"Breathe slowly," he whispered against her ear. "Keep it steady…" he slowly released his hands from hers. "And fire."

The pistol jerked as Julie fired, but she held it steady and was surprised that she was still standing once she realized she had pulled the trigger. She stood still and just breathed slowly at first, and then she pointed the gun to the ground and grinned from ear to ear. She turned toward Eric.

"Oh my gosh, I did it!"

Eric laughed and took the pistol from her. He laid it on the table and took her hand.

"Let's see just how well you did," he said as they walked toward the deer. Julie surveyed the felt-covered plastic animal. She ran her hand over several small holes around the area she assumed was where the heart would be, the bulls-eye.

"How do I know which one is mine?" she asked.

"It's right here," Eric pointed to a hole near the hind of the animal. Julie frowned as she looked back and forth between the intended target and the spot where Eric pointed.

"Are you sure?" she asked skeptically.

Eric nodded. "I'm sure, but for your first shot, it was darn good. You hit the deer, and that's more than most people can say." After letting that sink in, Julie smiled.

"What's next?" she asked, and they walked back to the table to begin round two.

Before they could get started, the fire signal sounded on Eric's phone.

CHAPTER 71

"Box 42, Station 40, Station 60, Station 70, paramedic 94. Kitchen fire, 902 Schoolhouse Lane."

"What does that mean?" Julie asked as she followed Eric quickly to the back door of the house.

"A kitchen fire at a house in St. Brendan near the elementary school. St. Brendan, Easton, and Tilghman have been called." Eric answered her as he motioned for Gunner to go into the house and closed the door before heading around front. They hurried to the truck and climbed in.

"Is it ok if I go?" Julie asked.

"Yeah, as long as you stay outside of the safety perimeter that's established."

"Can I take pictures?"

Eric nodded. "Same rules apply."

"Got it," Julie answered as she checked the settings on the camera she had left on the seat of the truck. Naturally, she had brought it with her that morning not knowing what Eric had planned for the day. "I'll stay out of the way."

"You can take the truck after I jump out at the station," Eric told her as he turned onto the main road toward town, his headlights flashing. The other cars on the road hurriedly pulled to the side to let him pass.

They arrived at the station, and Eric parked the truck but left it running as he undid his seatbelt and opened the door. Hesitating before getting out, he turned back to Julie and leaned across the seat. He kissed her on the cheek before climbing out.

"Be careful," she called, but he was in too much of a hurry to answer, adrenaline kicking in. Julie sat still, tightly biting the insides of her lips and holding her breath, as she watched him go into the station. Once he was out of sight, she slid into the driver's seat and closed the door. She waited for all of the trucks to pull out before she followed, at a safe distance behind, to the location just a couple blocks from the firehouse.

Coming to a stop a few houses down, Julie cut the engine and grabbed her camera before exiting the truck. Several people stood in nearby yards, watching the fire engines roll to a stop in front of the house and the firefighters emerge with their gear. Some of the onlookers were told to step aside as the fire chief and police officers on the scene set up a perimeter with cones and yellow tape.

Julie walked cautiously toward the house as the black smoke billowed from the windows. A little boy, about five, wailed in fear as he was rocked back and forth in a woman's lap in the back of an ambulance. A paramedic wrapped a blanket around the mother and son who had run from the house with no coats or shoes. A man, also coatless but wearing white waterman's boots, was talking to the chief and motioning toward the house. Julie couldn't hear what he was saying, but she assumed he was giving details about how the fire started. Julie discreetly took pictures of the family members as the paramedics attended to them.

Suddenly, and without warning, a great noise erupted from the house as a window blew out, followed by a rush of flames. The firefighters shouted to each other as they hurried to extinguish the fire and prevent it from jumping to the neighboring house that stood only several feet away. It was then that Julie noticed that some of the men had gone inside the burning home. She felt a rush of dread as she looked around for Eric and remembered something he told her one night. He rode the truck, as opposed to the engine, which meant that he didn't work the hose; he went into the burning building. She tried to remember who he told her was the saintly protector of firefighters. St. George? No, it was an unusual name. St. Florentine? No, but something like that. She closed her eyes and tried to recall the conversation. She shook her head with no avail and went straight to the top instead.

"Please, God," she whispered. "Please keep him safe."

Opening her eyes, Julie remembered why she was there and went to work, taking pictures. At least it would occupy her thoughts while Eric risked his life.

Even though the day was cold, she watched the men emerge from the house bathed in sweat. She zoomed in and snapped shots of their weary expressions and the lines the sweat carved through the black soot on their faces. Their clothes were also covered in smears of soot, and ash clung to their helmets. They worked tirelessly for over an hour to combat the smoke and the flames that threatened to spread throughout the house and endangered the houses around it.

Eventually, the fire began to die down, and she saw Eric exit through the front door. As if covered with a strange war paint, the black on his face was smeared from where he had wiped his brow, his eyes, and around his mouth. His helmet was pulled low over his forehead, and he was hard to recognize, but her body instinctively knew him and began to relax. He reached for a bottle of water offered to him by one of the other men and guzzled the entire thing before tossing the empty bottle into a pile of debris that had collected outside of the house.

Spotting Julie across the street, Eric said something to one of the men and headed in her direction. He wore a slight smile as he approached her, and she could see the weariness in his eyes.

"Your first fire?" he asked and motioned toward the house. Julie nodded. "It can be intimidating," he said quietly. Again, she nodded.

Eric's smile turned to concern. "Are you okay?"

Finding her voice, Julie answered quietly, "I'm okay, but what about them?" She looked at the family standing at the back of the ambulance.

"Remember what I told you about St. Brendan when you first got here?"

Julie turned her gaze toward Eric and raised her eyebrow.

"We're family here. They'll be fine. They'll have warm beds to stay in tonight, and by tomorrow afternoon, most of the town will have offered them refuge and donated whatever they need."

"That's good," Julie said. "Is it bad, the damage I mean?"

Eric shook his head. "Just fire and smoke damage in most of the house. The kitchen is pretty much gone, but overall, it should be structurally ok. A lot of their stuff will be ruined." He shrugged and turned toward the family, gathered in and around the ambulance. "It's unfortunate, but it could have been a lot worse."

Julie understood his meaning all too well. Life is fleeting, and at any moment, one's world can be completely shattered and never feel the same again.

CHAPTER 72

December 4, 2014 - St. Brendan, MD

Julie woke up on a particularly cold Wednesday morning and wondered why she promised Helen she would meet her at yoga this morning. Helen pulled some strings and arranged for Julie to join the gym at a reduced price. Helen refused to share the details of the membership, and Julie was grateful to her friend, but she longed to stay, tucked, away, in her warm and cozy bed.

Sitting up, Julie arched her back and raised her arms over her head to stretch. She closed her eyes and tilted her head back as she lowered her arms and turned her head from side to side to loosen her neck. Opening her eyes, she reached behind the lamp on the nightstand to separate the blinds and see what kind of day it might be. Outside the window, the sunlight glistened in the sky as it was caught and reflected back by hundreds of swirling snowflakes.

Julie jumped out of bed and maneuvered around to the window. She opened it and reached out into the cold morning air, turning up her palm so the white crystals landed on her hand and melted into its warmth. She closed the window and raced into the bathroom to start getting ready for her outing into the snow.

CHAPTER 73

After yoga, Julie said goodbye to Helen and drove straight home to shower and change into warmer clothes. An early December snow was not unusual in Maryland, but the fluctuating temperatures meant that it never stayed around for very long. After blow-drying her hair with the dryer she found under the sink, Julie grabbed her camera and headed outside. She drove to the marina first and snapped several dozen pictures of the boats, covered with white blankets of snow. Since the snow wasn't sticking to any of the still-warm roads, and all traffic seemed to move as normal, she left town and drove to Oxford, another peninsula on the Chesapeake Bay in Talbot County. As she neared the town, she noticed the fire station on the left. The trucks were yellow, rather than red like the ones in St. Brendan, and Julie wondered why. She'd have to ask Eric later.

It's funny what you notice when you start paying attention to things that never interested you before.

After parking in a lot, on the very end of the small town, Julie began to take pictures. She loved the way the snow looked on the rocky ledge, outlining the small strip of sand in front of the historic Oxford homes. She photographed the snowy rug covering the town park and the crystals that sparkled on the slide that protruded from the wooden boat which no doubt provided hours of fun for children when the weather was warm. She climbed down to the beach and took pictures of the surf as it washed over the white fluff and took it out to sea.

While having a sandwich and hot chocolate at the Oxford Deli, Julie thought back over the previous three winters. She dreaded January and wondered where she would be when it arrived. Three years ago, the New Year brought with it the death of her parents. Two years ago, it ushered in the deaths of two of her friends and began a cross-country adventure that she could have done without. She managed to make it through the entire lonely winter in St. Louis last year, but she wondered where this New Year would find her and if she would be dead or alive. More than that, Julie wondered if it would find her alone.

She sipped her hot chocolate and thought about the feeling of Eric's hands steadying hers as she held the gun and about the way her body molded so perfectly to Eric's when he stood behind her and helped her with her stance. She felt a flutter in her stomach and wished she could push the feeling aside, but she could not. Now that Eric had entered her life, she wasn't sure how she would be able to live without him.

Julie closed her eyes and sighed. She tried to ignore the emptiness that now replaced the flutter in the pit of her stomach and the tear that formed in the corner of her eye. Julie was so tired of being alone, but what she felt for Eric was stronger than just the basic need to belong with someone. She was falling for him, and she knew that the best thing she could do was to put an end to it, today. But she also knew that one couldn't stop a freight train when it was heading full steam down the track.

CHAPTER 74

January 2014 St. Louis, MO

The first thing Julie did after buying her car on Craigslist, and adding the license plates she got from the man she met in Boulder, was to find a rental in Southampton, a neighborhood in St. Louis. Just outside the metropolitan area, it was filled with young families, couples, and single men and women just starting to make their way in the world. The rental was small, but it was roach-free and private. What more could she ask for?

She established herself in the neighborhood as a traveling photographer, and soon the young families with limited budgets were knocking on her door to have their portraits done for the New Year. Julie made a deal with the local community center where she taught photography classes after school for the local children. In return, she was allowed to set up a makeshift studio in one of their small meeting rooms. An added bonus was the free membership to the small gym, adjacent to the center, in payment for photos for their new web site. Julie hadn't been this content in a long time. She was making money doing something she loved, taking yoga and other exercise classes as often as she could, and making a difference in the community. The only catch was her strict rule against making friends.

Julie politely declined the many invitations to dinner, neighborhood get-togethers, and girls' nights out. After a few weeks, when she was having a hard time continuing to come up with excuses, word got out that Julie preferred to spend her free time alone. In the end, it was the Missouri winter that put a stop to the offers.

January slid into February with its blizzards and constant arrival of new snow. By March, Julie found herself actually growing tired of the snow, and she began counting the days until spring. She also began counting backwards and was beginning to get nervous about the amount of time she had spent in that one place.

She loved the feeling of being in a neighborhood with people who knew her name and greeted her on the street, but she knew that with familiarity, there was danger. She began using the computer at the community center to look for an affordable rental somewhere else, and after the long winter, somewhere down south was preferable.

CHAPTER 75

December 4, 2014 St. Brendan, MD

Julie made it home just in time. She was warming up with a cup of tea and was prepping the kitchen for some heavy-duty Christmas cookie baking when she heard the knock on the front door. She went to the door with an extra apron in her hand.

"Come on in, Abby," she said with a smile. "I'm so happy you're spending the afternoon with me."

The little girl bounded into the room and dropped her book bag by the door, kicking off her boots as if she lived there. Julie was pleased that Abby felt so at home with her. Julie's life felt so normal for the first time in so very long, that sometimes she was even able to forget that this time last year, she was avoiding all human interaction that took place on the other side of a camera lens. She suppressed the little voice that told her she was making things hard on everyone to whom she would have to say goodbye in the very near future.

When Julie agreed to watch Abby after school, so Kari could take Noah to the doctor, she thought they could take a walk, but the afternoon sun had turned the morning's snow into a messy slush that Julie would rather avoid. She opted for baking cookies instead. It was something she hadn't done since she was a child in her mother's kitchen.

"Mommy said that Noah's appointment won't take long, and she will be back as soon as she can," Abby said as she peeled off her coat, hat, gloves, and scarf.

"I hope she's not too quick," Julie said as she held out the apron. "We have a lot of cookies to make!"

The child squealed with delight as she took the apron and tied it around her waist. Julie led the way to the kitchen, and they went straight to work.

Abby talked non-stop the entire time they cut, baked, and decorated the assorted Christmas cookies, using the old metal cookie cutters Julie had found in a box in the pantry. Abby told Julie all about her school, her friends, and the assembly they had that day with real Irish Dancers, performing and bringing kids up on stage to learn the dances. Luckily the assembly went on as planned even though school started late that morning due to the falling snow. She lit up as she told Julie about her best friend who was invited to learn the Celtic steps. There wasn't a hint of jealousy in her voice, and Julie mentally praised Kari for doing such a wonderful job with her daughter. Abby was genuinely happy when good things happened to other people.

When Kari arrived, she and Noah stayed long enough to sample some cookies while Julie put together a big tray of Christmas trees, angels, stars, reindeer, and snowmen for them to take home for later.

While the women chatted, Abby wandered into the living room to look around. When she saw the stack of photos on the little desk, she couldn't stop herself from leafing through them. At the bottom of the stack was the picture of the deer tails disappearing into the trees and the print out of the story that Julie had written.

Abby read the story and was enthralled by the telling of it and all of the details about hunting that Julie wove into the story after the afternoon at Abby's house that day back in the fall. She peeked around the corner to be sure that her mother and Julie were still talking, and then she quietly folded the paper with the story around the picture and slipped it into her pocket. This story deserved to be read, and she knew just what to do with it to make that happen.

CHAPTER 76

For perhaps the first time as an adult, the morning snowfall put Eric in a good mood. He actually caught himself whistling, *Let it Snow,* as he thought about spending the evening with Julie in front of a warm fire and was disappointed when the flurries subsided mid-morning. He was busy setting up inventory for the December hunting season when his phone began whistling the call of a Wigeon, a green-headed duck native to the Shore. Eric's good mood vanished when he saw that the call was from Jerome. For no reason he could come up with at the moment, a feeling of dread crept upon him like the *Blob* from the movie remake he saw as teenager. It weighted him down as it crawled up his legs and over his body, settling into the pit of his stomach. He sat down on the bottom shelf and answered.

"Eric, man, glad I got you." Jerome's irregular greeting sent that blob farther up, and it tightened around his heart. "Look, man, I gotta take off, you know?" The caller didn't even sound like Jerome, but Eric knew that it was. "My old lady needs to get away, you know? Me and her, we gotta get outta here for a while, take a little vacation."

"Jerome, what's going on?" Eric was suddenly alarmed. He stood up and began pacing in the aisle.

"Nothin' man, I just gotta leave town for a while. My lady needs her man to focus on her right now, take *care* of her, if you know what I mean." Eric did not know what he meant, but he was beginning to get the message.

"Jerome, how can I reach you?"

"You can't, man. That's what I'm tryin' to tell you. I gotta be on the down low for a while. Maybe when I get back, we can go for coffee or something. Maybe at the café by the Naval Yard where we used to meet."

What the heck is he talking about? Eric swiped his hand down his face and pinched his chin. None of this made sense.

"Jerome, I don't und—" Eric tried to speak, but Jerome cut him off.

"I'm sorry, Eric. I really am. I know I'm your pathfinder, but you'll be okay without me. I gotta get through this sandstorm in front of me and clear my head. We might head out west, maybe to that Sundance place, do a little fishing, though I never was much of an angler. Anyway, you've got to keep your own scorecard for now. Sorry, man." Before Eric could ask what he meant, Jerome was gone.

Eric stared at his phone. What the heck had just happened? One thing was certain; Jerome's investigation had been compromised, which meant that Julie was in danger.

CHAPTER 77

June 2014 - Philadelphia, PA

Get out while you can.

Those were the words the voice in the back her head kept repeating to Officer Mindy Berman. Those and *I owe it to him.*

Mindy was frustrated that she and her Uncle Jack were no closer to solving the mystery than they were months ago. Mindy entered the door to her apartment, dropped her keys on the table in the entranceway, and kicked off her shoes. She changed into comfortable clothes and went to the kitchen.

Opening the freezer, she grabbed a Lean Cuisine and the plastic freezer bag, containing everything she had concerning Frank's death, including all of her notes and findings from the murders of Tina Marsh and Chad O'Donnell and the disappearance of Melissa Grant. It also contained the mysterious, anonymous letters. As she ate, she flipped through the paperwork. After she threw away the cardboard carton and washed and dried her hands, she slipped on her gloves and took out the notes to look at them once again.

Mindy stared at the letters and tried to connect them to the information she had collected in the file. She tried to find a different meaning than the one that kept her awake at night. That seemed to be only one explanation, and she didn't want that to be right. Would somebody in our government really do such a thing? Would this be so important to hide that they would kill innocent people? A chill raced down her spine as she thought about the answer. People in high positions often did anything they felt was necessary to protect their place in the world.

Mindy's uncle had learned that Lissa Marshall was a waitress at Murphy's Irish Pub when she was killed. She had dropped out of school when she learned she was pregnant, but nobody who knew her had any clue who the father of the baby was. She gave birth to a healthy baby girl but gave her up for adoption. None of her friends or co-workers knew the sex of the baby or who adopted it. She lived alone, having parted on bad terms with her roommate after an argument in which Lissa refused to name the baby's father, according to a former co-worker. The former roommate's name and whereabouts after the argument were unknown. Only Lissa's name was on the lease.

A short time after the delivery and adoption, Lissa was murdered in a mugging. Nothing in her past connected her to the Grants, and her record was clean. How did she get mixed up with someone in the government? Or were they barking up the wrong tree? Perhaps no government officials were involved in this after all. It could have been anyone with power and money, although who outside of the beltway could have pulled all the strings in this cover-up? And what more were they covering up? With no further contact from their tipster, and no way to find out who the biological father was, she felt like she was still at square one.

Giving up for the night, Mindy put the contents back into the envelope and replaced the freezer bag in its hiding place. How was she supposed to solve a crime where there was no evidence and no witness other than a missing person? Mindy slammed the freezer door and turned off the lights. She made sure the front door was bolted before heading to bed with her ten-millimeter automatic Glock by her side. So far, she was the only person involved in this case who was unquestionably still alive. She wanted to keep it that way.

CHAPTER 78

March-October 2014

Julie stretched out on the beach and closed her eyes as she took a deep breath of the warm, salty air. It felt so good to just lie there and enjoy the moment. She had spent the past month on the road, determined to enjoy the freedom that owning a car gave her, while still guarding her privacy. She took the role of a traveling photographer to heart and visited many sites between snow-covered St. Louis and the golden sands of Miami.

After spending the rest of February planning her course, checking weather predictions, and locating places where she could stay a night or two, Julie was ready to say goodbye to Southampton and the comfort of her little house and friendly community. She was truly going to miss free, unlimited access to the Internet, but she had met too many people and made too much of a footprint to stay any longer.

The Ozarks hadn't quite given her the taste of spring she was seeking. Temperatures were still in the thirties and forties every day, and most of the state parks and hiking trails were closed, but Julie captured some stunning photos of Buffalo National Park and River. She had done her research ahead of time and knew that the park would be open as long as it was accessible. The wilderness was a far cry from the cities she had been living in for the past year, and she hoped to someday visit the area in the summer when she could take advantage of not only the scenery but also the outdoor pursuits. For the first time in her life, she wanted to learn to kayak and go white water rafting and do every thrilling thing that she never considered doing before being on the run.

By the time she reached the Kisatchie National Forest in Louisiana in mid-March, the temperatures were in the low seventies, and Julie drove with her windows down, feeling a freedom she hadn't experienced in what seemed like years. As she drove throughout the state and into the Bayou, she took pictures of the marshes, willows, magnolias, whooping cranes, and other forms of wildlife she had only seen in zoos or on television, and the sights filled her with awe. And though she told herself that seeing a poisonous snake or an alligator was not on the agenda, she couldn't deny the thrill she felt just thinking about the possibility.

Spending just a day in the French Quarter gave Julie a small taste of New Orleans. She arrived at sun-up and didn't leave until after sundown. She tried to soak up as much of the atmosphere as possible in that short amount of time. She snapped pictures of the ironwork on the buildings, a jazz band warming up for a show, and the masks hanging in the storefront windows, and she wondered what this city was like a month before at the height of the famed Mardi Gras celebration. Ironically, the Cathedral in New Orleans was named the St. Louis

Cathedral, and Julie was mesmerized by the colors that surrounded her inside the church. There were flags, representing every country by which New Orleans had been ruled throughout its history, as well as ten enormous stained-glass windows depicting the story of St. Louis, King of France from 1226 until 1270. She could have stayed inside for hours but allowed herself only the time it took to pray for protection and guidance.

After spending a day in the big city of New Orleans, Julie went back to the shadows and stuck to the back roads of Mississippi. She traveled into the Wildlife Management Areas north of Biloxi, being careful to stay on Route 10 and not enter any areas requiring her to check in with a ranger. With the warmer weather, she had the choice of staying the nights in any cheap hotel or sleeping in her car at a truck stop. She found that most truck stops were well lit and felt safe, and after the first couple of nights, she learned to fall asleep to the sound of a humming engine from a nearby eighteen-wheeler. She took the highway to Mobile, Alabama, but skipped the city itself and opted for photographic sites away from the general population. The exception to her rule was a visit to Bellingrath Gardens where she skipped the house tour and went straight to the grounds. The spring flowers were in bloom, and Julie took both macros and landscape photos of the rows of Easter lilies, hydrangeas, marigolds, fuchsias, impatiens, delphiniums and the most magnificent azaleas she had ever seen. They reminded her of the ones in front of her home back in Hampden, and she stopped for just a moment to think of her mother, whose hands so lovingly tended their small gardens.

From Mississippi, Julie headed to the Sunshine State where she visited Apalachicola because she was intrigued, when she saw it on the road map, by its use in a favorite Tim McGraw song. It was in that beautiful port city on the water where Julie developed an overwhelming case of homesickness. The rich maritime history and culture reminded her, more than any place she had been, of the Mid-Atlantic Coast. Julie took pictures of the boats, hauling in the end of the season oysters, and the homes along the waterfront with their breezy wraparound porches framed by swaying palm trees.

Julie's skin was golden brown from the hours she spent in the sun after the long St. Louis winter. Her confidence grew as she managed to find shelter from the storms in her life and solace in her work and solitude. Never taking chances, she learned to enjoy the life she was making for herself even if it meant a life of being alone. She felt like she had aged twenty years in less than two, but she had aged in the ways that count. She was wiser, stronger, and happier. Yes, she was still prone to a panic attack now and then, but she had learned how to cope with them.

Julie spent the summer in Florida, celebrating her birthday alone at a beachside bar. She traveled from beach to beach enjoying the heat and the sunshine before working her way up the Eastern seaboard toward Maryland. Though that old feeling of dread sometimes found a home in the pit of her stomach, she was determined to conquer her fears and deal with the homesickness that was creeping into her bones like the coming fall that would soon overtake the summer. She had no idea where she would go once she arrived in the Old Line State nor to where she would move on from there, but she knew she wanted to be 'home' for the holidays.

CHAPTER 79

December 7, 2014 St. - Brendan, MD

It was Christmas in St. Brendan as far as the town and its guests were concerned. The entire village was decorated with lights and greenery, and people from all around the area came to see the parade of fire trucks, floats, and marching bands stroll down Main Street waving and throwing candy. Julie was itching to be down the street, sitting on the sidewalk with her neighbors watching the festivities, and while she knew better than to take the chance, the thought of another weekend hiding in the little cottage was driving her crazy.

Putting on the heavy coat, bought at the local thrift shop, the fashionable hat Helen knitted for her, and a large pair of sunglasses, she left the house and headed for the music and clapping ahead.

I'll just stand quietly behind the crowd and peek over their shoulders as the parade goes by.

She carried her camera with her, more out of habit than anything, as she headed down the street toward the excitement.

"Julie, I'm so glad you're here," Kari said dramatically when she caught site of Julie coming up the street. "I just realized I forgot my camera and was running home to get it, but I'm so afraid that I'll miss Abby when she rides by in the parade."

The newest Little Miss St. Brendan had been talking for weeks about riding in the parade in a flashy convertible with the magnetic sign proclaiming her title. Julie smiled as she recalled the fancy dress that Abby had modeled for her, along with the tiara she wore to Julie's three different times to show her how it looked with each hair style she was trying out.

"Would you please take some pictures for me?" Kari begged, her hands folded in front of her chest and her puppy dog eyes blinking away.

"Sure," Julie said, hoping Kari wouldn't hear the regret in her voice. *So much for staying behind the crowd.*

As the fancy blue Mustang rolled by, Little Miss St. Brendan waved as hard and fast as her hand could move and even blew a kiss to her little brother, Noah. Julie caught it all on film without missing a single bat of Abby's eyes as the little girl's family and friends cat-whistled and called her name. Rich, a member of the fire department, gave up his spot on the antique brush truck in order to drive his daughter in the borrowed convertible. Julie made sure she captured his picture, too. His pride was evident by the smile that beamed from behind the wheel as the locals and visitors alike waved to his beautiful daughter, sitting in the open-topped car. Not a beauty contest by any means, Little Miss St. Brendan, like all of the other Little Miss contests on the Shore, was a show of talent, poise, and most of all, knowledge about the dangers of and ways to prevent fire. Julie was sure that

Abby had been hearing horror stories about the fires that her father fought since the time she was born. The little girl's knowledge was quite impressive, and Julie was her favorite audience when it was time to practice for the judge's questions.

As Julie was sliding back through the crowd, she heard a familiar voice call to her.

"Melissa, is that you?"

Julie's blood ran cold, and she froze in her spot between two strangers who had been kind enough to part to let her pass through. She closed her eyes and held her breath. She tried to summon whatever hidden super power she might possess—invisibility, time stopping, the ability to outrun a locomotive. Nothing worked. Julie stepped out from between the strangers and kept walking without turning or acknowledging the woman. Perhaps she was calling someone else.

"Melissa Grant." The woman walked up to Julie and grabbed her arm. When Julie was forced to turn toward her, the woman opened her arms for an embrace and held onto Julie's arms. "I thought that was you," she said with a smile.

"I'm sorry, do I know you?" Melissa tried not to look Mrs. Watson, her seventh-grade math teacher, in the eye.

"Of course, you do, dearie. Don't you remember me? It's Mrs. Watson from St. Thomas Aquinas School. I taught you, oh, how many years ago was that…twenty, twenty-five? And I watched you grow into the beautiful young woman you are until you moved after college." Mrs. Watson's smile faded, and she looked at Julie with sympathy. "I'm so sorry about your parents. I still miss seeing them in church."

"Ma'am, I'm sorry—"

"And where are you living now?" she interrupted. "You moved to, Philly, right? Or somewhere near there?" Mrs. Watson looked away and slid her jaw to the right, just the way Julie remember her doing back in school when she was deep in thought.

"No, I'm sorry, ma'am. My name isn't Melissa." Julie tried to wiggle out of the woman's embrace, but Mrs. Watson held onto her too tightly and forced Julie to look her in the eyes. After a moment, she let go, and shook her head.

"I'm very sorry," Mrs. Watson said slowly never breaking eye contact. "I must be mistaken."

"I'm sorry, too," Julie whispered as she turned and walked quickly away. She felt Mrs. Watson's eyes on her the whole time she hurried down the street and knew that the woman had not been fooled.

PART FIVE

Nothing in life is to be feared, it is only to be understood. Now is the time to understand more, so that we may fear less.

Marie Curie

CHAPTER 80

December 7, 2014 St. - Brendan, MD

After his call from Jerome, Eric had confided in his mother that Julie was in danger. They took turns keeping an eye on her, careful not to arouse any suspicion. They both wanted to protect her and knew that if she ran again, she would be gone to them forever. At noon, Helen briskly walked into the shop and caught Eric's attention as she moved to the back room and subtly motioned for him to follow. He excused himself from his customer and trailed her into his office.

"Something happened at the parade. I think she may have been recognized."

"Parade?" Eric asked in astonishment. "What was she doing at the parade?"

"I don't know," Helen answered, her eyes full of fear. "She wasn't going to go, but I think it had something to do with Abby. Kari must have asked her to take pictures, and you know Julie, she probably wanted to avoid having to explain why she wasn't going."

"Okay, so what happened?" Eric wanted his mother to cut to the chase.

"Some woman, I didn't recognize her, stopped Julie. She had her arms around her like she was hugging an old friend. I couldn't hear what she was saying, but when she let go, Julie quickly took off toward the cottage." If there was more, Eric didn't hear it. Without saying a word, he flew out of the office and through the storeroom, out of the front door, and down the street. Knowing he would have a hard time penetrating the line of cars backed up from the parade, he ran as fast as he could down the crowded sidewalks and onto Maple Street.

By the time he reached the house and used the spare key to let himself in, Julie was packed. She was standing at the kitchen counter with a pen in her hand, finishing what looked like a letter. When the front door slammed, she darted for the back door, but before she could make it through, Eric's arms were around her. She fought to get loose, but Eric refused to let go.

"I would've been here sooner, but I had to run all the way from the store since the road is closed. I'm here now. Everything is going to be okay." He spoke quietly and soothingly, hoping to calm her down. He could feel their hearts racing through their clothes.

Julie stopped struggling and dropped her head. The tears began to flow as she turned toward Eric and let him pull her into his arms. She cried on his chest and clung to the front of his shirt with clenched hands. He let her cry and waited for her to speak. After a few minutes, she lifted her head and looked into his eyes.

"It's no use, Eric. I was writing a letter to you to tell you that I can't stay here. It's time for me to go."

"Go where? Wherever it is, I'll go, too."

Though there was longing in her eyes, she shook her head and gave him a sad smile. "If only you could, but I have to go alone."

"Julie, there comes a time when we all have to stop running. You taught me that. I would still be holed up in that store twenty-four-seven feeling sorry for myself if it weren't for you. Let me help you now."

Julie shook her head. "You can't, Eric. Nobody can. The last people who tried to help me all ended up dead. I could never live with myself if—"

"It won't happen to me. We can do this – together."

Julie heaved a long sigh, her shoulders drooped, and she looked down at the buttons on Eric's shirt. She closed her eyes and ran her hand over her face. Running her fingers through her bangs, she looked back up at Eric.

"And just how do you propose we do that?" Eric heard the challenge in her voice but saw the pleading in her eyes. He couldn't stand it any longer. Eric gave into his feelings and did the only thing that felt right.

He leaned down and kissed Julie, pulling her tighter, in a way he'd never kissed anyone before, not even his wife. Gone were the chaste goodnight kisses and the friendly hugs. He kissed her with a passion and a desperation that he had never felt. It didn't take long before he felt her melt into him and encircle him with her arms. He ran his hands up her back and through her hair, and she cradled the sides of his face between her palms. Eric slipped his hands under the hem of Julie's shirt and splayed them on her back, the softness of her skin and the warmth of her body pulsating though his hands. He silently pleaded with her, using his thoughts and caress to try to banish all thoughts of leaving him from her mind. He enjoyed the taste of her and the feel of her body pushing against him until he forced himself to pull away from her mouth. He rested his forehead on hers, attempting to control his impulses. They stood there, breathless, instinctively clinging to each other in a tight embrace, unable to move.

"Now, do you promise not to run?" Eric whispered. Julie didn't respond.

"I won't lie to you, Julie," he said, their foreheads still touching. "I don't know how, but I do know that together we can work this out. From now on, total honesty and trust, okay?"

Julie took a deep breath and release a long sigh. She pressed her lips together and closed her eyes then opened them and turned her gaze to Eric. "Okay," she whispered.

Eric released her from his embrace, but his body felt lost without touching her, so he took her hand as he led her into the living room to talk about how they could keep her safe. He truly prayed, for the first time in years, that God would grant him this one request—that he could keep Julie safe.

CHAPTER 81

December 2014 - Washington, D.C.

Robert Mason stood in his boss's office, wiping a piece of lint off of his Kiton suit straight from Saville Row. He was growing impatient as he waited for the second most powerful man in the world to arrive at work. This nonsense had gone on long enough, and he was tired of dealing with it. He was also, for the first time in his life, a little nervous.

"Good morning, Robert," the Vice President smiled as he entered. "Margaret told me you were waiting to see me. Anything important on the agenda for today?"

"Something personal." Robert turned from the window and faced the former Air Force heartthrob who raced through women's hearts as fast as he raced his jet.

"Should I sit down?" His voice grew cold.

"Perhaps you should," Robert conceded.

Vice President Malone sat down and pushed a button under his desk, turning off all forms of known surveillance in the room and, as far as he knew, blocking anything unknown.

"Proceed," he told the man who had risen with him over the past thirty years.

"She's gone," was all Robert could muster.

The vice president raised his brow. "Gone? As in…"

"Off the grid," Robert sighed. We've received no word of her since last winter. She seems to have made it as far as St. Louis and was there for quite some time under a new name. After that…" he shrugged.

"That's it?" Malone imitated Robert's shrug. "She's just gone?" He rose from his seat and walked around the desk to stand face to face with Robert, who shrank as his boss towered over him. "You're supposed to have a handle on this. You've been telling me it's all under control. Where the hell is she?"

Robert took a step back. "We're still working on it, Sir." He rarely, if ever, used the term in private, but he had never seen Malone this angry.

"Well find her. I will not let some nuisance from the past destroy everything I have worked for. Do. You. Understand?" The vein in his forehead pulsed as he leaned closer to Robert's face and jabbed him in the chest with his finger.

"That 'nuisance is your—"

"Don't you dare." The Vice President put his face as close as possible to Robert's. "She is nothing to me. Take care of her," he sneered behind his clenched teeth.

"Yes, Sir. I'm on it." Robert turned and left the room with his tail between his legs.

Vice President Malone walked back to his chair and pushed the intercom button on his phone. "I do not wish to be disturbed, Margaret." She acknowledged his request, and he turned the chair around to the wall and closed his eyes.

CHAPTER 82

December 12, 1987

It started out as an evening of innocent fun. Peter Malone was getting together with his Greek brothers to send the last single member of their fraternity's graduating class off to his proverbial death. Money was no object to most of them, and they rented out Murphy's Irish Pub in Alexandria for a bachelor party to end all bachelor parties. The taps were practically run dry from the amount of drinks that were poured, and the men, all in their early thirties, behaved like the college boys they once were.

Around two in the morning, the bartender told the men it was time to go home. Keys had been collected at the party's commencement, so taxis were called to drive them all to wherever they needed to go. Peter Malone was still flirting with the pretty cocktail waitress, a college girl at least ten years younger than the loving wife who waited for him at home. Offering to walk her home, he waved off his buddies as they climbed into their cabs. Declaring that there was no need to escort her, the young woman looked at the senator's son with stars in her eyes, and Malone knew what she was really saying with her coy looks and come-hither body movements.

When they reached the apartment that she shared with another college co-ed, Malone followed her in. When she protested that they might wake her roommate, he reminded her that she had mentioned earlier that her roommate was away for the weekend. Enamored by the handsome young man with a political dynasty behind him, dating back half a century, and the ability to make aerial maneuvers unlike most others, she slipped off her shoes and offered him a drink in exchange for walking her home.

Malone grabbed her hand and pulled her against him. Though he could barely stand at that point, and his thoughts were becoming jumbled, he wrapped his arms around her and tightened his grip.

"That's not the thanks I was hoping for," he slurred as he pressed his lips against hers, the smell of stale beer and whiskey breathed hot on her mouth.

Lissa tried to push Peter away. Yes, she'd been flirting, and yes, she liked the attention he'd paid to her all night, but things were getting out of hand. She knew that she should have shoved him into a cab and been done with him. Now she found herself pushing him away with all of her might, clawing at his neck and face, attempting to keep his legs from spreading hers apart. When one of her fingernails scraped across his cheek, he hauled back and slapped her across the face, hard, sending her reeling into a short bookcase and then onto the floor. She tried to scream, but he was on top of her in an instant, his hand on her mouth. The rest of the memory was blank, for both of them. Lissa allowed her mind and body to go to a dark place she never knew existed, and Peter Malone's white-hot rage controlled him in a way he never knew it could.

An hour later, Senator Malone stood in the room, looking at the broken bookcase and unconscious girl. Peter sat in the corner sobbing.

"You, stupid fool. How could you do this?" his father asked.

"I didn't mean to," Peter cried. "I was drunk."

"I don't mean that, you idiot. We've all done that. I meant, why the hell did you involve me?"

Peter felt like he'd been slapped. He put his head in his hands to hide his shame.

"Is this how you act when turbulence hits? It's a wonder the Air Force lets you fly that piece of tin. Thunderbird pilot, my rear. You wouldn't even have that coveted position if it weren't for me." The Senator looked at his son with disgust.

"Get up," his father kicked at his legs. "Get out of here. Go home and tell your wife that you passed out drunk at the bar and somebody called a cab. There's one waiting for you out front. Tell her you don't remember anything else but think you got in a fight with some local guy trying to crash the party. Is that understood?"

Peter nodded. "What about…" he gestured toward the girl on the floor.

"I'll make sure she gets help. Now go before somebody sees you or your wife calls the police."

After Peter left, the senator searched for the girl's purse. He dumped the contents onto the couch and shoved her apron full of tips in his pocket. She was still alive but pretty badly beaten up, and he doubted she would live until her roommate's return. Her cheek was swollen, and blood pooled on the floor below her ear. The senator surmised that her roommate would return, see the girl and the empty purse, and assume she had been followed home, beaten and robbed, and left for dead.

It was a shock to Peter and his father both when Peter received a letter six months later, demanding help for the girl and the baby that was on the way. If they didn't help, she threatened to contact the press. Once again, Daddy came to the rescue. The girl was paid a heavy sum to give up her baby and never contact Peter again. Wanting no part of that night, she agreed, but for a very high price. Two weeks after delivering a healthy baby girl and handing her over in an adoption arranged by the senator himself (a secret kept from the new parents who were only told that the baby's mother was a teenage girl from another state), Lissa was shot in a robbery while walking home from work late at night. The crime was never solved.

CHAPTER 83

December 3, 2014

Meg dropped the flash drive into her purse before performing her ritual of straightening her desk, drawing the blinds, turning out the lights, and locking the door. She was working late this evening, supposedly finalizing the agenda for the upcoming Congressional meeting, but she was actually working on her own agenda tonight. For years, she watched out for Melissa Grant from afar, keeping tabs on her whereabouts and maintaining a watchful eye over those who would hurt her. Throughout that time, Meg had amassed quite an astonishing and damning collection of falsified documents, intercepted phone conversations, blackmail schemes, and murder plots. She never saved anything on her computer, home or office, but she did have everything neatly organized and dated on her encrypted flash drive.

Meg's husband, Jeremy, was planning an elaborate Christmas vacation for the entire family, a two-week cruise out of Baltimore that would have them celebrating the holidays in the Caribbean. Meg's boss didn't care. Heck, no elected officials in the nation's capital worked over Christmas. The upcoming meeting between the vice president and congressional leaders would be the last piece of business they would attend to this year, before going home to their families, leaving their lovers and all thoughts of work behind. While Meg looked forward to spending some quality time with her family, she worried that Melissa would be located and killed while they were out of the country and oblivious to the state of the world for a whole two weeks. Now was the time to act, before it was too late.

With one last letter to mail, Meg was going to expose the man behind the grand conspiracy to kill Melissa and rid the world of all traces of his crimes. She knew that once Officer Berman received the final clue, things would start moving quickly. Once she detected that Officer Berman had decoded the message and was investigating Peter Malone, she would mail the flash drive to the Attorney General and be done with this charade. She just hoped that the information reached the AG before Berman became another victim of the vice president's plot to hide his past and secure his future. But until she felt the timing was right, Meg would hold onto the drive and pray that Melissa and everyone else around her was safe. She'd been able to put it off for months, years really, but she knew that the past was closing in on them all, and Melissa would not be the only one in danger once the truth was out.

CHAPTER 84

December 5, 2014 - Philadelphia, PA

Home as last, Mindy thought as she rushed into her apartment. Another letter had been delivered, and the end of her shift had finally arrived, allowing Mindy to go home and open the envelope. She threw off her coat, gloves, and hat and grabbed her crime scene gloves. This time, she didn't bother changing her clothes or eating dinner first. She had waited months for further contact from the informant and was beginning to think that he or she had decided to stop communicating with her, or worse.

Using a sharp knife, Mindy carefully sliced open the envelope and pulled out the piece of paper from inside. Her heart skipped a beat, and she gasped as she looked at the letters glued to the page. Gripping a nearby chair, she eased herself down while trying to keep calm. Her mind and heart raced as she began putting all of the pieces together. Lissa Marshall had given birth to a baby around the same time Melissa Grant was born. Marshall was murdered shortly thereafter. Melissa was raised in a happy, healthy home and went on to become a maternity nurse. After her parents died in a car accident, she decided to look for her birth mother. An attack was made on her life that very day, which meant that someone was watching her every move, someone with access to the best surveillance in the world, someone who had access to professional killers and federal judges. Who could that someone be?

Only the mysterious letters glued together to form a phrase gave her any clue, and in Mindy's mind, it pointed to just one possibility. The letters read:

GRANT IN DANGER
FIND: CODENAME T-BIRD

As a police officer, a former military brat, and a history and trivia buff, it didn't take long for Mindy to put the pieces together. Though she could be wrong, Mindy felt certain that the message referred to one, specific individual who gained his notoriety as an Air Force Thunderbird pilot before jumping out of planes and into politics. Now what on earth was she supposed to do with this information? She hid the letter with the others and tried to figure out what to do next.

CHAPTER 85

December 7, 2014 St. - Brendan, MD

Julie and Helen cleaned up the dishes after their Sunday dinner while Eric started a fire for his mother. The temperatures were fluctuating every day between the forties and fifties, but there was always a damp chill in the air no matter what the thermostat read. As Eric reached for the newspaper to crinkle it up for the fire, he saw the headline for the story he had read over breakfast that morning.

Vice President Malone to visit St. Brendan next weekend.

The article went on to tell about a meeting between Vice President Malone and congressional leaders that was taking place at the famed Revolutionary Inn that weekend. They would be discussing a compromise on national education requirements that the administration was trying to push through. Though a former cabinet secretary and former vice president both lived in secluded homes in and near St. Brendan, the town was not usually the top pick for government meetings, though Margaret Thatcher, Queen Elizabeth, and Henry Kissinger had all stayed at the Inn.

Eric assumed that the location had been chosen for this series of meetings because of its close proximity to D.C.

Eric dreaded the arrival of the Secret Service over the course of the next week. He had already received an official letter from the U.S. Government telling him that an armed guard would be stationed outside of his gun shop during business hours as well as when the shop was closed. He cursed the many new gun laws that had been passed over the last ten years and wondered how badly this would hurt his business. He crumpled up the paper and threw it into the fireplace.

"You're going to have a keep a low profile this week," Eric told Julie when he walked back into the kitchen. "There's going to be extra security everywhere and probably press all over the place."

"I was thinking that maybe I should go away for the weekend." She held up her hand when Eric started to protest. "I'm not leaving, just taking a short trip, maybe to the beach. Just for the weekend." Eric wasn't sure whether to believe her. She avoided eye contact and nervously licked her lips.

Eric shook his head. "No can do. I can't leave the store with all of this going on. Heaven forbid anything should happen and I'm out of town."

Julie stopped drying the dish in her hand and looked at Eric. "I didn't say *you* were going anywhere. I said *I* was going."

"Not without me, you're not. We're in this together, remember?"

"Eric, just because I allowed you to stay last night," she turned to Helen and emphasized "*on the couch,*" then turned back to Eric, "doesn't mean that we have to be joined at the hip. I can go away by myself for the weekend."

"There's no way, Julie," he began.

"You can't tell me what to do," she challenged him as she put the dish and towel on the counter and drew herself up to full height. "I will go where I want, when I want."

Helen stepped in, "That's enough, you two. Eric," she addressed her son, "you have to trust Julie and let her live her life."

"Thank you, Helen," Julie said smugly.

"I'm not finished yet," Helen turned to Julie. "You have to remember that you were recognized. It's not safe for you to go anywhere alone. If you want to go to the beach, then I'll go with you. End of discussion."

Eric and Julie exchanged a look, acknowledging that neither was prepared to argue with Helen. Satisfied that Julie would be safely out of town, Eric opened a drawer and took out another towel, then reached for one of the wet plates. "Let me help you with that," he said to Julie. "The Skins game is starting."

"The Ravens, you mean." She smiled and snapped her towel at his leg. Eric eyed her with suspicion. She might think she had him fooled, but he wasn't going to give her the chance to run.

"Watch those dishes," Helen scolded. "They're as old as Eric is. I'm going to sit down." She winked at Eric and left the kitchen.

Eric dried the dish in his hands and took Julie's from her, placing them both in the cabinet. He then took her towel and dropped both towels onto the counter. He put his finger in front of his lips with a silent shush and pulled her to him. Julie wrapped her arms around him, and they shared a kiss.

"So, about that couch," Eric said as they ended the kiss. His eyes sparkled with mischief.

Julie playfully pushed him away and headed to the living room. "It's quite comfortable isn't it? I'll be sure to have it made up for you when you and Gunner arrive tonight."

Eric watched her stroll into the other room and smiled. He knew he had it good, and he was willing to wait for better. Julie had made it quite clear that she wouldn't make any kind of commitment, sexual or otherwise, until she knew it was safe for everyone involved, and Eric hoped that day would come soon. He spent too many years taking the future for granted. It was time to start living the life he almost never had.

CHAPTER 86

December 10, 2014 - Philadelphia, PA

Officer Mindy Berman was walking through the violent crimes division when a fellow officer called her name.

"I got a woman on the line, asking for you by name, who claims she knows where Melissa Grant is. You want it, or should I send it up to Cold Case?"

Mindy froze in her tracks. "I'll take it," she said, and she actually started to tremble. Was this for real? Did someone know what she knew? Could this be the informant? She picked up the phone with a shaking hand as she remembered Frank's mysterious phone call his daughter said he had received before he drove off to his death.

"Detective Berman," she answered and then waited.

"Yes, Ms. Berman. I, um, I think I know where you can find Melissa Grant, the missing nurse." The woman on the phone sounded nervous, and Mindy felt a glimmer of hope that this might be the real thing.

"Go ahead, ma'am, what can you tell me?" Mindy grabbed a pen and a pad of paper.

"Well, I think…No, no, I'm sure of it." The woman was beginning to sound more confident. "You see, I used to teach Melissa when she was in middle school. I know that was a long time ago, but I never forget a student, and we attended the same church until she graduated from college." Mindy indicated she was listening and let the woman continue. "My husband and I recently retired, and we were spending a few days on the Eastern Shore. Are you familiar with Maryland's Eastern Shore, detective?"

"A little," Mindy told her as she moved the mouse on her computer and watched the screen come to life.

"Well, we were in this quaint little tourist town called St. Brendan, a place we've always loved. We were there for their annual Christmas parade and celebration."

"Isn't it a bit early for a Christmas parade?" Mindy asked as she began typing in the name of the town.

"It's a town tradition. I guess they hold it early so that people aren't too tied up when the holiday gets closer. Anyway," she continued, "I saw Melissa at the parade. She was taking pictures of one of the little girls riding in it."

That sounded strange to Mindy, and she started to lose hope that this woman saw the right person.

"Pictures?" she asked.

"Yes, when Melissa was younger, she was always taking pictures. She was the photo editor of the middle school yearbook, and the high school one, too, I believe." She paused as if trying to remember for sure.

"It's okay, Mrs., I'm sorry, what did you say your name was?"

"Watson, Jane Watson. As I was saying, Melissa always had a camera with her, and as I watched this woman taking pictures, something about her struck me as being so familiar. Then it clicked. No pun intended," she chuckled before becoming serious again. "Her hair was blonde, and she had a hat on, but I've known Melissa since she was in the first grade, and I knew it was her. She denied it, but—"

"You spoke with her?" Mindy stopped typing and held the phone with both hands.

"Yes. She acted like she didn't know me and said I was mistaken, but I saw the look in her eyes. I *know* it was her. Anyway, I know that she's been missing, and I pray that I'm doing the right thing by calling. I don't believe she would ever have had anything to do with hurting those other people, but I felt I had to call. I thought, if she's in trouble or in danger, maybe it would help…"

Mindy assured her that she had done the right thing and asked her a few additional questions and a follow-up phone number. After she hung up, she turned back to her screen. She almost fell off her chair when the words in the first Google hit jumped off the page at her:

Vice President Malone to lead compromise talks with congressional leaders at the Revolutionary Inn in St. Brendan next weekend.

Mindy leaped from her seat and ran to her sergeant's office. She burst into the room, interrupting a meeting he was having with another officer.

"I'm sorry, sir, but it's an emergency. I have a story for you that you aren't going to believe."

CHAPTER 87

December 10, 2014

After school on Monday, Abby tiptoed across the store while her father talked to Mr. West. She had been planning to pin up a contest entry for quite some time and hadn't had the chance. Actually, she'd been carrying two stories in her book bag, patiently waiting for the chance to enter them. One story was the one she had worked so hard on and was very proud of. But the second story was a secret. Nobody else knew she had found it and decided to do something nice for someone who was always doing nice things for her.

Listening to her father and Mr. West's conversation, Abby was very grateful that they had come to the store today. 'The Contest' was taking place in two parts, and the first part ended tomorrow. She had made it just in time. Abby wandered back to the counter and tugged on her father's sleeve. "Ready, Dad?"

Rich and Eric said their goodbyes, and Abby led her father out of the store before he had a chance to peruse the entries on the board.

Abby was so excited by what she heard Mr. West saying as they left the store. At the end of the day, Eric and Nathan would gather all the photos and stories and

take them to the newspaper office in Easton. The staff
would read the entries and decide on the best story. The
story would be featured in Friday's paper, and the name of
the winner would be announced.

CHAPTER 88

Friday, December 17, 2014 - St. Brendan, MD

All week, Eric woke up on Julie's couch, around four in the morning, and headed home where he slept a little more before heading to the gym. Eric always left before sunrise and sometimes parked on Main Street and walked down to the house just to protect Julie's reputation. He had been raised to believe that a woman's reputation was the most important thing she owned, and in a town as small as St. Brendan, word got around fast. Most people knew he and Julie were seeing each other, but Eric didn't think anyone needed to know anything more than that.

Eric arrived home just as the morning paper was being delivered. 'The Contest' winner would be announced today, but Eric had other things on his mind. He tossed the folded paper onto the kitchen table as he passed by, and Gunner lazily collapsed onto his favorite rug after circling it several times. Eric had been trying to remember all of the clues from Jerome's cryptic phone call. He was missing something, and it was frustrating him. He tried to get another hour of sleep, but bits and pieces of the conversation flashed through his head. He gave up trying and threw on a pair of shorts and a t-shirt and headed to the gym where he could think clearly.

After pushing himself harder than usual, Eric left the gym around six-thirty and went home for a shower and something to eat. After his shower, he made himself a cup of coffee with the single cup brewer his mother had given him for Christmas the previous year. He poured himself a bowl of cereal, and then sat down to read the paper. The above-the-fold article was another story about the congressional meetings being held at the Inn that weekend with the Vice President. Eric briefly skimmed the article before opening the full front page to see 'The Contest' winner announcement. When he saw the headline and the picture that was submitted, a beautiful shot of seven white tails disappearing into the threes. Eric skimmed the article, his hands momentarily freezing as he reached the conclusion and read the name of the winner. He dropped the paper and jumped up from the table as if a match had been held to it, and the fire was spreading rapidly up the page.

Grabbing his keys, Eric dashed for the door with Gunner on his heels. He let Gunner jump into the truck ahead of him and backed out of the driveway. Gravel spit out from under his tires as he turned the wheel and sped back toward town, leaving the story in the newspaper lying on the table.

The Hunted

I spent the entire day hoping for the perfect shot. I tried one location after another, and I let many opportunities pass by. Should I go for the biggest prize or the easiest? Should I wait in one spot for something to come to me, or should I go looking for it? These were questions I asked myself. Deciding on the latter, I drove from place to place trying out different areas, different techniques. Then, I saw what I had been hoping for.

In an open field, there stood not one, not two, but seven whitetail deer. They looked at me with wary eyes as I lifted my armament to my eye. I focused on the biggest one, a buck with an eight-point rack, and I took aim. He just continued to stare as if daring me to shoot him. The others, too, stood their ground.

Why didn't they run, I wondered. Were they tired of running? Tired of being chased? Did they just want the hunt to end? I watched them, and it occurred to me that we aren't that much different, those deer and me. All we want is a chance to live without fear, to have a home we don't have to leave, to love without end.

Suddenly, they were alert; someone else was coming. They leapt at once and ran toward the woods as I took aim and shot with my camera. My heart raced away with them, and my mind called out to them to come back. But they could not come back, for the hunter will never give up until the hunted is gone.

-Julie Lawson

CHAPTER 89

Julie made herself a cup of tea and opened a container of Greek yogurt before grabbing a spoon and a banana and sitting at the table. Though a light breeze blew the pine needles across the small back porch, the sun was bright, and the last forecast she heard the night before was calling for above normal temperatures. Julie was beginning to look forward to her weekend away with Helen and only wished they could leave today instead of the following morning. Helen had already agreed to volunteer for a church dinner being held that night, and though she offered to back out, Julie insisted that she keep her commitment. The bright side was that she and Eric would be apart only one night instead of two.

Julie never thought she would meet someone like Eric, and for the past two years, she wouldn't even let herself dream of the possibility. Though her every instinct told her to run, that not even Eric could protect her, she couldn't bear the thought of leaving him, nor of turning his life into the rat chase that hers had been ever since that fateful day when she escaped death for the first time. Eric was everything that Julie ever wanted in a man and more. She felt her eyes mist up as she thought about how much her parents would have loved him. She was content with the belief that they were looking down on her now with love and happiness. Perhaps it was they who had orchestrated Eric's entrance into her life. How else could she explain the miracle of his needing her right when she needed him?

Julie was careful to always keep the doors to the cottage locked. She was about to put a spoonful of yogurt into her mouth when she heard pounding on the front door. By the time Julie reached the door, Eric was shouting for her to open it up. Where was his key, she wondered, as she pulled open the door. He rushed inside and wrapped her in his arms. He was sweating, and she could feel his heart racing. Julie tensed and waited for Eric to tell her what was wrong.

"Don't panic," he said as he turned back to the door and locked it. He took her hand and led her back to the kitchen.

"That's not a good lead-in, Eric," she said as he gently glided her onto a chair. "What's going on?" She took a deep breath and braced herself.

"The Contest," he began.

"They announced the winner today, right? Is that what this is about," she smiled and placed her hand on his arm. "Eric, you scared me. Why is that so upsetting?"

"It's you, Julie. You won."

Julie frowned and looked at Eric. She was bewildered. How could that be? She hadn't entered. He had to be mistaken. Suddenly the meaning of his words dawned on her. Someone had entered her story. Her eyes widened with panic, and she stood up and began pacing around the room.

"Oh my gosh, oh my…" she dropped back into the chair and put her face in her hands, shaking her head. When she lifted her eyes back to him, tears began to flow. Eric stood up and went around to her. He knelt down and pulled her to him.

"How?" she whispered. "I didn't—"

"I don't know. Someone must have entered it for you, but who could have done that? I can't imagine that my mother would have."

Julie's head shot up. "Abby. I watched her one afternoon, and she was acting very secretive when she left. I bet she found it and entered it. She helped me with the details and must have thought I'd appreciate it." Julie looked at Eric. "I never intended to enter. It was for, for me to imagine that I could, but not to actually do it."

"I understand, but now it's done. What do you want to do?"

Julie was quiet for a long time, and then she pushed back the chair, stood, and walked to the back door. She gazed out at the bare trees that lined the small backyard and for the first time, she admitted to herself just how much she wanted to stay, how tired she was of running, how much she wanted this town, this man, to be her home.

"Nothing," she said with an exhalation as she turned back to Eric. "I'm going to do nothing. I don't want to be interviewed or have anyone make a big deal out of it. I will just let things be and pray for the best. I can't do this anymore, Eric. I can't keep running and hiding. I want a life, and I want it here, with you."

"People will wonder about the meaning of the story. They might ask questions. The paper will want pictures of you accepting the prize."

"And I'll come up with an answer to their questions, but no pictures. Maybe Abby can accept it for me."

"We'll come up with answers together," Eric told her.

He went to her and placed his hands on her shoulders. He looked deeply into her eyes. A tear slid down her cheek, and he kissed it away.

"No more tears, then. I'm here, and I will never let anything happen to you. I love you."

Julie smiled up at Eric. "I love you, too."

His hands dropped to her waist and circled around her as she lifted her lips to meet his. They kissed, not with passion, but with love, and then Eric held her in his arms and whispered in her ear that, no matter what, she would never be hurt again.

CHAPTER 90

Some members of the Secret Service arrived in St. Brendan around noon on Friday. The vice president's personal detail would be with him when he came to town, and several men had been in town for a few days, doing surveillance and sweeping any places that Vice President Malone or the congressional leaders might go.

The most recent arrivals were just checking into the local hotel. The vice president's Chief of Staff, Robert Mason, was due to arrive in town that evening, and would be staying at a bed and breakfast near the posh Revolutionary Inn. He would have preferred being at the world-famous resort with the elected officials, but he understood propriety and knew that the American people would not appreciate him paying $300.00 per night just to be near the vice president and the congressional delegation.

One of his staff checked into Mr. Mason's room for him in order to ensure that it was secure and had everything that his boss would need or want. He placed a stack of newspapers on the desk with the local paper on top. He knew that Mr. Mason would want to read the town's news when he arrived so that he could make it seem like he knew everything that was going on in the sleepy little town. It was important to always make the voters feel special, and Mr. Mason had a knack for that. He would be sure to inform the vice president if there was anything special taking place in the town about which he should know.

CHAPTER 91

"I don't like this," Helen protested. "Maybe Julie and I should leave now. I'll call Betty and let her know that I can't be at the dinner tonight."

"Absolutely not," Julie insisted.

They sat in Helen's kitchen, the women drinking tea and Eric drinking a strong cup of coffee. Helen knew that Eric was reluctant to go to work, but he had no choice but to be there all weekend. She was grateful that he and Julie had finally let her in on the secrets about Julie's past. What a nightmare that poor girl had been living.

"I don't like it either," Eric said, "but Julie won't budge, and I won't force her." They sat next to each other, holding hands. Helen had grown to love Julie as much as Eric had, and she worried about her safety. However, she admitted to herself, that she was more worried about Eric. How could he ever survive if he lost another love? It would be too much for both mother and son to stand yet again.

"I don't understand," Helen looked at Julie pleadingly. "Why won't you go? Why put yourself in danger like this?" Helen was in agony. She was worried about Julie, but she was also concerned for her son. She wanted to remind Julie that they were all in danger, but she couldn't put any more on the poor girl's conscience. Julie reached for Helen's hand.

"Helen," Julie spoke soothingly, "I'm sorry. I don't want to worry or upset you, but I have to do this. I have to face whatever is going to happen, not just for me, but for both of you. I have to let this play out, no matter what." She looked at Eric and gave him a weak smile. "If we get through this day without anything going wrong, you and I will enjoy a wonderful, relaxing weekend at the beach and then deal with any fallout once we get back."

Never one to let her emotions get the best of her, Helen cleared her throat and picked up her teacup. She stood and walked to the sink. Eric and Julie sat in silence while she rinsed the cup with her back to them. Finally, Helen turned around and dried her hands on a tea towel she had picked up from the counter.

"Then it's settled. We pray for safety tonight and head to the beach tomorrow."

"Yes," said Julie, "and then we come back. To live our lives."

"Together," Eric added as he patted the top of Julie's hand with his.

"Together," Julie affirmed, smiling up at Eric.

Helen sighed and walked to the table. She placed her small, bony hand on top of Eric's. "Together," she said with resolve.

CHAPTER 92

Officer Berman drove over the bridge that led to the peninsula where St. Brendan was nestled on the Chesapeake Bay. When she read that the vice president was going to be there that weekend, she obtained permission from her sergeant to go look for Melissa Grant. Was it a mere coincidence that Melissa and Vice President Malone were going to be in the small town at the same time, or had fate stepped in and lent a hand in bringing them together? Or worse, had the vice president discovered Melissa's whereabouts and arranged for the meeting to take place so that they could meet? That seemed unlikely given the attempts on Melissa's life unless the vice president was trying a different approach this time. Mindy didn't know the answer, but she sensed that Melissa was in grave danger, and she knew that just by being here, she could be putting herself in grave danger as well.

When Mindy stormed into Sergeant Farrell's office one week earlier, she had no idea what she was going to do, but she knew there was a reason this had fallen into her lap. She felt compelled to see this case to a close for Frank Morris, for Tina Marsh and Chad O'Donnell, for Officer Kelly, who had given his life trying to protect Melissa, and for Melissa Grant who had unknowingly started the clock on a time bomb that was about to blow up in the little

Eastern Shore town after almost thirty years of ticking. Mindy pleaded with her sergeant to let her leave right then and head to Maryland, but he insisted on taking things slow.

"We're talking about the second most powerful man in the United States, heck, the world," he said to her. "You can't just barge into this woman's life and tell her that you think her father is the vice president, and he may be trying to kill her. Just what do you think would happen next?"

Mindy didn't have an answer for that. All she had was a set of circumstantial evidence, most if it from an anonymous source. Drawing the blinds and locking the door, they stood at the whiteboard in his office and laid out the timeline and the facts, as they knew them.

Lissa Marshall gave birth to an unknown child and gave him or her up for adoption. She was murdered two weeks later.

Melissa Grant, maternity nurse in Philadelphia, was born on August 10, 1987, in the City of Baltimore, birth parents unknown. She was adopted by James and Ann Grant. The possibility of Robert Malone being her father hung in the air but couldn't be verified. It was a theory that Mindy was willing to bet her life on, although it was quite a gamble considering the only evidence she had was a cryptic note written with letters cut from a magazine and an innocuous code name.

On January 1, 2013, Melissa started a search for her birth parents. On that same day, an attempt was made on her life. Within less than a week, three people associated with Grant were dead, and Melissa had disappeared. Not many people on the planet had the resources or the ability to move that quickly, especially for a personal, and not national security, matter.

On April 8, 2013, Frank Morris was killed in a car explosion that was ruled a gang-related homicide. He had just ordered a subpoena for Grant's adoption records. The request was denied by a federal judge. Furthermore, the records subsequently disappeared altogether.

Beginning on April 9, 2013, Mindy received several cryptic letters, from an anonymous source, warning her to back off and then switching gears and dropping clues that alleged that Vice President Malone was a danger to Melissa Grant. There was no known connection between the two, and Mindy could make only one correlation—the possibility that Malone was Melissa's birth father.

Almost two years after she disappeared, in December of 2014, Melissa was identified as a photographer in the town of St. Brendan, Maryland, by a woman who knew her well.

Where had she been for the previous two years? Presumably, computer genius Chad O'Donnell had helped her escape, but how had she continued to elude so many government and law enforcement agencies once Chad was dead? Had the vice president, or someone close to him, been tracking her movements since then? It seemed implausible since she was supposedly still alive. How could she have eluded them for that long?

There were more questions than facts, and Sergeant Farrell was reluctant to let Mindy do anything that could endanger her life or embarrass the department with a wild goose chase, especially since the target of the chase was reportedly about to announce his bid for the presidency. It was only Mindy's absolute certainty of a connection that finally changed Farrell's mind. She was allowed to go to the town and look for Grant, but she was not to let on, in any way, who she was, why she was there, or what she suspected. Of course, she told herself, sometimes circumstances beyond one's control could dictate a change in plans.

Mindy drove to the town and pulled into the parking lot of the only hotel other than the famous inn on the other side of town. She already knew, from her previous phone call, that there were no rooms, but she was going to give it a try anyway. When her attempt at cajoling was not getting her anywhere, she relented and decided to just look around town. She could find a room back in Easton where there were a number of hotels that, hopefully, were not all booked by government officials or members of the press.

Mindy had no idea where to start, but she did have the name of the street where Grant was last seen, retreating toward a house where she may or may not have been staying. Officer Berman parked her car in a public lot and began walking, following the Google Maps App on her phone, toward Maple Street.

CHAPTER 93

Robert Mason checked into the Old Mill Bed & Breakfast on Crabapple Street at six that evening. After a long day in Washington, Mason was glad to finally be at the hotel. He got his room key from his Secret Service agent and went to freshen up before dinner. He was to meet the vice president and the speaker of the house at the Inn at seven. Mason used the bathroom and then sat on the bed and called his wife to let her know it might be a late night, and he would call sometime over the weekend if he could. A small wave of guilt washed over him when his youngest child, a seventeen-year-old daughter, picked up the phone, and he thought of what Melissa Grant might have sounded like at that age. He shrugged off the feeling as he waited for his wife to pick up the line. Thinking of Melissa Grant as a problem that must be solved, rather than someone's daughter, was the only way Mason could face himself in the mirror. It was the same thing he told himself about her mother after he learned about the rape and her subsequent death. Having to deal with that 'problem' was just the first of many such 'problems' he had cleaned up for the former Senator and his son.

After disconnecting the call, Mason reached across to the desk and picked up the newspaper on the top of the stack that had prepared for him. It was his responsibility to keep the vice president on his toes, so he needed to know what the pulse of this little town was, so that Malone could issue some sound bites, showing his knowledge of the area. Mason skipped the article about the meeting since it had already been sent to him by his Google News feed the evening before. He opened the paper and scanned the story that was part of a local contest. Could this be just a coincidence? A woman with the same name as the last known alias used by Melissa Grant wrote a story about being hunted. Can it be her? Mason abruptly stood up from the bed and let the paper drop to the floor as he picked up his phone from the comforter. He fumbled with the device as he quickly tried to find the number.

"I need the background and current location of someone living in this town, a woman going by the name Julie Lawson," he barked into the phone. "I don't know if she's in a house, a hotel, or sleeping in the gutter, but find out for me, and find out now. It's a matter of national security." Mason slammed down the phone and began pacing while he waited to be called back. Dinner would have to wait.

CHAPTER 94

Jerome Williams and his wife, Corinne, were at a ski resort in Maine when Jerome logged into the Internet from a hotel computer. He had been out of touch for several days and was curious about what was going on in the world. The first article to come up, under national news, was a story about the president's upcoming trip to China. The second story stopped Jerome's heart as he immediately realized its possible ramifications.

Jerome decided to throw caution to the wind and do what he knew was right. After running back to his room to consult with Corrine, who was in complete agreement with his decision, Jerome made a phone call to Washington, D.C. Hearing his story and recognizing its implications, the person on the other end promptly transferred him to a higher office. Jerome hoped that he had not made matters worse for himself and everyone else by alerting the U.S. Government to the danger at hand. Could he trust his contacts in the federal bureaucracy? Just how far through the government did the vice president's web of deceit extend?

CHAPTER 95

Things were slow in Bass & Bucks, a good thing for Eric whose mind was elsewhere. Nathan had been sent home, and Eric had rearranged, inventoried, and straightened more than he thought was possible. He was grateful, and relieved, when six o'clock arrived and he was able to close up and head to Julie's. She was just turning off the oven when he used his key to open the front door. Eric breathed a sigh of relief at the sight of her. Though she promised not to run, the possibility lingered in the back of his mind throughout the day.

Julie turned from the oven, and Eric watched her face light up as he entered the room. His heart skipped a beat as it occurred to him, for about the hundredth time, how far and how hard he'd fallen in the past two months. He crossed the room and picked up Julie in one swift motion. She squealed as he spun her around in the small kitchen and then planted a kiss on her lips. He lowered her to the ground, and she tightened her arms around his neck.

"I never thought this day would end," Eric whispered into her hair as he held her close.

"Neither did I," Julie agreed. He released her, and she carried a bowl of salad to the table. "I hope you're in the mood for seafood. Shrimp was on sale this week." Eric lifted the lid off the steaming pot and let the warm, seasoned air fill his nostrils.

"Sounds good to me," he said as she took two baked potatoes out of the oven.

Eric went to the cupboard and took down two wine glasses and retrieved a bottle of white wine from the refrigerator that he had brought by earlier in the week. He poured their wine, and Julie finished putting the dinner on the table.

"How as your day?" Julie asked as she sat down.

"Long. Yours?" Eric asked, raising his brow.

"Quiet," she said. "Thankfully."

Eric nodded, acknowledging her meaning. They reached for each other's hands, and Julie led them in saying grace.

"You were able to get mom to go to the dinner?" Eric asked.

Julie nodded. "She didn't want to leave, but I assured her that you were on the way. We're all packed and ready to leave for the beach first thing in the morning."

"I dropped Gunner off to stand guard until she gets home."

"Good. I think she will sleep better, knowing he's there with her."

"I agree. This is great by the way," Eric said, biting into the homemade biscuit.

"It should be. It's your mom's recipe. She taught me to make them, and then we each baked a cherry pie, one for the dinner and one for our dessert."

Eric smiled. "My favorite."

"That's what your mom said."

They polished off the bottle of wine and ate a long, lazy dinner before cleaning up and going into the living room. They rummaged through the collection of old movies the Baileys had amassed over the years and chose to watch an old classic, *Casablanca*.

"I guess Hitchcock is out," Eric grinned as he looked over the rest of the collection.

"Not tonight," Julie agreed.

After queuing the movie, Eric retreated to the couch with Julie, and they snuggled together under a blanket. They were lying side by side with the glow of the television and the fire from the gas fireplace softly illuminating the room.

"These old classics are such a part of my childhood," Julie mused. "My parents loved old movies, and we watched all of them, everything from Bogart to John Wayne and Hitchcock. But I have definitely steered away from horror and suspense movies over the past couple years."

Eric leaned forward and kissed her lightly on the head, pulling her more tightly to him. "Let's hope there's no more horror or suspense in your life from here on out," he said quietly.

"I hope so, too," she whispered, and he wondered if her response was partly to him and partly to God.

Experienced in staying in the shadows and not making a sound, the secret service agent outside the window watched them for a few minutes before slinking away to make a call.

CHAPTER 96

"Shouldn't you be heading out?" Julie asked when she walked into the living room and saw Eric still stretched out on the couch on Saturday morning.

For the first time since he'd been staying overnight, Eric was not in a rush to leave that morning.

"I probably should be, but it's Saturday. I thought I'd be a little lazy this morning." He sat up and stretched his arms over his head. Julie, already showered and dressed, walked toward the kitchen. "You're up awfully early," he called after her.

"I couldn't sleep, and you're not fooling me, Eric," she called back over her shoulder. "You don't know the definition of 'lazy.' Go to work. I'll be fine until your mom calls."

"It's only 6:30. I don't need to be there for a couple more hours."

Julie watched him fold the blanket and sheets and carry them to the bedroom. She walked to the kitchen and stood in front of the sink, looking out the window. She shivered. Eric came up behind her and wrapped his arms around her, nuzzling her neck.

"Cold?" he asked. She shook her head.

"It's the fog. Something about it really gets to me."

Eric lifted his head and peered out into the thick morning mist. "You get used to it," he told her. "It's a little odd for December, but it was pretty warm yesterday. It must have cooled down overnight." He released her and began making himself a cup of instant coffee.

"If I keep staying here, we're going to have to invest in a real coffeemaker."

"Maybe Santa will bring you one for Christmas," she teased as she reached for the canister of tea bags.

Eric watched Julie drop her tea bag into the hot water and place it in the microwave. She went to the refrigerator and reaching for her morning yogurt.

"How can you eat that? It looks utterly disgusting."

"I like it." She pretended to be insulted and continued stirring her fruit and honey into the white cream that turned purple as she blended everything. "Maybe you should try it. It's good for you."

Eric reached for a bowl and a box of cereal he kept in the cabinet. "I'll stick with my Froot Loops, thank you."

After they ate, Eric kissed her goodbye and headed to his house to change.

"Don't forget to bolt the door behind me," he called.

"I'll do it in just a minute," Julie told him. "Have a good day."

Julie smiled as she began washing the dishes, but her smiled faded as she looked into the eerie backyard. She wondered how long it would take before this thick blanket was lifted from the earth.

Once again Julie shivered, and the thought occurred to her that the yard appeared to be draped with a greyish-white shroud as if the house had been entombed by a gauzy funeral cloth. Suddenly a familiar feeling crept up her arms, and goose bumps rose on her flesh. She unintentionally dropped the spoon from her hand and jumped as it clanged against the stainless-steel sink. The house was eerily quiet, but Julie knew she had heard something. Whether it was a real sound or a click in her brain telling her danger was near, she did not know.

Julie slowly turned to see if Eric had come back inside, but she saw no one. Chills ran down her entire body and her heart quickened with the sensation that she was not alone. She stood at the sink with a direct line of sight to the front door and watched in horror as the knob slowly turned. She glanced at the deadbolt. Why hadn't she locked the door as soon as Eric left?

Whoever was turning that knob would be inside the house within seconds. Instinct kicked in, and Julie moved quickly to the back door. She fumbled with the lock but resisted the urge to turn and look behind her when she felt the rush of cold air signaling that the front door had opened. She unlocked the door and fled into the mantle of fog. She was already on the dirt path to the trail when she realized Eric's gun was safely tucked under the mattress of her bed. So much for all the time they spent practicing her shooting skills.

CHAPTER 97

Mindy Berman was gulping down the continental breakfast at the EconoLodge on Route 50 in Easton when she noticed the rack of newspapers on the wall in the hotel breakfast room. She grabbed Friday's issue, with the story about the vice president coming to town, and opened the paper to look at the below-the-fold story about a local writing contest. In an instant, Mindy dropped the paper and fled from the room, leaving a half-cup of coffee and unfinished bagel behind. She had no way of confirming that Julie Lawson and Melissa Grant were one and the same, but she wasn't going to take any chances. *Let the hunt begin*, she thought as she ran from the room.

CHAPTER 98

Julie took the path that led through the trees to the trail. She debated which way to go. She was closer to the end of the trail if she turned left, but she would be going in the direction of the police department if she turned right. Before she could really make up her mind, she heard the slam of the back, screen door. Without any further consideration as to which was the best way to go, Julie took off to the right, adrenalin kicking in and propelling her to just run, no matter which way.

The morning was chilly, but what Julie felt was cold fear. As many times as she and Eric had walked on the trail, she felt as if she was on it for the very first time. The fog made the trees seem closer, the day darker, and the path almost indiscernible. She tried to visualize exactly where she was and how far was left to go, but she couldn't remember which landmarks came in what order. Was she near the Sycamore Street path where the police department was or the graveyard? The tombstones that had so fascinated her the first time she walked the trail now filled her with dread, and she prayed that she wouldn't accidentally wander into the garden of graves.

Julie could see nothing ahead of her; the fog seemed to be thickening rather than fading, and she fought her way through the heavy air, hoping she could find the right path to lead her to help and safety. The sun was up, but the light was unable to penetrate the shroud that surrounded her. When the path curved, Julie missed the change in direction and continued going forward. She didn't realize her mistake until she felt a shift in the ground under her feet and looked down at the narrow planks running out over the creek. She swallowed hard, held her breath, and tiptoed onto the pier, praying that she hadn't just made a fatal mistake.

CHAPTER 99

Robert Mason had never encountered a natural phenomenon such as the fog that now hindered his progress. He waited all night in his car down the street from Melissa's rental house until that local man, identified as Eric West, left. Once the Secret Service Agent informed him that she had been located and had been seen around town with the local shopkeeper, Mason took matters into his own hands. If you want something done right, you have to do it yourself, he decided. One professional, military-trained hit man and a highly respected government spy had both let Grant escape their grasp. Mason knew that he alone could make this right.

After informing Vice President Malone that he had important business to take care of, Mason ordered take out from a local restaurant and drove to Maple Street, where he parked in the lot of a small bakery on the opposite corner. He braved the cold and spent the night in his car, unwilling to let Grant slip through his fingers again. Using his government issued car, not even the local police dared to stop and ask him what he was doing in the lot that night. He was forced to leave his car when the damned fog began to roll in early the next morning. Keeping to the shadows, he made his way on foot down the road to the little house. West's truck was still parked in front, and to Mason's surprise the vehicle's doors were unlocked. He quietly opened the door and slipped inside the cab. Going through the glove box and the rest of the cab, Mason searched for a gun, assuming that West owned one and probably kept it handy. However, his search yielded no weapons.

He stayed hunched down in the front of the truck until he saw the glow of lights from inside the house, shining like far away beacons in the fog. Silently slinking out of the vehicle and sneaking around to the side of the house, he waited until he saw the man leave. As soon as the truck was out of sight, Mason looked around and tiptoed up onto the front porch, hidden by the murkiness like a curtain conceals a stage. He chuckled at the thought and its irony. He had indeed become an actor, playing his role to perfection, fooling people throughout the government to join in the hunt for an innocent young woman who he had turned into a shrewd and cunning spy, hell-bent on destroying the vice president. A small, but deadly task force had been employed to use every resource the government had at its fingertips to find her and stop her from terminating the VP's career, from machines to software to people, they spared no expense to access security cameras, facial recognition software, identity tracking software, spies, agents, and even judges. They all knew better than to question orders from that level of government, and quite frankly, over the years, bureaucrats and even voters had stopped questioning elected officials altogether. Their power had become boundless.

Mason turned the knob on the front door and was amazed to find it, too, unlocked, such a trusting little town oblivious to the danger within its midst. He glanced into the bedroom that stood empty, the open bathroom door concealing no one. He looked toward the kitchen and felt the cool draft coming from the back of the house. Rushing toward it, he discovered the back door open, and the house empty.

Peering into the fog, he saw just the slightest movement among the trees, a flash of blue, a woman's sweater? He listened to his inner voice and went to where he saw the movement. There, he found a well-traveled dirt path. He followed the path through the small cluster of trees and came out onto a paved road, or was it a walking path? With his limited vision, he assessed the area and decided it was indeed a walking path. Which way should he go? He listened for the smallest sounds and then took a chance and headed to the right.

CHAPTER 100

As Eric drove home to change, he thought about the list of words he had written down after his last conversation with Jerome. He had been trying, off and on, to make sense of them, and suddenly an idea clicked inside his head. He pulled the truck over to the side of the road and dug out his smartphone. He started typing the string of words into a search bar. There had to be a common link, and he felt like a fool for not trying this sooner. *Sandstorm, Sundance, scorecard, damn, what were the others?*

Deciding to go with what he could remember, he hit *Go* and sat up straighter in his seat, shaking his head when he saw the first hit, a page in Wikipedia: *Secret Service Code Names*. Confused, yet sensing he was on to something, Eric clicked on the link and scanned for the words he recognized from the conversation. They jumped out at Eric as he thumbed the screen to scroll through the list.

Spiro Agnew – Pathfinder

Nelson Rockefeller – Sandstorm

Dan Quayle – Scorecard

Al Gore – Sundance

Dick Cheney – Angler

"Son of…" Eric yelled as he tossed his phone onto the seat and spun his tires in a U-turn.

All of the names that Jerome so carefully mentioned were used for vice presidents, and the current vice president was less than a mile from Julie right now. Eric still didn't understand the connection to Melissa Grant, but he wasn't about to waste time. Julie was in danger; he felt it to the bottom of his soul. He hit the speed dial on his phone, grateful that he had never changed the order of numbers in his contact list.

"D.C. Attorney General's Office."

"Sandy, it's Eric West, please put Martin on the phone. It's an emergency."

The receptionist connected Eric to the D.C. Attorney General who listened to his account of the past two years and promptly alerted the U.S. Marshals.

CHAPTER 101

Officer Berman called her sergeant and informed him of the latest development as she drove toward the small town of St. Brendan.

"It's time," Sergeant Farrell told her. "We have to tell somebody. This is much bigger than you can handle."

"Then call the locals down here," Mindy told him, "but do not call the Feds. I don't know who we can trust, and quite frankly, I don't trust anyone."

Farrell assured her that he would take care of things and that she needed to stand down and wait for backup.

"It's no longer our case, Mindy. Once I make this call, it's out of our hands."

"The hell it is," she told him as she ended the call.

Farrell knew that this had become more than a case to Berman. It was personal, and she would stop at nothing to see it through. He placed a call to an old friend in the Tactical Operations Division of the U.S. Marshals Service and led him on a hyphenated journey that started in Alexandria, Virginia in 1986 and was about to come to a head in St. Brendan, Maryland today.

CHAPTER 102

Julie, or Melissa as she had been known until twenty-three months ago, walked as far as she could go and looked down at the frigid water at the end of the dock. There was no boat tied here, nowhere to hide, and as luck would have it, she was beginning to be able to make out the boats tied to the other docks in the creek. The fog was lifting, and Melissa would no longer be invisible.

The snapping of a twig caught her attention, and she turned back toward the trail. Standing at the end of the dock was a man in a suit, looking down at the small stick that had given him away. He looked up at Melissa, and his face twisted into a sick sort of smile.

"We meet at last, Melissa Grant." He sneered as he spoke her name.

"Who are you?" she demanded.

"Nobody you know, but somebody you should fear," he taunted her. Melissa sensed his glee in their meeting. He took a step onto the dock.

"I've been watching you for a very long time, pretty much your entire life as a matter of fact." He moved toward her one step at a time, and it felt to Melissa as if the whole scene was taking place in slow motion.

"Who are you?" she asked more forcefully this time.

"I am Robert Mason, Chief of Staff to the Vice President of the United States." He paused and pulled himself up to full height to show his importance. When he took another step toward her, Melissa glanced over her shoulder at the water and wondered, *how cold is it this early in the season?*

How long she would last in it before hypothermia set in? Could she make it to the nearest dock? She looked toward the dock in the distance, panic welling in her chest.

"Go ahead and jump," Mason said. "Make what I have to do even easier."

Melissa turned back to him and found her resolve. "What did I ever do to you? Why have you been after me all this time?"

"Do you really want to know? Do you really want all f the sordid details? You don't have any idea what you're asking." He was less than three feet from her now, and her already accelerated heart felt as if it might burst through her chest.

Keep him talking. Help will come.

"I think I deserve to know the truth," Melissa told him with as much firmness and confidence as she could muster.

"The truth? You can't handle the truth!" He laughed at his own joke, a hideously high-pitched laugh that conjured up images, in Melissa's mind, of Jack Nicholson as both the colonel in *A Few Good Men* as well as the mad man in *The Shining*. "I've spent the last twenty-six years trying to hide the truth. I've been protecting Peter Malone since I was nothing but a lackey, trying to get in the good graces of his father, Senator Colin Malone. I did what he asked even as it turned my own stomach. Then I went to work for Peter and realized the leverage my knowledge gave me, how I could use it to my advantage to gain any position I wanted. And just when Malone's popularity hit an all-time high for a vice president, you had to start asking questions."

"What questions?" Melissa demanded. "I don't care about vice president Malone. I couldn't care less about his popularity. What does he have to do with me?" She was shouting now, and her voice carrying as the fog diminished.

"What does he have to do with you?" he screamed at a fevered pitch. "He's your father!"

CHAPTER 103

Washington, D.C.

Phone lines were ringing throughout the U.S. Marshal's office as agents listened to and then reported on the wild story involving the vice president of the United States. First, a sergeant from the Philadelphia Police Department called with outrageous accusations that he believed the vice president was involved in a string of hits, allegedly tied to the parentage of one of the victims. The Marshal had taken notes and passed it on, trying to convince his superiors that the sergeant was credible, but the story was not given much weight.

However, a second call came in to another department just minutes later from the D.C. Attorney General's office, making the same accusations, and then a third call was taken from a ski resort in Maine. Subpoenas were issued immediately for cell phone records, Homeland Security records, and the sealed adoption records of one, Melissa Grant. For a city with the reputation of moving at a snail's pace to get anything accomplished, evidence mounted against the vice president and his staff at a breath-taking rate.

CHAPTER 104

St. Brendan, MD

Eric skidded to a stop in front of the cottage. He jumped out of his truck and yanked open the back door. Lifting up the back seat of the truck, Eric thanked God for the gun cases he sold that attached securely to the underside of the bench seat, only visible when the seat was lifted, thus opening the top of the previously concealed case. He grabbed the rifle and raced up onto the porch where the front door stood open.

"Julie!" he screamed as he ran into the empty house. He sprinted to the kitchen and found the back door open to the cool morning air. He knew instinctively where she would go and wasted no time tearing across the back yard and through the path to the trail. The last of the fog was clearing as he followed his gut and turned in the direction where she had almost broken his nose. For some reason, he was sure that the nine-millimeter pistol he had given her was still in her nightstand drawer.

CHAPTER 105

"What did you say?" Melissa asked, her voice barely above a whisper.

"Vice President Malone is your father. He knocked up your mother when he was on a drunken binge at a bachelor party, not his own as he was already married, which was the problem. That and the fact that she apparently wasn't a willing participant in the carnal act." Melissa gasped. "Yes, Melissa, you were the most unwanted of the unwanted, except that your mother didn't do what she should have done. She didn't get rid of you. But don't think you were so special that she couldn't bear to abort you. No, your mother was just another greedy wench, like so many before I've had to deal with for the senator and his son. She tried to blackmail the senator, your grandfather, so he told me to take care of her. I paid her a hefty sum to agree to give you away."

Tears streamed down Melissa's cheeks as she listened to this complete stranger deal her blow after blow.

"She signed you away before you were even born, then went back to her oh, so glamorous life as a cocktail waitress. But that wasn't enough for the senator. He knew she'd be back for more. They always came back for more. I was called once again to intervene. About a month after you were settled into your nice suburban home with your loving parents, your mother was killed in a mugging on her way home from work one night. Pity. She was such a pretty girl." He glared at Melissa and took another step. They were close enough for her to see their breath curling between them. "I've had the privilege of monitoring your every move since you were born. The day you decided to look for your birth mother, I was ready."

"Does the vice president know about this, all of this, you trying to kill me for the past two years?"

"Every. Little. Detail," he enunciated with a smile that chilled her to the bone. "And now he's waiting for word from me that you won't ruin his plans to get the party's nod to be our next president. He doesn't want any loose ends."

Knowing what was coming, Melissa braced herself. When Mason thrust his hands toward her throat, she grabbed his arms and pulled him towards her. She banged her head against his bent face and hit him in the nose as hard as she could and then raised her knee, hitting him hard where it would hurt the most. He instinctively reached down and grabbed his crotch even as he screamed in pain and blood ran from his nose, and Melissa raised her foot to kick him over into the water. He was too quick, though, and grabbed her ankle, twisting it around until she was holding onto to the pylon and screaming for help. She kicked back and forth trying to loosen his grip while she held the pier and balanced on her other leg. Mason found the strength to stand using her leg and then her body as a lifeline to pull himself up. His hands on her body made Melissa want to gag. The blood from his nose ran down

the front of his designer suit. He moved his hands to her
face and began pushing her backwards towards the water.
Julie knew she was going to go over. She had no leverage
with which to fight him off. Her only hope was that he
would be unprepared for what she was about to do.

CHAPTER 106

Helen's heart beat erratically when she turned onto Maple Street and saw Eric's truck, haphazardly parked in front of the cottage, the front and back doors of the cab both left open. She slammed her car into park and leaped from the front seat, screaming for both Eric and Julie. She ran through the house but found it empty. Racing back to her car, she grabbed her cell phone from the console of her car and called 911. She prayed that Eric hadn't been too late as she frantically asked for help.

Hearing another vehicle pull up, Helen turned to see an unfamiliar car with out-of-state tags come to a stop in front of the house. The neighbors started to gather in the street, the buzz of their voices rising in alarm. A petite young woman with blonde hair pulled into a bun emerged from the car, holding out a badge.

"Officer Berman, Philadelphia Police." She walked toward Helen. "Do you know the woman living in this house?"

Helen hesitated but then nodded her head.

"Where is she?" the officer asked.

"I, I don't know," Helen stammered, and though she truly didn't know, she wasn't sure if she should answer.

"Ma'am, I'm here to help," the woman said soothingly as she laid a hand on Helen's arm. "Melissa, or Julie as

Amy Schisler

you may know her, is in grave danger. Please, do you know where she is?"

"I don't," Helen said. "I just got here. We were supposed to be going to the beach for a weekend away. Eric, my son, his truck was here when I got here. I, I don't know where he is either."

"Ma'am, what is your son's relationship with Melissa? Does he know...." Mindy stopped, and Helen sensed her question.

"He knows everything," Helen admitted. "Please, help them."

The officer looked around Helen toward the house and then back at the older woman. "I'm sure going to try." Helen watched the woman take off at a run, pulling a Glock from her waistband as she headed toward the back yard.

CHAPTER 107

Eric heard Julie's screams and stopped momentarily to locate from which direction they were coming. The dock, he was sure she was at the dock. He sprinted toward it, relieved that she was still alive, but horrified at the sound of her screams. There wasn't much time.

Eric rounded the bend, and the dock came into view. Julie was struggling with a man in a suit. From what Eric could see, she had fought him in the same manner she had fought Eric, but this time, the man was fighting back. He had her bent over backwards pushing her towards the water. Julie was struggling to keep her balance but losing her grip on the pylon. Eric raised the rifle and looked into the scope then lowered it back down and cursed. They were moving too much. He didn't trust himself not to hit Julie. He took off down the path to the pier and watched in horror as Julie let go of the pylon and fell toward the water. He heard a loud thwack before the man followed her into the creek.

CHAPTER 108

Melissa had one last chance. She let go of the pylon and reached out to grab the man's suit. Holding on for dear life, she pulled him toward the pylon, and he hit it hard before falling into the creek with her. As she hit the frigid water, pain shot through her body and took away her breath. She gasped, and water filled her lungs, causing her to gulp in more. She clawed at the murky creek that surrounded her as if she could grab hold of it and pull herself up to its surface, but Mason was on top of her, pushing her down to the muddy bottom. Seaweed waved to her and mingled with a rusty brown fluid that mixed with the water around her.

Just before she lost consciousness, Melissa sensed movement ahead. Raising her eyes to the light above her, she saw a figure coming towards them. Her last thought was that her father, James Grant, had come to take her home. She surrendered to the cold and to the weight of the water and to the man who would not give up until she was dead.

CHAPTER 109

Eric ignored the pain that shot through his body as he hit the cold water. Mud rose up around him as the man and Julie sunk to the floor of the creek. Eric grabbed the collar of the man's suit coat and ripped the him away from her. As his body turned over with the motion, Eric saw the lifeless eyes below the large gash that was open across the man's forehead. Blood flowed from the gash and from the man's nose. Eric let go and watched a trail of blood follow the man's body as it rolled on the creek floor and came to a stop against the pier.

Eric grabbed Julie's lifeless body and dragged her through the water. As he reached the surface, several arms were reaching down to help him lift her up onto the dock. Rich grabbed Eric's arms and pulled him out of the water, sitting him down on the dock next to Julie. Abby stood nearby, crying as Kari and a woman Eric didn't recognize performed CPR on Julie. Eric tried to go to her, but Rich stopped him.

"Hold on, man, let them work. Here, you're gonna need this." He handed Eric one of Kari's handmade quilts, and Eric suddenly felt the cold throughout his body as the rest of his buddies from the fire department seemed to appear out of nowhere. Truck tires screeched to a halt on the access road, and an ambulance, siren blaring, careened to a stop beside the chief's car.

Helen rushed over to her son and knelt down beside him. "Are you okay?" she asked with the concern of a mother.

Eric wrapped his arms around her, pulling her into the quilt with him but never taking his eyes off of Julie. "I don't know yet."

Helen nodded and turned her gaze to the young woman lying on the dock.

At that moment, Julie's body began to spasm. The woman rolled her over, and creek water spewed over the side of the dock. Julie coughed and started to shake uncontrollably. Eric tossed off the quilt and leaped to her side. He pulled her to him as she coughed and shivered. Someone threw a dry blanket around them both, and Eric found himself once again weeping for the woman he loved. But this time, he wept tears of joy.

CHAPTER 110

As the crowd of friends, neighbors, and rescue personnel gathered around the couple on the dock, the sound of propellers filled the air. The crowd looked up and saw a fleet of helicopters heading toward the south side of town. Within minutes, a second ambulance pulled up alongside the trail on the access road that led to the dock. As Melissa was being lifted onto a stretcher, the onlookers heard a sound behind them in the water as Robert Mason surfaced next to the dock. Eric spun around, ready to fight, but Robert Mason was not going to fight back.

Floating alongside the dock was the body of a man in a suit with a large gash along his forehead above dark, blank eyes that seemed to be staring up at the sky. Kari grabbed her daughter and shielded her from the hideous sight. Eric, Rich, and a few of the other firefighters reached over the side of the dock and attempted to lift the body up, but it was too heavy and bloated even for all of them working together. A rescue boat would be called to fish the man from the creek.

Melissa was in shock, and there was no telling yet how much damage her brain had sustained while under water. As she was lifted into the back of the ambulance, Eric ran to her side.

"You're not leaving without me, Sam," he told the driver.

"Go to the other bus, Eric. They'll want to transport you and check you out, too."

"I'm fine, and I'm not leaving her side." The men locked eyes, and Sam knew there was no use fighting. The police were trying to clear the scene as Sam extended a courtesy from one rescue member to another and moved aside for Eric to climb in next to Melissa.

As the ambulance pulled away, Officer Berman introduced herself to the Chief of Police, a grey-haired man with the skin and build of a farmer or waterman.

"Sergeant Farrell explained the situation as best he could, given the limited amount of information that you have. I think you'll be very happy to know that those choppers that just flew overhead are on their way to the Revolutionary Inn. Shall we?" Chief Prince brushed his hand through the air, gesturing for Mindy to lead the way from the dock and accompany him to the Inn.

CHAPTER 111

The field in front of the Revolutionary Inn was often used by the Maryland State Police to land the medevac chopper in emergencies. Instead of the medevac, the field was filled that day with Federal tactical helicopters transporting U.S. Marshals. The operation was delicate, to say the least, but the marshals were given explicit instructions to hold the vice president and his staff for questioning. Though the U.S. Marshals have the constitutional right to arrest anyone accused of a crime, the Senate sergeant at arms was on his way in order to cover all legal bases. The Constitution holds that only he can arrest the president, and the arrest of a vice president was constitutionally undocumented, and up until now, unprecedented.

As Chief Prince and Officer Berman rode to the Inn, the Chief filled Mindy in on the briefings he had received so far.

"According to charging documents, the vice president and certain members of his staff have committed crimes against the Federal Wiretapping laws, abuse of Homeland Security surveillance systems, unlawful use of military personal, and blackmailing a Federal Judge. Charges of stalking, harassment, and ultimately murder are pending."

"Will any of it stick?" Mindy asked. Chief Prince shrugged.

"Hard to tell. He is the vice president, and no doubt, his lawyers will be the best money can buy. But the ACLU and a whole host of Victim's Rights Groups are bound to be clawing their way into the fight, not to mention all of the other candidates vying for his position, now and in the next election."

"And the proverbial nail in the coffin?"

"I'd say that's Melissa Grant and exactly how much she knows, can remember after today, and her credibility."

Both officers grew silent as the cruiser was waved onto the Inn's property by a Federal Marshal, and they witnessed all hell breaking loose.

CHAPTER 112

"You can go in now," the doctor told Eric. Another ER physician had examined Eric and declared him to be in fine health.

Eric wasted no time blowing through the curtain of his cubicle and heading to the closed room at the end of the hall in the emergency department. An armed guard stopped him and asked for ID before letting him enter, and Eric handed him his entire soaking, wet wallet before pushing open the door and going in. Julie, or Melissa, appeared to be asleep as several machines beeped and pumped around her, their wires and tubes connected to various parts of her body. Eric went to her side and took her hand in his. She opened her eyes.

"Hey… there," she whispered.

"Shh, don't try to talk," Eric told her as he stroked her head and ran his hand down her cheek.

"I… need… to… tell…" she said breathlessly.

"Not now," Eric told her. "You need to gain your strength."

Melissa slowly shook her head. "He… can't…. get… away…. Need… to… tell… what… he… said…"

The door opened behind Eric, and a man entered the room with his badge held up for them to see.

"Mr. West?" Eric stood up and nodded. The man extended his hand. "Special Prosecutor Thompson. I started working for the AG right after you left. I would like to speak with you and Miss Grant."

"She's not up to talking," Eric said, but Melissa tugged on his hand.

"I… want… to… talk," she insisted quietly.

Though it took some time, Melissa took them through the events on the dock. She remembered everything despite the doctor's cautioning that she might not. Eric listened, stunned at what he heard. Special Prosecutor Thompson listened, asked follow-up questions, and made notes.

"Miss Grant," he leaned in, "I need to ask you about the past two years, where you've been and how you were able to elude the men who were looking for you."

Here it comes, Melissa thought and closed her eyes.

"Will I be arrested for breaking the law?" Her voice was still low, but her words came more easily now.

"If you are, I know just the right lawyer to defend you." Eric said and squeezed her hand.

The prosecutor smiled. "I can't make any promises, but I'd say that there were most definitely extenuating circumstances."

Melissa nodded and quietly, with Eric's help, told the prosecutor her amazing story.

CHAPTER 113

Word was received that several staff members, as well as Homeland Security employees back in Washington, were being rounded up and taken in for questioning, or in some cases, being served arrest warrants. Vice President Malone was being questioned by Federal Marshals when the Senate Sergeant at Arms of the United States walked into the Presidential Suite at the Revolutionary Inn, followed by Special Prosecutor Thompson. Trying to maintain his cool and act as if nothing out of the ordinary was taking place, the vice president stood and extended his hand to his old friend. Ignoring the outstretched hand, the Sergeant at Arms looked the vice president in the eye and spoke these words,

"Mr. Vice President, you are under arrest for conspiracy in the murders of Tina Marsh, Chad O'Donnell, Officer Ryan Kelly, Detective Frank Morris, and the attempted murder of Melissa Grant. Other charges are pending."

PART SIX

In three words I can sum up everything I've learned about life: it goes on.

Robert Frost

CHAPTER 114

Christmas Eve, 2014 - St. Brendan, MD

The sun had set on the Chesapeake Bay, and the little town of St. Brendan was just beginning to return to normal after the shocking events of the previous week. Boughs of holly and garlands of pine hung to and from each lamppost, and white lights twinkled in the shop windows. The air was crisp, but no snow was predicted. A white Christmas on the Shore was a rare event. All was quiet in the town as loved ones gathered in their homes or in one of the local churches to celebrate Christmas. The news from Washington was unimportant to the citizens of St. Brendan that night.

An early Christmas present had arrived for Melissa Grant that morning when she received a call on her new cell phone, clearing her of all potential charges. The vice president was arrested, and a Grand Jury trial was scheduled. His entire staff was fired including his secretary, Margaret Gallagher Turner, who came to work for the vice president after many years with the National Security Agency.

While at the NSA, she became quite an expert at listening in on calls, hacking computers, and intercepting confidential information. She was a steadfast Patriot and abhorred abuses of power by those in government, but what she detested the most was that people in power had been able to get away with murder, specifically, the murder of her best friend. Her attorney was hard at work to obtain a plea bargain based on her anonymous tips to the authorities and her compliance in the case against her former boss, Peter Malone. The flash drive, she turned in as soon as she heard the news, was full of compelling evidence of years of abuse of power and conspiracy to commit murder on the part of the vice president and members of his staff. Unfortunately, her family's plan to take a holiday cruise had been suspended since she was not allowed to leave the country.

Officer Mindy Berman was to be given a Commendation of Merit by the Philadelphia Police Department as well an award from the D.C. State's Attorney's Office for her perseverance in solving the string of Philadelphia murders, including the death of Detective Frank Morris, and for locating and saving the life of Melissa Grant. A quiet ceremony was being planned in the Nation's Capital to honor her work in bringing down the vice president and his co-conspirators. She was thinking of leaving her job in Philly and taking a position offered to her by Chief Prince with the St. Brendan Police Department. It would be a lot slower and substantially less pay, but Mindy felt ready for a change. And with her biological clock ticking, she liked the idea of finding the right man and settling down to raise a family on the Eastern Shore, away from the violence in the city.

Eric and Melissa had done a lot of talking over the past couple weeks. For the first time in a long time, Melissa could think about her future and plan the rest of her life, or as the case was now, their life. Eric was going to continue running Bass & Bucks, but he was thinking about taking on a few legal clients on a case-by-case basis. Melissa extended her rental agreement on the Bailey cottage and was planning to be re-certified as a nurse. She was in the process of transferring her money into a bank account with her real name on it and had bought a fancy smart phone and new laptop. She was more than ready for Melissa Grant to re-enter the world. Rich, Kari, Abby, and Helen were all privy to the contents of the Tiffany's box that was wrapped and waiting under the tree and were anxious for Melissa to be a permanent resident in St. Brendan's.

Eric and Melissa gazed at the twinkling lights as Lisa, Mark, and their twin boys carried in bags of presents from Helen's den. Everyone was full after a bounteous meal of turkey, stuffing, mashed potatoes, rolls, and other side dishes they each had contributed to the holiday dinner. Eric's arm went around Melissa's waist, and he pulled her to him and kissed her. The little boys gagged in protest, and Melissa smiled as she leaned back and looked into Eric's deep green eyes.

"Stay right there," Lisa commanded as she raised her camera and focused on Eric and Melissa. "You look perfect," she said to her brother and the woman he loved.

And for the first time in almost two years, Melissa posed for the camera.

EPILOGUE

New Year's Day, 2015 – Bethesda, MD

Melissa was a bundle of nerves as she and Eric pulled into the driveway. She clasped her hands in her lap and trembled as she watched a front curtain move to reveal a little girl, looking out at the truck as it came to a stop in front of the three-story house in the upscale town. Eric switched off the engine and turned to Melissa. He took her hands in his and fiddled with the half-karat diamond on the ring on her left hand. Melissa tried to smile as she squeezed his hands.

"It's going to be okay," Eric soothed. "I'm here, and you've waited for this day for a long time."

Melissa nodded, "I know. I'm just so nervous. I don't know what to say to her, how to thank her for, for things that I didn't even know were happening. It's all so surreal."

Eric waited while Melissa composed herself with a few deep, cleansing breaths, and then squeezed her hands once more.

"Ready?" he asked, and she smiled.

"As I'll ever be," she answered.

They let go and reached for their respective door handles and exited the truck. Eric walked over to Melissa

and put his arm around her waist, and she thanked God
that he was there. They had attended New Year's Mass
that morning before making the two-hour drive to the
Western Shore. It was the first time Melissa had crossed
the Chesapeake Bay Bridge in a long, long time. As they
drove along Route 50 towards the D.C. Beltway, Melissa
watched the signs go by, signaling the roads to Baltimore.
It didn't seem real to know that she could take any one of
them any time she wanted to now and go to her old
neighborhood in Hampden, see her childhood home, visit
her parents' graves.

The life she had lived for the past two years was
already becoming a distant memory—something more like
a plot in a book, a life lived by someone else, someone
named Elaine, or Christine, or Brandy, or Julie, but not
Melissa Grant. All except for the last two months, of
course, when she met Eric and discovered that the life she
had always hoped to live was within her grasp. She
glanced at him now as they walked up to the door. How
lucky she was to have found him. He looked her way and
smiled, his eyes telling her that he felt exactly the same
way.

Before she could ring the bell, the door swung open,
and the same little girl Melissa had seen peering from the
window was standing before them, wearing a fancy
Christmas dress, red with a white lacy collar and black
belt.

"I'm Emily," she said, "and you're Melissa." Showing
no hesitation or shyness, the little girl smiled brightly and
opened the door for them to come in. "Mommy, she's

here," Emily called as Eric and Melissa stepped into the foyer.

A woman came toward them. Melissa watched her advance down the hall, and her heart began to race. This tall, thin, brown-haired woman knew her mother, knew Melissa before she was even born, and spent her entire life trying to protect her. Suddenly Melissa was overcome with emotion. She began to shake, and her eyes welled up with tears. Meg came to her with outstretched arms and folded her into her embrace. Both women stood in the foyer and cried as a small crowd gathered.

"I thought this was supposed to be a happy meeting," Emily said in confusion.

"It is happy, silly," one of the teenaged girls with curly brown hair said. "Mom's just being Mom."

Meg released Melissa and grasped her hands to open their arms in a wide circle and gazed at Melissa with love and affection.

"My word, you look like her," Meg said as she swallowed. Fresh tears sprang to her eyes as she shook her head. "I always wondered if you would."

Letting go of Meg's hands to wipe her own tears, Melissa smiled.

"Do I?" she asked as she sniffed and reached into her coat pocket for a tissue. Meg nodded.

Introductions were made as Meg's husband, Jeremy, took Eric and Melissa's coats and hung them in the coat closet. Emily took Melissa's hand and led her into the living room.

"Mommy said you get to see the pictures first. She wouldn't let any of us touch them." She threw her mother a reproachful look and crossed her arms across her chest.

"You must be hungry, though," Meg said. "Would you like to eat first?"

Melissa glanced at Eric.

"It's up to you," Eric told her. They hadn't eaten since early that morning, and Melissa was sure he was hungry, but she respected his acquiescence. She knew he understood that she had a lot of questions, and this was her homecoming, so to speak.

Knowing she would be holding up everyone's meal if she said no, Melissa agreed to eat before looking at the album. They would have a lot to talk about over dinner, and the album was something to look forward to. She laid the book down on the coffee table as they moved toward the kitchen. Melissa glanced back at the black album just before she left the room and felt a ripple of excitement in her stomach. She couldn't wait to see what was inside of it. She knew, beyond a doubt, that a picture was worth a thousand words.

ACKNOWLEDGMENTS

When writing a mystery novel, in particular, I, the author, am able to take liberties in creating people, places, events, and even technology that will aid in the telling of the story. However, as a reader, I am easily irritated when details don't make sense or crime scenes come across as something from a cartoon. In order to ensure that the story flows, the characters are likable and believable, and the facts are correct, I depend upon friends and family to help out. In this regard, I am lucky, because I have a wide circle of people who can give me the specific feedback I need.

Thank you, readers and experts, Mindy Berman Beck (teacher and lover of mysteries), Joni Kolakowski (teacher), Aunt Maureen Parkhurst (Nurse), Mike MacWilliams (photographer), Sarah Muller (friend and avid reader), Mary Leve (teacher, avid reader, and great critic), Pam Enrico (my high school English Literature teacher and proofreader extraordinaire) and Corporal Nicholas White (Marine, fire fighter, and like a son to me). Most of all, thank you to my Godfather, John O'Neil, international ballistics expert. Without all of you, this book would not be possible.

To my husband, Ken Schisler (avid hunter and marksman), my Aunt Debbie Nisson and my mother and father, Judy and Richard MacWilliams (my number one proofreaders and biggest fans), and my daughters, Rebecca, Katie Ann, and Morgan (readers, critics, and one future attorney), I owe you a world of gratitude.

ABOUT THE AUTHOR

Amy has been writing all of her life as an author and freelance writer. Her first children's book, *Crabbing With Granddad*, is an autobiographical work about spending a day harvesting the Maryland Blue Crab.

Her debut novel, *A Place to Call Home*, was released in 2014 by Sarah Book Publishing. A second edition was published in March of 2015. *Picture Me, A Mystery*, published in 2015, was the winner of the 2016 Illumination Bronze Award as one of the top three eBooks of 2015. Amy's critically acclaimed novel, *Whispering Vines*, published in 2016, was awarded the Illumination Bronze Award as one of the top three Christian Romance books of 2016. *Whispering Vines* was also awarded the LYRA for the best ebook romance of 2016. She followed up her success with *Island of Miracles* in 2017, winner of a 2016 Illumination Award.

Amy released her newest children's book, *The Greatest Gift*, as well as her novel. *Summer's Squall* in 2017. Amy's novel, *Island of Promise,* the second book in the *Chincoteague Island Trilogy*, was released in June of 2018. All of Amy's books may be purchased in bookstores as well as online on all major print and ebook sites.

Amy grew up in Southern Maryland, received her Bachelor's Degree from Salisbury University, and graduated from the University of Maryland with a Masters in Library and Information Science. A former librarian and teacher, she now lives on the Eastern Shore of Maryland with her husband, three daughters, and two dogs.

BOOK CLUB QUESTIONS

1. In today's world, is it truly impossible to leave no footprint? How many of the methods employed in this novel do you think are feasible in the 21st Century?

2. Melissa made several mistakes that almost got her killed. What was her biggest mistake?

3. Though Melissa evaded her killer for most of the novel, and succeeded in escaping from the government time and again, she believed that her panic attacks showed weakness and lack of composure. Why was she incorrect?

4. Do you agree with the way Meg handled the situation when Melissa inquired about her adoption and set things into motion?

5. If Julie/Melissa had met Eric in one of the other places she hid do you think she would have let the relationship develop or was it as much the community that enabled her to let her guard down?

6. What would YOU do if you saw a formerly close acquaintance from years past who was wanted in a police investigation?

Made in the USA
Middletown, DE
24 June 2018